M000025137

WHEN BEAUTIFUL, JADED ATTORNEY RUBY RANDOLPH IS ARRESTED FOR KILLING HER SNAKE OF A LAWYER HUSBAND, NOBODY BLAMES HER—EXCEPT THE COP WHO LOVES HER.

Ruby Randolph is a street-smart lawyer with a dark past who finally makes it big, but she's snared in an abusive marriage. Privilege has its costs.

When her husband's shocking murder sets her free, Ruby vows to keep it that way at any cost. But when her former lover shows up at her door as the police detective investigating the case, freedom gets tricky. There's still heat between them, but can she trust him?

Hank Rider, an honorable, world-weary cop, knows better than to get emotionally involved in a case. But he can't forget what he once felt for Ruby as they re-ignite their steamy affair. When he discovers evidence against her, the line between duty and passion gets blurred, fast.

As the investigation spirals out of his control, Hank struggles through a long list of suspects who wanted Ruby's husband dead—including Ruby. A bankrupted law firm, a busted client-attorney privilege, an ex-con out for revenge, a corpse in an orange grove, and Ruby's own shady history conspire to make everyone a suspect.

"Claire Matturro's twisted, intense mystery layers one deception over another in rapid-fire delivery that will keep you reading until the wee hours. Forget sleep—this sizzling, sexy story will leave you breathless."—*Donna Meredith, award-winning author and associate editor of Southern Literary Review*

"Ruby Randolph is a red-hot force of nature... *Privilege* is a steamy tale of murder, betrayal, and bad behavior. But look closer, and you'll see that it—like its heroine—also has a bright glimmer of hope etched on its heart."—*Laura Benedict, award-winning author of The Stranger Inside*

"Only a lawyer [like Claire Matturro] would know the inner workings of a law firm. Only a great writer can make it so thrilling. *Privilege* is a great read."—*James O. Born, NYT best-selling author of crime and thriller novels.*

"The reader is kept off balance by the gritty characterization of lawyer Ruby Randolph. Is she a victim or the orchestrator in this intricate web of misdeeds? ... [A]n excellent story, well written, and with complex and satisfyingly flawed characters."—*Rebecca Barrett, author of Trouble in Paradise and Road's End.*

"Welcome to a read that is as steamy as a Florida swamp on a hot August night. ...Secrets and secret lovers make it a riveting page turner as each layer of this captivating mystery is slowly revealed."—*Andrew Nance, author of All the Lovely Children.*

"A dark and twisted past follows Ruby Randolph .... Drugs, financial abuse, and murder all play a role in this intense legal thriller that pulses with action—and plenty of heat— under the Florida sun. Ruby learns the hard lesson that Karma always comes round again and the dead will rise from their graves."—*Carolyn Haines, USA Today best-selling author of the Sarah Booth Delaney mystery series*

PRIVILEGE

Claire Matturro

Moonshine Cove Publishing, LLC
Abbeville, South Carolina U.S.A.

Copyright © 2019 by Claire Matturro

This book is a work of fiction. Names, characters, places and incidents are products of the author's imagination or are used fictitiously. Any resemblance to actual events, locales or persons, living or dead, is entirely coincidental.

ISBN: 978-1-945181-59-7
Library of Congress PCN: 2019940431

All rights reserved. No part of this book may be reproduced in whole or in part without written permission from the publisher except by reviewers who may quote brief excerpts in connection with a review in a newspaper, magazine or electronic publication; nor may any part of this book be reproduced, stored in a retrieval system or transmitted in any form or by any means electronic, mechanical, photocopying, recording or any other means, without written permission from the publisher.

The front cover is copyrighted by the author, Claire Matturro, who is the sole copyright holder.

About the Author

Claire Hamner Matturro, a Romantic Times book award winner, has been a journalist in Alabama, a lawyer in Florida, an organic blueberry farmer in Georgia, and taught  at Florida State University and University of Oregon. She now lives with her husband in SW Florida. Her books are *Skinny-Dipping* (a BookSense pick, Romantic Times' Best First Mystery, and nominated for a Barry Award); *Wildcat Wine* (nominated for a Georgia Writer of the Year Award); *Bone Valley* and *Sweetheart Deal* (winner of Romantic Times' Award for Most Humorous Mystery), all published by William Morrow, and *Trouble in Tallahassee* (KaliOka Press). She remains active in writers' groups and contributes to *Southern Literary Review, Compulsive Reader*, and the Alabama Writers Forum.

Visit her at www.clairematturro.com.

To RG and KB

Acknowledgments

I want to acknowledge and thank Mike Lehner for his unparalleled and selfless help with this manuscript. Mike was sounding board, brain-stormer, content and copy-editor, friend and supporter. He had the thankless task of hunting down my many typos, correcting my rather loose sense of punctuation, and catching the plot inconsistencies. Any errors that survive his skillful, careful, and time-consuming efforts are all my doing, not his.

I also want to thank my brother, William Hamner, a career law enforcement officer with a distinguished history, including a long stint as a detective. He did his best to keep me accurate on police procedures. Any lapses are my own doing by way of poetic license.

Finally, last but most assuredly not least, I want to thank William Matturro, my husband, for his unfailing love and support.

PRIVILEGE

Prologue 1972

The first thing Ruby asked Gardner Randolph was whether she could trust him.

She needed help and the big guy over at the jail said Gardner was the best criminal defense attorney in the city. So, there she was, standing in front of his desk, hungry and with no shoes.

When Ruby asked if she could trust him, she watched his face, figuring that's where his real answer would play out. He studied her, taking her all in, and a gleam flared up in his eyes.

How powerful he seemed sitting behind his big oak desk, leaning back and ogling her from his deep red leather chair. How clean he was. How good he smelled. She stood still and straight, not flinching one bit. Just because she was homeless and dirty now that Billy had burned the trailer down didn't mean she couldn't look him in the eyes. And wait for him to answer her question.

He smiled at her then. "I'm Gardner Randolph. But you know that. Sit down. Tell me how I can help you."

Ruby kept standing. She liked looking down at the man in the clean white shirt from where she stood. "I need help. With some, er, things." She'd go back to that trust thing later.

"What sort of things?"

"My boyfriend's in jail."

"Boyfriend." Gardner laughed. "Well that takes some of the fun out of it."

Ruby didn't like him laughing and didn't like the way he made a point of staring at her chest. She wished she was wearing a bra. Hell, she wished she owned one.

When she didn't answer, Gardner asked, "Where?"

"County. Look, I could need a lawyer too. Both of us, you know."

"Are you a juvie? You look young."

"No, I'm eighteen."

"The boyfriend?"

"Twenty-two." As she answered him, she pulled her long, chestnut-colored hair off her neck, making a ponytail holder with her hand. Her hair was heavy, and though the office was air-conditioned, Ruby felt hot. Maybe that was because the lawyer in the clean shirt kept looking at her, letting his eyes do a full body inspection, and not hiding in the least what he was doing.

"I pass, or what?" she asked.

"Men must stare at you a lot. You're beautiful."

"Yeah, look, that and two bits, you know, will get me coffee. Can't you help me, or not?"

"Tell me about it."

"Thing is, I gotta know, can I trust you?" Ruby wasn't going to let him ignore the question a second time.

"Anybody ever tell you about lawyer-client privilege? I can't tell anyone anything you tell me. It's protected under a specific statute in Florida."

"Yeah, but that's jes' if you *are* my attorney, isn't it?"

"Smart girl. Got any legal training?"

"Yeah, I got some real good legal training. You hear a lot from the boys over to County, hang out long enough. You gonna be my attorney, or what?"

"Yes. I am now officially your attorney. You can trust me. Tell me your sordid little story."

"My boyfriend got popped for amphetamines, a few 'ludes, some pot, not too much. It's mostly the speed. Cops had a warrant 'cause he offered some speed to a narc. Pretty stupid story. Brought that narc right to the trailer. When they busted him, he punched a cop, hurt the one cop pretty good and broke his collar bone slamming him down across the table. Got away for about half a minute. Jes' long enough to knock over a damn candle—our power was shut off—and burnt down the whole damn trailer."

"Cops get the drugs?"

"Yeah. He didn't burn the trailer down quick enough."

"Too bad. What's his defense?"

"That it wasn't his. The speed wasn't his. Rest was, nickel stuff, county jail time stuff. The speed is different. Wasn't his, you know."

"Well that's certainly original anyway." Gardner sighed.

Ruby saw it register in his face. He thought they were just stupid druggies, that's all. He looked away from her and went back to studying papers on his desk. Damn, he was losing interest.

"You don't got to get sarcastic. Look, I know it's real stupid. I couldn't of made it up though 'cause I'd've made up something better. Thing is, they weren't all his drugs."

He looked up at her again. "Whose were they?"

"Jes' tell me that attorney-client thing again."

"Just, j-u-s-t. With a U and with a T. Just."

"What?"

"Attorney-client privilege. Florida law, clear as a bell, chapter 90 point something in the statutes. I'll look it up for you if you want. I'm like your priest. You can tell me anything and I do not repeat it. To anyone. Plain and simple. I don't tell what you tell me. If I do, The Florida Bar goes after me."

After studying his face while he spoke, Ruby felt satisfied. He wouldn't lie about the law because she could look it up. "Stuff belonged t'a guy named Harlan LaSalle."

Gardner leaned over his desk toward her. "And what's this Harlan LaSalle got to say about it all?"

"Nothing. He's gone missing."

"Gone missing?" Gardner frowned. "So he can't deny they were his drugs. Even if that was a defense."

"Maybe'd be better if we didn't bring Harlan into this, you know? And I wouldn't be count'n on me much either."

"Is this Harlan some kind of local drug dealer? On the cop's radar?"

Ruby twisted a strand of hair around her fingers, wondering what or how much to say. Then, surprising herself, she blurted out, "No. He was a college professor. Taught biology at USF." Wishing she hadn't used the past tense, she shut up.

" *Was* a professor." Gardner stared at Ruby so hard she felt herself blush. "What is he now?"

"Missing. I told you."

Gardner scribbled something on a note pad on his desk and then cut his eyes back at Ruby. "Look, I'm *your* attorney, okay, we weren't really clear on that. Already there's a conflict of interest. I can't represent your boyfriend."

"Nope, there's no conflict. He's the one in jail. He's not gonna point to Harlan or me. Understand? You gotta do what you can."

"You have to tell me the whole story." Gardner looked straight at her with his nails beginning to tap, tap, tap on the desk. His fingers were long, and thick, and well manicured.

He was eager, that much Ruby could tell now. But the tapping bothered her. She folded her arms across her chest. "I don't got to do nothing. I'll tell you what I'll tell you."

"I need to know everything. All of it. That's part of the deal." Gardner stood up. "Look at me. Trust me. You need help. First thing, let's feed you, get you a shower, some decent clothes, maybe a pair of shoes. Then you sleep. I got a second bedroom. When you wake up, you tell me the whole story."

"Yeah? What if I jes' cop your good silver?"

"It's just—J-U-S-T. With a T. And I'm not leaving you alone in my house."

***

The second bedroom in Gardner's house had a lock on the door. The first few nights in his house, Ruby used it.

By the fifth night, Ruby didn't bother. If he'd repulsed her in some way, yeah, she'd have kept locking it, or not been in the bedroom in the first place. But the thing was, he excited her. His confidence, his power, the way he looked at her. The way he left her alone every night. She thought about those long, thick fingers, and how very clean he was. How perfectly he pronounced each word he said.

On the sixth night, Gardner knocked on the door. She told him to come on in. He was in a robe and smelled of mint and some other spice she couldn't name. Ruby pushed herself up in the bed and looked right at him.

"You don't have to do anything," he said. "It's not a *quid pro quo* thing."

She didn't know what *quid pro quo* meant and didn't want him to know she didn't. So instead of asking, she kicked the sheet off her legs and rolled forward enough that she could peel off the new T-shirt he had given her to sleep in.

Standing over her in the bed, he looked down at her. Ruby was wary, but willing. He leaned in, fingered the ruby pendant around her neck, a necklace she always wore, the one thing she'd been able to keep. "Pretty," he said, "cold and shiny." His fingers slipped down from her neck, stroking steadily till they found her breasts.

She rose toward his touch, arching her back and parting her lips. "All right then," he said, "let's find out what you like."

Chapter One: Locked Doors and the Law Firm, 1987

"It's not the worst thing I've done." Ruby Randolph looked out the conference room window of the law firm, then closed her eyes for a moment and wondered what she was doing.

"Damn straight," Gardner Randolph said, and laughed. "I can testify to that." He leaned over the rosewood table to a vase of silk flowers and knocked off a clump of dust.

Ruby opened her eyes and watched out the window as a young woman pushed herself along the sidewalk in a wheelchair. The woman's lawyer, a stocky man in a gray suit, strutted along beside her, waving his arms. "She got half of what she deserved."

"So? You convinced the jury to cut her award way down. That makes you a good lawyer. But not her lawyer. She was the plaintiff. Your guy was the defendant. Get it?" Gardner stood up, stretched a bit, and walked to the door. "What'd she say to get you upset?"

"Nothing. She was nice."

"Sure, they're always nice once they get the check in their hands."

"Why'd you come in here? Making sure I got the settlement papers signed and sealed?"

"Case is over. Forget it. Come down to my office, I have a new malpractice file I want you to take. Let me get back to my criminal defense work."

Ruby shook her head. "I have a hearing in an hour. I need to go over the file again."

"What hearing?"

"Jacob's West Palms case. You know, that endless construction loan default case with seven co-defendants and three cross-defendants."

Gardner's grip on the door knob tighten. "I know it," he said. "Good old Jacob Stanley. Bills more hours than any partner and never sets foot in a courtroom."

"That's what he's got me for. Anyway, I have an hour to figure it out."

As Ruby edged by him in the doorway, Gardner moved toward her. He was so close she could smell the sandalwood in his Aramis aftershave and the Altoids mints he ate by the handful. She flattened herself against the door frame as he stepped closer and touched the side of her face with his fingers. Tilting toward him, Ruby inhaled. Give the devil his due. Her husband did smell good.

Gardner ran his fingers down her face to her neck and trailed them under her collar. Ruby leaned into the scent of him and for a moment she almost didn't despise him. He asked, "You need the whole hour?"

She jerked away. "That and more. Let me go."

Blocking her way, Gardner reached out and cupped his hands over her breasts, one hand against each, rubbing the fabric of her blouse against her bra, creating a small friction against her skin. All but involuntarily, she pressed against his fingers and her breathing quickened. Even now, he could do this to her. But when he pressed his body hard against her pelvis, Ruby pulled back and shoved his hands away.

"Damn it." She smoothed out her blouse, brushing out the wrinkles from Gardner's hands with the flat palm of her own. "You know what it costs to dry clean and press this kind of silk?"

Gardner laughed. "Then come in my office and take it off."

"Like hell." Ruby pushed past him.

"You have a hearing, you do something with your hair before you go. Don't be going into court with it hanging down your back like that. I mean it."

Ruby walked down the hallway without looking back at him.

Once in her own office, she shut and locked the door. Humidity seeped into the room, outwitting the non-stop air conditioner. August on the Florida west coast and everything outside was sticky with heat. Even inside the artificial cool, a dank warmth collected in the corners. Her hair coiled out from her face in a disheveled tangle. Working without a mirror, Ruby pulled it back into a knot and anchored it with a large silver barrette she took out of her desk. Gardner had given her the barrette. Her name was engraved on the inside of the back and on the front, a delicate spiral of seed pearls outlined a single emerald. It was expensive and specifically designed for her and she hated it. But it got the long, hot mess of hair off her neck. She reached for the case file and mentally began to formulate a legal argument.

***

Walking back after the hearing, Ruby paused in front of the law firm, her blouse damp and her suit jacket wrinkled over her arm. She tried to rally her energy as she stared at the building. The firm had dark oak double doors in front with an elaborately decorated but quite serious deadbolt lock. A sign, four foot high with a marble facade, proclaimed the name of the law firm: Vincent, Ambruski, Stanley, and Thompson, Professional Association. The VAST, P.A., building itself was two stories, square, uninspired architecturally.

Located a few blocks from the courthouse, the firm's lot fronted a main street in Desoto Cove, Florida and ran deep enough that the back boundary was a road, little more than an alley, through a once grand 1920s neighborhood fallen into ruin and cheap rentals. The lot was overgrown with drooping bougainvilleas and hibiscus. Brazilian Peppers crowded the sides, only partially hiding the yellow stains from the sulfur water splashed on the walls by the sprinkler system.

The building felt like a prison to Ruby. The front doors, though lacking the mechanics of heavy jailhouse doors, seemed to possess the same clanking and locking qualities. Tired as she was from the day and the thick heat, she walked the extra steps around the lot to use the back door.

* * *

From an upstairs window, Nathaniel Thomas Vincent, the firm's founding partner, studied Ruby as she paused outside the front of the building. As he watched her square her shoulders and pick up her briefcase, Nathaniel took in the tightly knotted hair, the long-sleeved white blouse and long gray skirt.

Ninety-five degrees and she's dressed like a nun. *Why's she try to hide her looks?*

"Damn," he muttered, craning his head to follow her until she walked out of his line of vision.

Nathaniel turned back from the window and glared at Nancy, the firm's office manager and head bookkeeper. A tiny woman with spiked black hair, she stood in front of his desk and squinted her narrow eyes at him.

"I got your attention now?"

He nodded.

"Somebody pried open the locked box in my desk last night and stole $235 out of our petty cash."

"Oh, hell," Nathaniel said, more upset at the odd look of satisfaction on Nancy's face than the theft. "You have any idea who did it?"

"Yeah. One of my girls saw, but she won't tell anybody but me. Afraid she'll get fired, given the current mood of you partners. And you won't like it."

Nathaniel hadn't liked much about the law firm this last year and a couple hundred bucks constituted more irritation than injury when they were losing thousands. "Tell me."

Nancy stood rock still, her arms crossed in front of her chest, but her eyes never wavered off Nathaniel's. He remembered what she'd said when Gardner hired her: "I'm as mean and smart as any of you." That was the closest she'd come to saying anything personal to him.

"Come on," he said. "Tell me."

"Jacob. Jacob Stanley."

Nathaniel shook his head. "You know what that man takes home. You cut the checks yourself. Why'd he steal from petty cash?"

Her eyes narrowed further until they were tiny slits. "It goes up his nose."

Nathaniel knew the rumors, but he wasn't going to discuss them with Nancy. "You bring me those month-end totals today, before you leave the office for the night."

"Firm didn't make its expenses. Again." Nancy turned her back on him and walked out, but she left his door standing wide open.

He shut the door and stood behind it for a moment as he ran his hand through his thick, white hair. *What's next?* The firm trusted its finances to a woman who never smiled and flunked her CPA exam four times before she quit trying. And now she was hiding the pea in the shell before anyone even knew they were playing that game.

***

Ruby sat across from Gardner and kept her chin up, looking over his head toward the big plate glass window. He sat straight-backed in his damn red leather chair like he was royalty. And waiting for her to bow down.

Don't let him do this to you.

"You listening to me, or what? Here," Gardner spun a file across his desk toward Ruby.

She caught it just before it slid off on the floor and held it a moment without looking at it.

"Read it, okay. Then we talk."

Ruby skimmed the complaint and attached exhibits. "This doctor did a hysterectomy on a pregnant woman and you want me to defend him?" The band of pressure around her forehead tightened. She wanted more aspirin, but wouldn't let him see her take them.

"Damn it, Gardner. I'm your wife. You're supposed to be on my side."

"I am. There's plenty of righteous billing in that file and nobody expects you to actually win, okay?" Behind his oak desk, Gardner leaned back while Ruby flipped the pages, frowning.

"Let's settle it." Ruby shut the file. "I'd say their demand for the malpractice policy limits is about right."

"Come on, Ruby, you know how it works. Do the discovery. Make sure the plaintiffs aren't coke heads or child molesters, something the jury wouldn't swallow. Get the doc's side of it. Then if nothing defendable turns up, we settle."

"No. I can't handle a new case right now."

"You just finished the wounded beauty queen case, okay? Your billable hours are down, not to mention your actual money-in figures. You need this case."

Ruby slid the file across Gardner's desk at him. "I need to get home before dark."

"Why? It's not like you cook or anything."

"Give it to Tally. You're always bragging on her billable hours, so let her bilk it."

"Her billables are way over your numbers. That's why I'm giving this file to you. If you want to beat her out for being the first girl partner this year, you need to catch up by the annual meeting in December. Come on, it's easy billing. Just discovery work. You're not actually going to try it."

"No. I'm not taking the hysterectomy case. It needs to be settled, quickly, before the plaintiffs' attorney gets ideas of grandeur."

"Ruby, take the damn case. Work the discovery. Wife, or not, you're the associate and I'm the partner. Get it?"

Ruby rose out of her chair, went to the large window in Gardner's front, ground-floor office and looked out at the firm's sign. Outside, a redbird flitted in the yellow hibiscus framing Gardner's window. Through the glass and concrete, she could hear the bird singing.

Ruby turned from the window and without looking back at him picked up the file.

"And, Rue, hon, don't settle it till I tell you to."

Son of a bitch. You watch me.

Chapter Two: The Real Prison

After a three-hour drive to the Union Correctional Institute in Starke, Ruby stood in the visitors' reception area signing forms. Already weary, she eased into the line of Saturday visitors waiting to cross through the metal detector under the watchful eyes of the guards. Once through, she trailed a guard into a large room, took a chair at a table and waited.

Billy came in a few minutes later, thin, pale, shadows under his eyes, but erect as ever. He still looked like an athlete and she admired that about him, that he stayed in shape.

He sat at the table, looked her in the eyes, and asked, "What?"

When Ruby made small talk, some gossip, a lot of sports stuff, he didn't respond, but he kept his eyes right on her.

Ruby reached across the table and took one of Billy's hands and kissed it, turned it palm up and cupped it against her face. He pulled his hand away.

"You let me lose you," she said in a half whisper.

"Man, don't pass it off on me."

"If I'd had any idea how it would have gone, I'd have—."

Billy cut her off. "Do we gotta run over this every time you see me? You took care of your own ass, okay?"

Ruby put her hands into the loose pockets of her pants to quiet them and looked down, away from Billy. Neither of them spoke or moved and Ruby figured she might as well leave. But then Billy reached across the table between them and took a handful of her long hair, held it up to the light and let it fall, strand by strand.

Lifting her hands out of her pockets, Ruby turned back to Billy. "I'll get away from him, just wait. You'll be out by Christmas, if not sooner. We'll work something out."

"Man, it's gotta be lights out for him. He knows how you tried to grubstake yourself. Difference here, both of us know. But I don't hang it over your head. Hell, I liked you for it. Gardner, see, you roll over wrong one morning in bed and he don't like it, then your ass is history." Billy leaned toward her, his face as close to Ruby's as the table would let him.

"I can get away from him," she said, feeling a little breathless. "Something's going on. I don't know what yet, but I will. He won't turn me in. There's the attorney-client privilege he'd have to get around."

"Rot with him." Billy jerked away from her so forcefully the table jumped and made a loud clank on the floor.

"You don't mean it. You know you don't." Ruby reached out and took his hand again, kissed the palm. Warily watching the guard glaring at them, she took Billy's index finger in her mouth and stroked it with her lips. She stopped when the guard rushed toward her. "You remember, don't you? Time was you'd have done anything for me."

He hooted, a half snort, half laugh. "It's not the ticket anymore. Besides, it ain't real to you now."

She left quickly after that.

Outside, eager to leave the prison and shake off Billy's anger, Ruby inhaled deeply. Poorly aimed sprinklers had left puddles of water collected on the parking lot asphalt. Steam rose off the puddles and the lot smelled like sulphur, but that was better than the sick-sweet smell of nervous sweat and the ineffective Lysol of the visiting room. Ruby kept her head down as she walked across the sweltering lot, dodging sad-faced strangers heading toward cars or the bus stop.

He was right. She didn't feel that energy between them anymore. Ruby could remember lying awake at night, her jaws aching with the effort of not saying Billy's name, her skin raw and itchy with the absence of his touch. But that was years ago. Now, her visits were habit. That and obligation. Fifteen years was a long time for nothing more than visits across a table in a guarded room. She owed Billy and she'd have to help him, but he need never touch her again as far as she was concerned.

Chapter Three: The River and Hank

On the drive back to Desoto Cove from Union Correctional, Ruby pulled off Clay Gully Road into a clearing by the Myakka River. An old haunt for her, the spot was usually deserted. She parked her car in the shade and walked down to the river, moving among the cypress and live oaks, dodging the green triangles of poison ivy, until the banks cleared into a coarse beach on the tea brown river. Gnats gathered around her face along with mosquitoes gearing up for dusk.

Ruby walked, her head down, studying the patterns in the sand, seeing dog tracks and people's foot prints. Honeysuckle, fooled by the shade and the cool of the river, bloomed past its season. Inhaling its scent, Ruby calmed down.

When she heard someone moving along the shore's edge toward her, she turned, studying a man as he approached her. Jeans, T-shirt, baseball cap. He was picking up stuff as he walked, his movements efficient and quick like a young man, hands moving, dumping beer cans and crumpled plastic into what looked like a busted Styrofoam cooler. The sunlight flitted off the water and through the trees, making his skin variegated shades of brown and tan. He looked up and saw Ruby.

He nodded at her, then bent down to dig out something rusty from the dirt, which he threw in the cooler with the rest of the mess.

When he was a few feet away from her, he put down the trash and rubbed his hands on his jeans. They studied each other for a moment.

"People are pigs," he said, and picked up the cooler with one hand and an empty Big Gulp plastic cup with the other.

"Yes, they are." She began picking up the trash around her, moving toward him, and dumped a handful of garbage into the cooler in his hand. "But I'm not."

His baseball cap was low on his forehead and his eyes looked black in the shadow of the brim. The hair struggling out from under the cap was graying. Not so young after all.

With his free hand, the man reached toward her face and Ruby jerked back so quickly she almost lost her footing. He moved to steady her, but she found her balance and stepped back.

"Sorry," he said. "Mosquito. On your chin."

Ruby felt the itch begin. Like the bites on her arms, making small welts she knew better than to scratch. She waved her hands across her face and shook her arms.

"That time of day," she said, listening to the buzzing. She wanted to take his cap off and see what color his eyes were in the light.

"My canoe's over there." He pointed. "I got some bug spray, you want some. Cutter's."

Ruby turned back and saw his canoe beached under the overhang of a live oak.

The man walked over to the spot and she followed. He pulled an empty bag out of the bottom of the canoe and shoved the busted Styrofoam and garbage into it. Then he washed his hands off in the river and dried them on his T-shirt.

When he pulled the Cutter's out of a backpack, he sprayed a heavy dose of the liquid on his palms and fingers and approached her, waiting.

Ruby held her bare arms out to him and he rubbed the spray into her skin, moving his hands up and down to her wrists. He ran his hands over hers and she caught him studying her ring finger. She was glad she didn't wear her wedding band when she visited the prison and there was no tell-tell spot on her pale finger to mark its absence.

The man re-sprayed his finger tips with Cutter's and ran them under the edge of the capped sleeves of her shirt. He dabbed a bit of the bug repellant from his fingers at the pulse points in her neck, as if he were putting perfume on her.

Ruby's skin practically sang from the man's touch as warmth spread through her. She arched her back and moved closer to him. The insides of his hands were coarse, like a workman's, but he moved them gently on her skin so that the sensation was both rough and soft.

"Don't know about putting it on your face," he said, and offered her the can.

She shook her head. "Thank you."

"You canoe?"

Ruby nodded.

"My truck's down at the next landing. Couple miles by river. I stopped here when I saw that crap of a cooler jammed in a root. Guess I got carried away picking up the trash."

Ruby waited.

"You want, you can canoe down with me. I'll carry you back here in my truck."

She hesitated, glancing back at her car to calculate the distance and time to get inside and lock the doors. "How do I know you're not a Ted Bundy?"

"Same way I know you're not a Lizzy Borden."

"I don't seem to have an ax, do I?"

"No, ma'am, you don't." He grinned, looking almost like a boy. A boy with a Saturday stubble and graying hair.

But the ma'am got her. *You just know sometimes.* He would be tender and she was starved for something gentle.

Ruby walked to the canoe, stepped carefully over a cooler in its center and sat down in the front. He guided the canoe off the bank and the narrow boat lurched as it took to the river. Treading through the shallow water, he stepped into the back and shoved off, steering the canoe toward the center of the Myakka. She picked up the extra paddle and dipped it into the water, feeling the tug of the river against it. She was glad they were canoeing against the current. The short trip would be slow.

Overhead, the clouds picked up pinks and purples from the reflected sunset and darkened about them. She paddled with a steady pull of the oar against the current, feeling the muscles in her arms stretched and used. She held her back straight and imagined the man watching her.

They didn't speak. Over the quiet of the river, the notes of the bronze bull frogs sounded like the plucked strings of a banjo. As she listened, other night noises echoed around them and the light began leaving the day.

At the landing, he stepped out of the canoe a few feet from shore and pulled it onto the sand. Ruby watched the flex and bunch of his muscles as he tugged the canoe safely past any drift. She stepped out and, without being asked, gathered up his backpack and the bag of garbage he'd collected.

She dropped the backpack by a truck, assuming it his and carried the garbage to a trash can by a dock. By then, he'd brought up his cooler and loaded it into the back of the truck.

Together they carried the canoe to the rack on top of the truck and he tied it down.

He opened the cooler and offered her a beer.

Ruby wanted something stronger, but didn't ask, shaking her head on the beer.

"Water, then?" He offered an old-fashion canteen toward her and she took it.

The water was tepid and against its blandness, she could taste a hint of whiskey. He must have carried straight whiskey in it the last trip, she thought, and wished she had some now.

He held the passenger door open for her and she stepped into his truck. As he crawled into the driver's side, he pulled his hat off, shaking out a full head of hair. He drove back to her car without speaking. She couldn't make out his eyes in the dark inside the truck.

When he parked beside her car, she sat in the cab for what began to feel like a long time.

"Don't make me be the first to ask," she said.

He reached over and took her hand, held it a minute in his own, and then lifted her hand to his lips and kissed the inside tips of her fingers.

"Hank," he said, putting her hand down in his lap, keeping his fingers on top of hers. "I hang out some at Bull Feathers. Probably be there later tonight."

Ruby knew the place. She leaned over Hank in the front of his truck and kissed him, opened mouth. He pulled her hand up to his chest and they pressed together as well as they could in the cramped cab. Ruby wondered if she still smelled of the prison, or if the Cutter's had worn it off her. Hank smelled of sun and the river.

When he moved her hand down to his belt buckle, she pulled back from him.

Only a suicide would have unprotected sex with a stranger in a truck by the river, though she pressed her hand against his fly and felt the temptation play on her skin where his hands had touched her.

"Ruby." Taking her hand back, she got out of the truck and into her own car, and drove home.

***

Gardner put his thumb between his eyebrows and kept it there as if to smooth the furrow. The bar was crowded. Tonight there was a band and as Gardner rubbed his eyes, the dance floor seemed to dissolve into the wet circles on the table. Nothing was fresh and the bar was no cooler than the night outside. Though he had given up smoking years before, Gardner borrowed a Marlboro from the bartender. Half-way through he was dizzy, nauseous from it and ground out his cigarette until he completely flattened even the filtered end. He didn't like this place and he was too old for the crowd. A New College hang-out, with music he couldn't stand and girls with spiked hair and black lipstick. *Who the hell did they think they'd attract with that?* He eyed one woman, hardly more than a teenager, with safety pins in her ears.

Creepy bar.

But Tally was right. Nobody from work would see them here and they could dance. Though the music sounded like grinding gears and dying animals, he could at least hear a primitive beat in it.

He and the kid next to him talked sports and the heat, while the kid looked over Gardner's head, checking the crowd. Gardner knew Tally arrived when the kid stared toward the door and said, "Oh, wow."

"Well, here's my date." Gardner wanted to brag, hey, kid, look, an old man like me, forty-five, and I still got it, as Tally moved toward him.

Tally, the law firm's only other woman associate besides Ruby, bent over him, all but hiding his face with her dark hair as she kissed him on the mouth. Not shy or subtle one bit. He liked that, even if the bitch did think his wife was just a little speed bump in her way.

"Don't talk. Dance," she whispered, pulling him toward the make-shift dance floor and draping herself over him.

Gardner was furious because Ruby had gone to Starke that morning to see Billy. Served Ruby right if he didn't come home till late tonight. See what Tally had to offer besides those volleyballs on her chest. He rubbed against her, close enough now to smell her make-up.

***

Feeling grimy from the prison, Ruby stood in the hot shower of her own house until the water ran cool against her skin. She was relieved that Gardner wasn't home, but she didn't want to be alone. Turning the shower off, she dried and wandered into the bedroom. She switched on the radio and Whitney Houston's "How Will I know?" blared out.

She poured herself a shot of vodka from a bottle on the top of her vanity and stood naked in front of her closet, sipping it. She thought of Hank. Of his hands. His jeans. That something about him which promised he'd move her.

Finishing the drink, Ruby dressed in tight, white jeans and a red silk T-shirt, no bra. She turned sideways, looking at herself in the mirror.

Too obvious.

After pulling off the silk T, Ruby turned back to the mirror and studied the ruby pendant around her neck. Classic, simple, elegant. She'd cried when Billy gave it to her, cried at its beauty and because it was his goodbye gift. He was being sent half way around the world the next day, to a jungle where people he didn't know would try to kill him.

Ruby had worn the necklace every day since then. Even Gardner liked it. When she told him her father gave it to her before he died, he'd believed her and understood why it was the one possession that she'd been able to hang on to, something she hadn't pawned or lost during the bad years.

But that was a long time ago and Billy seemed to hate her now. Ruby remembered his face at the prison, ugly in the way he looked at her. She walked over to the jewelry box, unclasped the necklace, and dropped it in among the things Gardner gave her over the years, other stuff she didn't wear or much want.

She was done being sentimental about Billy. Besides, there was this new guy, Hank, waiting for her at Bull Feathers.

Ruby put on a linen camp shirt with carefully placed pockets and a looser fit, and kicked the red silk T aside as too trashy without the bra. *Just 'cause you started out trailer trash didn't mean you had to stay that way.* But she kept the tight, white jeans on, tucking the shirt in, checking out her butt in the mirror. *Yeah, in a Bull Feathers crowd, that'd catch some stares.*

Then thinking about Bull Feathers, a downtown bar and a place lawyers liked, she wondered if she should go. She'd been surprised when Hank said he hung out there. He wasn't a lawyer, that much she knew, and she considered the risks of meeting him there. Gardner might even be at Bull Feathers, or some other lawyer who'd know her and would spread tales. Going there wasn't a smart move.

But she sipped another mouthful of Absolut, slipped into her sandals, and headed out. She hopped into her car, a ridiculous sporty thing Gardner talked her into buying, and drove the causeway back into town in record time.

Ruby took a stool at the bar and ordered her drink. Absolut vodka. A double. She looked around, saw Hank sitting in the back, made sure he saw her, picked up her drink, and sipped. Quick service. She appreciated that.

The vodka hit her empty stomach with jarring precision. Just as she'd wanted it to. Hank ambled up and took the seat next to her. The bartender put a glass of water in front of him and raised an eyebrow. Ruby caught the nod Hank gave him. *A regular.*

Ruby hung her head down a minute, trying to inhale enough air to clear her mind. When she gulped a mouthful of air, she got enough second-hand smoke to make her cough. Hank pushed his untouched glass of water toward her and she drank it until her coughing stopped. When the bartender brought Hank's drink, Ruby ordered another one for herself. A caution light flared in her brain, but she drank her vodka until the warning shut down.

"I'm a lawyer." She braced for a negative come back.

"Yeah, you got that real smart girl look to you." He smiled when he said it.

"So what do you do?"

"I'm a cop."

She snickered. "Well, that about balances it out, doesn't it?"

"Yeah." He laughed too. "Nobody likes either one of us."

Ruby focused on him. *No use being bashful now.* A used face and a strong one, but etched with fatigue. In the artificial light of the bar, she could see his eyes were a dark brown.

"You from here? I mean originally?" he asked.

"No, nobody is. I came here from Louisiana. Not New Orleans, but a place you've never heard of. Bogalusa. But at least I'm not from Ohio."

"Me neither. I mean I'm not from here. Or Ohio." He eased in closer to her, almost touching her. "That's the whole trouble with this city. Nobody's from here. Everybody treats it like one giant hotel room."

Ruby smiled up at Hank. Clever. He was trying to impress her. She liked that. Still, she hated the way they were talking, like people meeting in a bar, picking each other up. This was different, something they'd already started on the Myakka River. The bartender put another drink down for Hank and looked at her. She shook her head. Maybe she should have eaten something before the vodka.

Hank swallowed part of his drink fast, touching her now with his body as he crowded against her. "How long you been a lawyer?"

Damn it, they were past this stage.

"You ask me what my sign is and I'm out of here."

He finished his drink. Ruby let him pay for both of them, and they left. She followed him to his place in her own car.

Ruby took no note of the house, just followed Hank in, right straight to the bedroom, no more chatter or pretense.

Hank slipped her clothes off her while they stood. When she was naked, he sat her on the edge of his bed, and undressed for her with the same sure, deliberate movements she remembered from the canoe. He moved like he enjoyed having her watch him taking his clothes off, like he was proud of his body.

When he was naked, he touched her shoulder, and she lay back on the bed, catching a pillow under her head, and closing her thighs against the warmth she felt, letting it happen, but slowing it down.

She'd known at the river he would understand how to touch her. The unease she'd sensed in him at the bar was gone. She recognized by the way he moved and handled her that he trusted his hands, his tongue, his cock, his own instincts. He was tender with his touches, and as that gentleness flowed over her body, she appreciated how he was careful to reassure her. This would be how he communicated with her, then. With his body.

Trust me, his hands and tongue said, I won't hurt you.

That's what Ruby thought anyway.

A little dizzy from the vodka, and tired from the day, she was passive under him. Letting him lead, letting him find what pleased her most, she opened herself to him. He nudged, and licked, and stroked at the edges, not missing anything, not even the backs of her knees or the sensitive skin on the insides of her upper arms. She could feel his control, how he waited for her, how he gauged her responses, until he began to use his fingers in a wet, silky stroke and she could no longer be passive. He pulled his fingers away and let her cool for a moment while he slipped a condom on. She sat up and took over, unrolling it down the full length of him with her lips, then using her mouth on his chest, biting his nipples.

They stopped being gentle.

Afterwards, he held her, running his hands over her hair, her face. Ruby curled into the crook of his body, closed her eyes, and reminded herself not to fall asleep.

She made it home fifteen minutes before Gardner did, but had enough time to shower again.

Chapter Four: Choosing Up Sides

Gardner slammed his briefcase down by the end table and watched to see if Ruby flinched. "Hell of a Monday, huh?"

"Don't know, kind of productive for me." Ruby fingered her drink and grinned at Gardner as if to bate him.

"Yeah, I bet. Real damn cute, settling that hysterectomy case against my orders. What'd it take after I said not to, a whole three days to work it out?"

"Less."

Ruby straightened up from slouching on the leather couch he'd bought as part of his renovation of their bay-front home near St. Anne's Circle, an expensive shoal of land nestled on east Coral Key and connected to the Desoto Cove mainland by the traffic-stalled Hernando Causeway. The two sliding glass doors between the outside and the den were open, letting in the night's damp, fishy heat, diffused and prevalent as mildew.

He shut the doors. "You have something against air conditioning?"

"Policy limits. That's what we settled for. Insurance company agreed right off, glad to get out of it. Plaintiffs' attorney was the one who had to be convinced." Ruby sipped Absolut vodka with one hand and rubbed her temples with the other. "Wanted to look at the doc's personal assets, like he wouldn't know how to set it up, make himself judgment proof."

"You think if you drank less, maybe your head wouldn't hurt so much?"

"You think you left me the hell alone, it wouldn't hurt?"

Sitting down beside her, Gardner put his hand on her thigh. She was still wearing her high-necked, sleeveless navy dress from work. He rubbed his fingers on the fabric stretched across her leg. When she pushed his hand off, he leaned back and studied her.

Her long hair hung in disarray around her face with wavy strands down her back, giving her a wild look. Something he'd loved when she was eighteen—that wild hair and feral look she'd get in her eyes. But she was almost 35. Time to cut the hair. Yet he had to admit that except for some lines around her eyes and a sharpness about her cheeks, Ruby looked like the skinny girl that came into his Tampa office fifteen years ago, needing more than his legal help. That first day he saw she was beautiful and within days he learned she was smart. And cunning. As he knew her better, he realized her native intelligence was a match for his own and this excited him. She had needed him and respected him. Intoxicating, that's what she'd been to him then, what she still was.

Gardner reached up and touched her bare arm as she brought her glass to her mouth.

At his touch, Ruby put her drink down. "You're up to something, aren't you?"

Gardner grinned. "So you've been paying attention."

"All that time in bookkeeping, all those computer printouts Nancy only makes for you. That night we stopped over at her house and you made me wait in the car. Yeah, I've been paying attention. What are you up to?"

"Rue, I'm taking over the firm."

"It's Nathaniel's firm, always has been, always will be."

"Like hell. You wait till the year-end partnership meeting."

"So how're you doing this hijacking?"

Hijacking. Yeah, he liked that term. Toss old Nathaniel out of the way and he was going to win it all, the firm and Ruby back on his side. He rubbed his fingers over her leg and inched up, wondering if she wore panties.

"I asked you, how're you going to do this?"

"It involves numbers, Rue. You'd never get it."

"Nathaniel'll stomp you, whatever you're planning."

"Damn you." Gardner yanked his hand off her leg and picked up her glass, slamming it across the porch and shattering it against a pot of peace lilies. "Stop saying that man's name in my house."

Breathing heavy and feeling heat in his face, Gardner watched Ruby get up and walk into the bedroom off the den. He followed her as she opened her jewelry box, took out a bottle of pills and downed two yellow Valium. Then she went to the pantry, got the broom and began to clean up the broken glass on the porch.

"Leave it for the maid, will you? We've got other things to talk about."

Ruby swept the broken glass into the dustpan. When she knelt to sweep up the last shards, the ends of her long hair brushed the floor.

"Damn it, do something with your hair. Now."

"Go to hell."

Gardner ducked as she flung the broken glass from the dustpan at him and went back to the bedroom.

He sat for a moment, thought of her body, sleek and muscled from the swimming and the gym, and her pale skin, smooth and cool under his hands. He'd been wondering all day what, if anything, she'd worn under that damn high-necked dress. He pushed off the couch and poured himself a drink. He'd give the Valium time to kick in. Then he'd make her forget that damn Nathaniel.

***

By the time Ruby stepped out of her shower, the Valium and vodka had worked their magic and the muscles at the back of her neck were easing up. After she tossed on a nightgown, she decided it was late enough to go to bed and slipped under the cover.

But before Ruby turned out the light, she listened for Gardner and wondered if he were prowling around in the house, or if he'd left while she was in the shower. Finally, she decided she didn't care and switched the light off.

The dark must have been his invitation, as soon enough the bedroom door opened and he headed toward her.

He pulled a candle out of the nightstand and lit it. Ruby almost laughed. He wanted to be romantic, after all the trash between them?

"Let's do something new, something you've never done before," he said, his voice low, husky, baiting.

There was something tempting about this. The vodka and the Valium played with her a little, made her forget for a moment who Gardner really was, the man she now knew him to be. There in the soft light off the candle, he looked like the man she thought she had married.

"Come on," he said. "Must be something you've never done before."

There were a lot of things Ruby hadn't done, but she said the first one that came into her mind. "I've never done a threesome."

Gardner sat down on the bed, put two of his thick fingers on her bottom lip and pressed down softly, pulling her mouth open.

Oh, that. Easy. Though hardly new. But she took his fingers into her wet mouth, reminding him she knew what to do with her tongue.

"There's nobody else here," he said and pulled his fingers free of her. "So that threesome is out."

Her lips still parted, Ruby began to move her head down to his crotch, but he stopped her, pushed her back on to her pillow. She wasn't scared. Instead, she was intrigued. On the bedside stand, the candle flickered, showing off shadows on the wall as she studied her husband's face. After all, she once thought she loved him.

But she didn't reach for him again. Instead, she propped herself up on her pillow and waited for him to make his next move.

"Good girl." He slid over on top of her, pressing her down into the bed as he cupped his hands under her hips. Sliding his fingers under her nightgown till he touched bare skin, he moved his hands, slowly, but firmly across her ass. Ruby lifted her hips from the bed, just enough to give him room to work. He kept staring right into her eyes and she couldn't look away or shut her eyes. His look was daring her, or mocking her, and she couldn't tell which. But she felt him, those strong hands, stroking her buttocks, pulling her apart, and, with those long fingers, he began probing. Still, she wasn't scared. Already little ripples of sensation danced through her body. She reached for one of his hands and tried to pull it from under her toward her breast. But he didn't let her move his hand.

"No, I told you. I want something nobody else has ever had from you. Something you never gave old Nathaniel."

Ruby tensed, finally registering the anger simmering in him, ready to strike her. She raised her arms to push him off.

"Not tonight, Rue. I told you, something new, something just for me."

And for a second longer, despite the fingers pulling at her ass, she didn't know what he meant. By the time she did, it was too late to stop him.

***

40

Nathaniel looked past the three men gathered around his desk to a portrait of General Patton, the old eagled-eyed genius himself. He looked back at the men. Friday night, and none of them wanted to be here. He didn't want to be here himself, but Nathaniel had summoned the other three named partners to a meeting after the building emptied out. Studying them now, he felt the first fear he could remember since the bullets ripped across his arm on that damned Omaha beach. He rubbed the scars he always kept hidden with long sleeves.

He wasn't going down again.

Nathaniel glanced at Jacob Stanley by the window and remembered what Nancy said about him stealing petty cash for cocaine. Jacob was acting more fidgety than normal, with his long strands of hair wiry about his sharp face and his shirt tail half-out, white flakes of dried spittle collecting in the corners of his mouth. Nathaniel could smell his aftershave across the room. Turning away from Jacob, Nathaniel looked at the other two men huddled in his cluttered office.

This is what they were now, in the recession of 1987. Going broke. Tired, getting old, and outnumbered, him and the three men he had respected enough to pull around him when he started his own law firm after years of working in a four-story Miami firm: Jacob Stanley, Fred Ambruski, and Dave Thompson. Fred, Nathaniel's first partner, looked coarse and worn out. Fred had aged past the point he would ever want to lead the firm if Nathaniel stepped down as chairman.

Dave Thompson, the youngest of them and once the heir apparent to Nathaniel's chairmanship of the professional association, slouched vacantly in a chair across from Fred. Jacob, sniffed, then wiped his nose and grumbled away from the window, narrowly avoiding the files littered about the floor.

"Gardner's a manipulative bastard and we've got to handle him." Nathaniel regretted recruiting Gardner out of a Tampa law firm after they tried a case together and he'd respected Gardner's persuasive skills with the jury. He remembered how they'd negotiated the terms over Gardner's kitchen table. When Ruby came in, needing help with her college homework, Gardner stopped everything, left Nathaniel sitting there, while he worked Ruby through a calculus problem.

Son of a bitch had sure changed, or maybe Nathaniel just read him wrong from the beginning.

For a second, maybe two, Nathaniel let his shoulders slump, then he straightened up. "I never realized how slick and dirty Gardner is. Guess I'm slipping in my old age." Nathaniel took his glasses off and rubbed the bridge of his nose where the heavy lenses made it sore. "Used to admire the bastard. Till it was my ox he was goring."

"He's got all the younger partners lined up against us, you know?" Jacob spoke fast and dodged a briefcase in his path. "Calling us the four old farts and blaming us for the revenue being down and the overhead up. They'll vote their pocket books at the December meeting."

"I'll be damned if I'm letting Gardner steal this firm from me." Nathaniel paused and looked in turn at Fred, Dave and Jacob. "I mean us."

"Dave?" Nathaniel turned to the younger man.

With what appeared to be a great effort, Dave raised his head a few inches. He had the dazed, somnolent look of a man well into his liquor. But Nathaniel knew Dave had not been drinking.

"What are you worried about?" Dave asked. "It's your firm."

"If they stick together and vote unanimously on the one man, one vote items, they can out-vote us," Nathaniel said, hating that he was saying the obvious to Dave. That was the system. Everything straight majority rule except two issues, forcing out a partner or revising the shareholders' agreement. Those they voted the number of shares they owned.

"Pie's only so big. Told you not to let in any more junior partners," Jacob said, skidding to a stop in front of Nathaniel.

"They'll never vote together. You know that," Fred said. "You can't get those guys to agree on anything, not donuts or bagels. Remember the ruckus over whether to fire all the law clerks when we couldn't make payroll?"

"It's different now. Gardner's got them by the short hairs. They'll vote how he tells them to," Nathaniel said. "Only thing saving the four of us, to terminate a partner, we vote the shares we own. We kept enough shares to block theirs, even if they vote to a man to kick us out."

"Plus," Dave said, "the shareholders' agreement requires them to buy back our shares. They can't afford to vote us out right now."

"Holy shit, Dave, wake up, will you? That's the point," Jacob said. "You don't think they'll have the stock re-valued? They can do that on a one-man, one-vote majority. That's right in the agreement. What do you think a CPA will say a share in a privately held corporation is worth when it's one credit line from bankruptcy?"

That was the beauty of it, what Gardner was doing. *Bring the firm to the edge of insolvency and kick us out for pennies on the dollar. If Gardner could turn one of the four of us, that is.*

"The building alone is worth —" Dave said.

Nathaniel cut him off before Dave embarrassed himself further. "This building is mortgaged beyond its value. I've put up most of my own assets to guarantee the last loans, even my wife's house on Sanibel." Nathaniel saw the point didn't sink in, but he knew Dave didn't get it because he didn't care, not because Dave wasn't smart enough.

"What are you going to do?" Fred rubbed his wedding ring and stared at Nathaniel. The "you" wasn't lost on Nathaniel.

"We're going to stick together, the four of us. Can't stop the five junior partners on the day-to-day votes if they can agree, but if we four all vote our shares together, they can't kick us out." He waited, letting everyone think on that. He knew they understood Gardner wanted to kick him and Dave out, but that Fred and Jacob could hang on a few more years. Maybe. Yet if Nathaniel and Dave went, Fred and Jacob wouldn't have the shares to stop the others from booting them out whenever they wanted to do so.

"I want to know where the hell the money went. I've been billing twenty-hour days for years," Jacob shouted and glared at Dave.

"It's the recession," Dave said.

"It's more than the recession," Fred said.

"You are going to stand with me, aren't you?" Nathaniel asked. "You and Jacob and Fred?"

Dave nodded a barely perceptible nod, then lowered his head again.

Fred coughed as he exhaled a mouthful of cigarette smoke and grunted.

"Sure," Jacob said, but he didn't let his eyes meet Nathaniel's.

"We done?" Fred started to get up.

"Yeah, I am," Jacob said. "I got a hot date waiting."

Nathaniel watched them get up and leave, practically ignoring him like he was just background noise to them.

***

The Friday night happy hour crowd milled about, though thinning, when Ruby stepped into Bull Feathers. Taking a seat at the bar, she caught the bartender's eye and then fished around in her purse until she found a plastic bottle of aspirin. Struggling with the child-proof top, she said, "Vodka Gimlet. Absolut. No bar brand." She put the bottle down and glared at him. "And I *can* tell the difference." The bartender moved off.

Ruby couldn't get the cap off the damn aspirin. She was trying to pry it off when Hank came up beside her and took the bottle. In one easy motion, he flipped it open and handed it back to her. She put the bottle to her lips and, using the tip of her tongue inside its open neck, counted out two and swallowed without water. She replaced the lid and put the bottle back in her purse. "I was hoping you'd be here tonight."

Hank slid in closer to Ruby, but didn't speak.

The bartender put down her drink and looked at Hank, who nodded.

"Okay, your turn. Talk," she said.

"Hello."

"How are you?"

"Fine."

"Fine? And work?" Damn it, she thought, we're still making bar talk.

"I told you, I don't talk about work."

"Or politics or religion, I suppose. Okay, fine, name your topic." Ruby took a long swallow of her drink and pushed some hair off her face.

"Fishing works okay."

"Fishing? Okay, let's see. What's my best fishing story?" Pulling down the same hair she'd just pushed behind an ear, Ruby covered the edge of her face, half hiding one eye, Veronica Lake style. "Ever been tarpon fishing out of Boca on one of those charter boat deals?"

"No, have you?"

"Of course. My law firm provides only the finest in client and judicial entertainment. A few of us took Judge Garcia out tarpon fishing two summers back. All-day boat complete with guide and stocked coolers. All we had to do was show up and wear sunscreen."

"Catch one?"

"No, I took a hit of Dramamine before we left and Judge Garcia and I split a six-pack before we even got out past the reef. I went to sleep. Woke up with my head in his lap just as we were coming back in. Old judge had a sheepish expression. Ever since he's treated me like I'm his favorite girlfriend."

Hank laughed, but didn't speak.

"So what's your best fish story?"

Hank thought for a moment, then lifted both arms up, spread his hands as far apart as they could go with his arms straight out. "This big, bigger. Got away."

Ruby grinned, the drink easing her nervousness just enough.

Hank chugged his drink like a frat boy starting a binge.

"Where are you from?" Ruby figured that was safe enough to ask.

"South Carolina. The mountains, up past Greenville, a place called Pickens."

Mountains. Ruby sighed before she could stop herself. She used to want to live in the mountains. She thought of her grandmother living at the edge of the Smokey Mountains in Tennessee and how the visits had stopped, but her missing the woman had not.

"Let's start meeting someplace else, okay?" She stood up. "Shall we get out of here?"

***

With one hand moving down his chest, one hand pushing up from his shoulders, Ruby straddled him with her thighs. She lowered herself to rub against his chest, the coarse hair damp and rough against her breasts as she pressed into Hank.

Her hands moved constantly, making no distinction between touching him and touching herself as she dissolved into him. The muscles in her legs quivered with tension. She felt as if she were evaporating, existing for only an instant as thin air blowing on his chest.

Afterwards, Hank slept. Ruby touched first her own arms, legs, then his. She slid away from him, rolling into separateness. She ran her hands down the space on the bed between them, delineating between him and her and the space that was neither.

Ruby stood up, facing the dark air inside the bedroom and thought of the files back on her desk. Of Gardner. Then, she thought of the mountains. Going there again. Once past Tampa, the drive would be a matter of cruise control and endurance.

Stay. Go. Either way, it's just a matter of endurance.

She looked back at Hank, sleeping on the bed curled up sideways, his dark hair framing his face on the white pillow.

He might be a cop, but he was a sweet man. For a moment before she dressed to leave, she wondered if there was anyway they might last together.

Chapter Five: The River and a Gun

Long. That's what Ruby looked like to Hank the first time he'd seen her on the Myakka. Long legs, long arms, long body, long hair. Coming toward him with that long stride, and later, carrying her weight without him having to ask. That night they first got together, when she hopped out of his bed, slapping on her clothes in a hurry, he thought, damn, married. He'd intended to stop it there. Now here he was, five weeks into it, breaking his rule about married women. He hadn't meant to get attached.

Thinking about her long legs, Hank watched Ruby drive into his yard, pulling her car out of sight behind a shed. Hiding it, he knew, and he thought of the vagueness and dodges of their relationship. He'd made himself not snoop, not ask, didn't pick up a phone book. Just let it be, he told himself. Whoever the husband was, he was out of the picture today.

He hugged her when Ruby came up to him, then kissed the tops of her ears and started to pull her into the house. But she shook loose of him.

"Got my hat," she said, "and my sunscreen. You promised me the beach on the river."

"Yeah. Okay." Hank wondered if she were already getting bored with his bedroom. "Got your bathing suit?"

"Don't need one." She laughed like a kid on a dare.

Hank laughed back, pitched a cooler into the bed of the truck, and they crawled into the cab of his pick-up. They rode without speaking. The morning was warm and would get warmer and Hank cut his eyes over to look at Ruby. She was wearing old jeans, faded to light blue, and a sleeveless cotton shirt. The tops of her shoulders were freckled. Hank covertly studied a scar across the top of her right shoulder, the visible part descending an inch or two under the shirt. That had been a nasty cut and though he'd seen it before, he hadn't asked about it.

Half an hour outside of Desoto Cove, he found the dirt road to what he thought of as his own beach on the Myakka River. It wasn't his, of course, and technically he was trespassing. But no one ever challenged him and he rarely spotted other people at the abandoned landing. An old dock collapsed at the edge of the water, fringed by live oaks and sabal palms. This time of day, the bugs would be light. He wished he could take Ruby camping over night or even up in the mountains.

The last night they were together, when Ruby had rolled out of his bed, he tried to pull her back to him, but she resisted and dressed. But after leaving his bedroom, she came back in and whispered, "I'm getting real fond of you." Then she turned and left in a hurry.

Real fond of you. Ditto.

Maybe more. Hard to say. And though he hadn't said anything back to her, he thought about it, wondered if she was opening some kind of door to something more between them. Like a relationship. Going out in public. Maybe talking about something more than the next time they'd be able to get together.

Could be, he'd say something to her about that today. He'd wait and see how things went. Both of them stared ahead as his truck bumped down the dirt road and neither spoke. Finally, the road ended at the landing, he parked and they both jumped out of the cab. He winked at her.

Before she winked back, Hank was already taking off his shirt. He liked the way sun felt on his bare skin. And truth be told, he liked showing off all that weight lifting. "Is your sunscreen waterproof?"

49

Ruby giggled, with that kid-quality he rarely saw in her blooming right out there under the full sun. She had her shirt off by the time he slipped out of his jeans.

"I'd like to have a photo of you. Naked, all right?" She giggled again.

"Don't have anything like that."

"Well, then, we'll get one."

That, and the way she was studying him, made him suddenly self-conscious. He reached over and unzipped her jeans, pushing them down some on her hips and tickling her belly with his fingers, feeling the flat, muscled strength there. When she let him, nothing coy about her, he ran his fingers low down on her stomach and circled, not too low, but good enough to get her thinking about it. Then he stepped back to let her finish undressing.

Ruby ran into the water first, splashing and swimming out to the center before floating, her face up to the sun and her hair drifting out behind her like a chestnut-colored veil on the river. Hank watched her, saw her flip over, caught the pale globes of her buttocks as she arched and dove under the water. He swam parallel to the shore, waiting for her to come back toward him in the shallower water. When she surfaced in front of him, he caught her, kissed her mouth and then her breasts, tasting the river silt on them.

The water made her buoyant and she pushed up on him until her legs wrapped around his hips and were opened to him. He slipped into her, forgetting the condoms in the bottom of the cooler and feeling the tight warm hold she had on him.

The drift of the river rocked them slowly against each other. Ruby rose and fell with the crest of the current, bobbing against him in the warm waters of the Myakka, gently and effortlessly. To stay afloat he had to tread water with his legs and that added to the bouncing motion of the river and their bodies. He didn't thrust, but let the current and her own strong legs work together for the friction he needed.

Ruby held one arm around him and with the other she circled her palm flat down in the river, also treading water. Hank took his arms from around her and she clung, so he paddled a few feet deeper in the river, where the added buoyancy made her feel weightless against him. He began to thrust his hips, pushing deeper into her. She met him with her own rhythm, building tension as the water made slap, slap noises when their stomachs hit. He forgot to tread water and they sunk into the tea brown river and came up, splashing and laughing, but still joined together.

***

After spending most of Saturday in his office and sniffing around in bookkeeping, Nathaniel came home, his spent energy reforming into anger as he thought about the jumbled numbers on the endless sheets of paper he'd reviewed. He slipped into his jogging shorts and shoes and stretched, breathing into the pulls. Even in the heat, he wore long sleeves, as if covering the damage on his arm made it hurt less.

Jogging into the late afternoon sun, Nathaniel felt the first burning in his lungs, but he knew it would pass. The scars from D-day ached as he pumped his arms and ran. He wasn't going down again.

Not just because some son of a bitch like Gardner Randolph had a talent for accounting and lies.

Not just because Dave, once his heir apparent, was still depressed over the death of his wife, a stupid water skiing accident over a year ago. She'd almost made it, hung on a few days in ICU, long enough to give them all hope. Long enough to extract a promise from Nathaniel that he would take care of Dave.

Having promised Dave's wife, he had to look out for him, even though Dave wasn't able to take over the firm. Anymore than Fred or Jacob could.

Nathaniel struggled for breath and reminded himself out loud: *I'm not going down again.* Not just because Fred was too old and didn't care, and Jacob a petty little coke head.

What made him choose these men for his partners? He hardly remembered anymore, not when the bigger question was what to do about Gardner and the law firm? His law firm. His. Not Gardner's.

Physically shaking his head as he ran, Nathaniel tried to throw off his worry. Inhaling the damp warm air was easier. Entering his second mile, his breathing steady and sure, knowing it would be easy until the fifth mile, Nathaniel knew the other lawyers joked about this, too—a skinny old man jogging five miles in the summer heat. Wait until their bodies turned on them. Wait till they woke up one morning with pot guts, their wives and old friends these strange people who couldn't remember where they left their glasses and their co-workers stealing the merits of their lives' works.

Even with the weight of bad decisions, Nathaniel could not ignore the beauty of the coming dusk. Mist rose off the bay, a visual humidity that softened his focus and hardened his breathing. The Florida sun in its westward spin lit the mist, depositing a glittering light on the trees and grass. Somebody's dog barked at the coming dark. He could smell the dinners being cooked from the houses rimming the path.

He had to come up with a way to strike back and soon. But he didn't want Ruby hurt in the fight. She was the Catch-22 in the whole damn mess. Her touch was the only pleasant memory from last July's firm retreat, where they spent money they didn't have, then fired all the law clerks at the retreat's mid-year meeting. Yet, before the blood-letting, the two of them walked on the beach at night, touching like old, dear friends. Ruby, holding his hand and telling him that everything she knew about being a trial attorney, she learned from him.

Not lovers anymore and that was all right. His decision. He was too old for her. He had a wife, Lena, that he loved and Ruby had a husband that she didn't love but was resolved to stay with for reasons Nathaniel couldn't understand. So, that was that.

What an odd dance he'd had with Ruby, from mentor to lover to friend. The first time he'd seen her, she was a skinny kid who needed Gardner's help with her calculus homework. Gardner put her through college and law school and then married her. Right after she graduated from law school, she started working with the firm and was assigned to Nathaniel as his associate. The first time she asked, he told her everything he knew about the practice of law.

When she started working with him, Ruby hadn't caught his eye. He didn't even think she was that pretty. Too tall, thin and angular. Too edgy. And, he tried to honor Lena and his wedding vows. But on a trip to the federal court in Atlanta, too hyped up to sleep before the hearing the next morning, they'd gone for a drink in the hotel bar. There'd been a band and people were dancing. They had their drink, got up and danced.

Later, he thought it was the way she slid, totally absorbed into the music, that pulled him to her, fluid and graceful in a way she was not ordinarily. Or maybe it was just the chance of being alone in another city with a young woman not his wife.

Ruby turned him down. Politely, even with humor, but with firmness. Nathaniel was relieved and undaunted. But the next time he had a trial in Miami, he took her along as second chair and asked her again. This time she said yes. The affair lasted for nearly a year, but his remorse, a raw kind of shame, bit at him. Nathaniel broke it off.

And, afterwards, somewhere along the line they'd become friends. Real friends.

Her husband was another matter. Why hadn't he left Gardner in that Tampa law firm when he saw how ambitious the man was, demanding an early partnership, angling for position right from the first. Then when Gardner found out about Nathaniel and Ruby, he started gunning for Nathaniel, even though by then the affair was over. Now maybe Gardner finally had him.

Imaging the shame of being voted out of his own firm, Nathaniel's heart pounded loudly and sweat stung his eyes. The burning in his lungs was bad now. It took all his concentration and will power to finish out the last half of the fifth mile. One more yard, and then just one more.

***

Ruby and Hank lulled on the beach as the sun began to cool. A mosquito landed on Ruby's arm and she rose from the blanket to slap at it.

"Cutters," Hank said, his voice low and drowsy. "Glove compartment."

Without saying anything, she jumped up and went to his truck. A few weeks ago, he'd have gallantly gotten the bug repellant and brought it to her. A little shift, but she noticed it. When she opened the glove compartment, a snub-nosed .38 was half-hidden under a pile of papers. She pulled the gun out first, then tucked the Cutters in her pocket.

Feeling the beer now more than the sun, she spun around with the .38 in her hand, eyeing various things and finally coming to rest on a "No Trespassing" sign nailed high on the bark of a tree. Lazily she swung the gun one handedly toward the sign. "Think I can hit it?"

Hank grunted.

"Seriously, I'll bet you. If I hit the sign, you owe me another trip to the river. If I put a bullet through the O, you owe me a trip to the river and a bottle of Bushmill's Irish Whiskey. Gift-wrapped."

"Put the gun down." Hank finally sounded awake. "It's not a toy."

"I know that."

He pulled himself up to a sitting position. "I mean it, guns and beer, bad match. Put it back in the truck." He sounded just a bit pissed off, which only egged Ruby on.

She inhaled, held her breath, and took slow, steady aim. As her finger tightened on the trigger, she kept herself still. And fired.

The bullet hit the sign, nicking the side of the O. A sudden flurry of birds squawking as they flushed from the trees nearly drowned out the echo of the shot.

"Damnit. Put it back." Hank jumped up, heading toward her.

She laughed. "Okay, you owe me another trip to the river and half a bottle of Bushmill's."

Chapter Six: Trapped

Ruby slept late the next morning, waking finally and groggily chasing the smell of coffee into the kitchen.

Gardner rose from the table to fix her a cup with milk and sugar. Placing it before her, he asked, "How do you feel?"

"Fine." Her arms were sunburned and stung like hell.

"Good, we need to talk."

After they drained the pot of coffee, they rose and went to the screened porch, where Ruby stretched out on the wicker chaise lounge. The lounge was positioned at an angle sideways along the wall and the pool, with only a narrowing triangle-shaped space between it and the back wall. A matching chair faced it. Gardner perched on the edge of the chair.

"How are your arms?"

"Fine." Wary, Ruby watched Gardner. He studied her back. Then he smiled at her, a soft, slow, big one, curling up his narrow lips and making laugh lines spring up around his eyes—the kind of smile that used to work on her.

"I'm not even going to ask how you got sunburned or where you were all day yesterday."

Ruby kept her mouth shut, but her heart thrummed out of sync in her chest. What had she been thinking anyway, a whole day with Hank.

"We're going to start over, you and me. We'll make this work." He leaned toward her.

Ruby made an inarticulate noise.

"You'll stop with whoever this is. It can't mean anything." Gardner dropped the smile and his voice was flat. "I know it wasn't Nathaniel, anyway. He was camped up in bookkeeping. I saw him myself."

Ruby said nothing, tensing her body, preparing.

"I don't want to know about this new guy." Gardner's voice rose, with a sharper edge. "Don't tell me anything. But from right now, it's over. Understood? You and me, we're going to get back together."

"Why bother, Gardner? Really? Tell me that, huh?"

"I told you, Rue, you and me. We'll be like we were when we first got married. Do you understand? We'll go away someplace. I can't get away from the firm right now, but we'll go soon. After Christmas. Someplace cold and romantic where we can snuggle in front of a fire. Just the two of us."

"It's too late for that."

"No. You'll see." Gardner slid from the chair to kneel beside the chaise lounge and put his right hand lightly on her sunburned arm. "Do you remember? What we were like in the beginning?"

Against her will, she remembered. She loved him then or at least thought she had. In those days, she hadn't started being afraid of him yet.

"Yeah. Sure. I remember, Gardner." She touched the side of his face, sorry they had screwed it up. "But it's too late." She dropped her fingers.

"It's not too late. I still love you."

"No, you don't."

Gardner's hand moved an inch down her arm, resting over a spot of blisters from the sun.

Ruby inhaled against the discomfort of his hand on the burn, but told herself to be quiet, not to piss him off. But she was tired of all this and couldn't hold her tongue. "I don't know what a psychologist would call it, but it's not love. Possession. Control, maybe. Obsession. But not love."

Gardner squeezed his hand around her arm, twisting and rubbing against the sunburn. Ruby gasped at the sudden pain as she pulled her arm away. When he did not reach for her again, she rolled as far away from him as she could on the lounge. He stood up and tensed.

Ruby swung her legs over on the side of the lounge opposite of Gardner and rose, placing her back to him and her face to the wall, cornered in the little spot of space between the wall and the lounge. She bent down a moment, breathing hard until the pain in her arm eased. Then she turned to face him, the wicker lounge between them. Squaring her shoulders and looking him in the eyes, she said, "I intend to be done with you. It's over. I'm leaving."

"Like hell, you will."

"I'm moving out. You keep the house. I don't care. And I'm quitting that damn law firm."

Trapped between the chaise lounge and the wall, she could either stand there or crawl over the lounge directly in front of Gardner. Unable to figure out where to go, Ruby froze with her back to the wall. With his right foot, Gardner began pushing the lounge toward her, forcing her to take a step back toward the wall in the narrowing triangle of space.

"I'm leaving you. Do you understand that?" She made her voice firm, though her breath was coming fast and shallow.

Kicking, Gardner slammed the chaise lounge against her legs hard and quick. The metal reinforcement bar along the edge crashed into both her legs right below her knees and Ruby cried out. She crumpled, penned against the wall, collapsing at her waist over the lounge. After gulping air, she struggled to stand up and pushed the lounge away from her with both her hands. Red welts stood out on her legs as she took a few small steps from the wall. Ruby shoved the lounge further away until she could walk around it, skirting Gardner by a few inches. "You just wait, I'll get away from—."

"Just in case you or that deranged Billy get any bright ideas, you should know I put it all down in writing. And I made copies of that tape of Billy, put them in a safe place. A little insurance."

Ruby closed her eyes against Gardner's face and his voice. So, he'd kept the tape after all, backing it up with a writing. Of course, why not? He put everything in writing. A man famous for his memoranda to files, his CYA letters, and file notes.

Damn. How could they have been so stupid as to trust him? Their lawyer, all his talk about attorney-client privilege, sacred as the confessions to a priest, inviolate, he said, encouraging them to talk. She and Billy believed him. And spilled their guts.

She remembered what her mother told her once: God pays you back for being stupid.

For years, she'd wondered whether it was an implied threat or real. He'd drag himself into it if he used what he had against her and Billy. Tape or not, he'd have to find away around the statutory attorney-client privilege and The Florida Bar ethical rules that protected a client's confidential information. But she'd been around the justice system long enough to know privileges could be and often were broken during legal proceedings.

Still, getting away might be worth calling his bluff.

"You'd get your own ass in trouble too, Gardner. Like I said, I'm leaving."

He laughed, a sudden rude sound. Then he winked at her in an almost coy gesture that made her stomach roil. "You forget, I know where the skeleton in the closet is. Or in the orange grove, that is."

Her heart pounded so violently she was dizzy as she realized he'd risk his own career to destroy her if she left him.

Yet, whatever trouble Gardner might end up in for breaching a confidential client disclosure could be nothing compared to what might happen to her. And Billy.

Not Billy. Not again. After fifteen years in jail, he was finally due out around Christmas. Prison overcrowding practically guaranteed his release this time if Gardner didn't play that tape for the wrong ears.

"You wouldn't dare." But her voice sounded feeble even to her own ears.

"Try me."

Ruby looked over the top of Gardner's head, surprised how bright it was outside of the porch. For a stunned moment, she studied the play of a few bees about the rich fuchsia flowers of the bougainvillea outside the screen. Nearby a lawn mower roared. Two mockingbirds lit near each other in a grapefruit tree a few feet outside the screened porch. The water in the pool looked cold and blue and smelled of chlorine.

Ruby closed her eyes and wondered if she could talk a doctor into a prescription for some narcotic painkillers for her arms. It was worth a phone call.

***

Ruby would have left Gardner the next Monday and gone to Hank, except for Billy and what that tape could do to him. Maybe Hank could help. But how could she ask him to step into her mess? When he called her at work, she told him to leave her alone and not to call her again. Not yet, anyway, she said, softening her voice. She'd be in touch she promised, not wanting to cut him off, but knowing he would be a danger and a distraction to her now.

Putting Hank aside, Ruby concentrated as the days passed and she and Gardner fell back into a guarded routine. She determined she'd decipher what was happening at the law firm and quickly. Living within her truce of habit with Gardner, she watched her husband, shadowing him in the firm, listening to the talk in the hallway, trying to figure out exactly what he was doing. Paying closer attention, eavesdropping, asking seemingly simple questions, stealing computer printouts from the partners when she could.

Ruby started putting it together.

It was about the money. The ebb and flow of the firm's income. The way it nearly stopped, started again, then slowed to a trickle, barely enough to keep the doors of the firm open.

When Ruby looked hard at the paper work, it wasn't difficult to see the history. The once steady cash flow at the firm ceased in the spring, then the partners fired the law clerks, a few associates, and several secretaries in July. After the mass firings and the highly motivated billings of the remaining attorneys, the financial situation eased up. Confidence among the attorneys returned. But now, in the early fall, inexplicably, the income crashed down to the point of crisis. When cash reserves were so low paychecks for the partners wouldn't clear, they agreed to work without pay. For the time being. Until the crisis passed and the money rolled in again.

The rumblings about money, like the tension in the hallways and offices, kept up its steady pace. Everybody had a theory, Ruby learned, and everybody blamed somebody else. Another secretary left. One of the assistant bookkeepers just didn't come in one day and hung up the phone when Nathaniel called her. Two of the associates left for law firms down the road. The younger partners huddled in groups which formed and reformed with differing alliances depending on the day. Fred and Jacob stayed in their offices, their doors shut.

Nathaniel skulked about the firm he had created. Ruby recognized they were avoiding each other, though she did not know exactly why. Dave was a cloud that moved between them all, a damp mist that hung in the air and dissipated when touched.

But now that Ruby knew about that strange ebb and flow of the money, she was confident she could find the counter-blackmail and her way out.

Chapter Seven: Hitting the Snake on the Head

The best way out of a burning building was to hold your breath, protect your eyes, and run straight through the flames for the door.

Ruby wasn't at all sure that was true, but she remembered Billy once telling her that.

Her brother also told her that if she saw a venomous snake, hit it on the head with something hard and get the hell away from it.

She wasn't sure that was true either.

But putting both pieces of advice together made her decide the best way to find out what was going on with the cash flow was to march right into the bookkeeping department and confront the fire.

She walked into the large, upstairs' room, ignoring the raised heads and puzzled stares of some of the women, and marched straight toward the head bookkeeper. Ruby towered over Nancy, who hunched over her keyboard and refused to look up. The other women bent back over mysterious columns of numbers on their computers, keeping their eyes to themselves.

"I'm afraid I just don't understand my month-end billing report," Ruby said, trying to sound friendly. "And I was hoping you could help me."

Nancy typed more numbers on her screen, then stopped and looked up at Ruby. "So it's my responsibility that you didn't take any accounting courses in school? I'm supposed to drop what I'm doing and teach you the basic principles?" She went back to typing.

"No, I just need to understand this report."

Nancy's fingers slowed over the keyboard, but she didn't speak.

After what felt like an interminable pause, Ruby bent down to the wall and put her hand on the electrical plug. Yeah, she knew every department had fourteen kinds of backup, but it'd still be a pain in the butt to restart and recover whatever Nancy was doing.

"Snatch that out and you'll never see another dime in your account." Nancy stopped typing and glared.

"So glad you have a moment to chat after all. This doesn't make sense." With that, Ruby flashed her monthly statement from bookkeeping in Nancy's face.

"Look," Nancy said, taking the report from Ruby, "This is all you need to know. Here's your money-in column, okay. That's the money your clients have paid that's been credited to you. Here's the firm average for the month for associates and for partners. You're below the firm average for both. That's what you need to worry about. Okay. Now go."

"No, I told you. This doesn't make sense. I added up my billing summaries from my time sheets and I billed out nearly twice this amount."

"So some of your clients didn't pay yet. Big deal. Happens all the time."

"Then I need a report that tells me which clients paid and which didn't. I can nudge the ones who didn't pay to cough it up."

Nancy handed the report back to her. "Look, I'm robbing Peter to pay Paul so this firm can pay its power bills and open its doors every morning. I haven't got time for your crap. Go away."

"It's not crap. If the clients aren't paying, then I'll call them myself. I just need to know which ones. We used to get that information every month."

"Yeah and it took me and my girls a lot of extra time to produce it and nobody looked at it. So now we don't give it to the associates. The

partners have it. Go run to Gardner and see if he'll show it to you."
Nancy went back to typing. Overhead, the muted sounds of a Frank
Sinatra song, barely audible over the hum of computers, drifted out of
the loudspeakers.

Giving up on Nancy, Ruby left the bookkeeping department. Next,
she might as well run straight to the snake. In another minute, she
walked past Gardner's secretary without speaking and pushed open his
office door.

"Gardner, I need to see your month-end reports on my bills. I want
to see why I'm billing out twice what shows up as my money coming
in." Ruby stood in the doorway of his office.

"Come in and shut the door," Gardner said. "And hello to you too."

'Hello." It occurred to Ruby they hadn't spoken to each other
today. She couldn't bring herself to flirt, but she did ask, "How are
you today?"

"Fine. You?" He sounded almost friendly.

"Puzzled. About my month-end report. I tried to ask Nancy about
it, but she blew me off."

"Sure and that's a big surprise." Gardner grinned at her.

"The thing is, I added up all the time I've been billing for the last
month. And it's more than twice what Nancy's reports indicate as my
money in. Some of my clients are not paying me and I want to know
which ones."

"Why?"

"What do you mean why? The firm seems to be broke again.
Rumor is Nathaniel's putting up his real property to cover the firm's
debts. Fred had to write a personal check to the court reporter last
week to get a damn transcript. Things were better in August and early
September. October started going down hill and now the money's not

coming in again. If my clients are stiffing me, I want to call them on it."

"Let it alone, will you?"

"That's stupid."

"That's a direct order. Do you understand me?"

"What the hell is going on, Gardner?"

"I told you back in August, you wouldn't understand. It involves numbers and, Rue, face it, you're not a numbers type of girl."

"Try me."

"Look, there's plenty of money or there will be. This is temporary. There's a reason. Just let it alone. Trust me, you'll be protected. In fact, you'll be in better shape than anyone else in this office."

"Except you, of course. People are looking around for other jobs, you know. Debbie and Betty already left. I don't suppose you particularly noticed, but they were great secretaries. And most of the associates are looking."

"Oh, yee of little faith. Let them go. You'll stay."

"Sure, I'll stay. Haven't you convinced me there's no air outside this law firm?"

But she thought, *when pigs fly, you bastard.*

***

Ruby was thrashing through her mail when the receptionist buzzed through on her office phone and said somebody named Hank was insisting he must speak to her, but he wouldn't say what it was about.

Ruby debated, but answered the phone. "I asked you not to call me here."

"Are you okay?"

"I'm fine. Now if there isn't anything else I can do for you, I have work to do."

She imagined Hank absorbing the coldness for a moment before he answered. "Ruby, what's going on?"

"Nothing. Nothing was ever going on. Now, please, it would be best for me if you don't call me again."

Ruby listened to Hank breathe for a long moment before he spoke again. "I'll meet you at the snack bar at Desoto Park. Half hour."

"No."

"See you there."

Desoto Park was on a man-made peninsula, dredged and filled in the curve of the Tamiami Trail as the highway followed the shoreline south. To hell with estuaries, fisheries, rookeries, just pump in some sand, add some concrete, pay someone to plant exotic trees after paying someone else to whack down the native mangroves at the shoreline—that was Desoto Park. Ruby hated that she liked the park so much, environmental injury that it was. But she could be there on foot inside twenty minutes.

She slipped out the back door and started walking.

Once at the park, she bought a cold beer at the snack bar, which also doubled as a rental center for wind surfers, small sailboats, and jet-skies. She twisted off the cap of the beer, waiting.

Mid-afternoon, a hot day in early November, late for the summer folk and early for the pale winter crowds, nobody but the man who ran the snack bar was there. Ruby drank her beer, sitting at a table while three sea gulls squawked and fought over some cold French fries tossed on the ground. When she finished and Hank hadn't appeared, she walked down the sidewalk to the tip of the park, her favorite spot, and sat on a bench and stared out at the boats anchored in the bay.

Ruby thought about Hank, though she tried not to. When this thing with Gardner was all over, when she didn't have to be on-guard, she'd give Hank a call. See what they could work out. But for now, she needed to convince him to back off.

Back off, yeah, that's what she had to make him do. Still, she thought of how he laughed when he swam naked, how he never tried to make her do anything she didn't want to do, how he knew without asking if she needed it gentle or rough.

A few minutes later, he eased in beside her with his sun-on-skin scent.

Though Ruby wanted to kiss him, she didn't. "What do you want from me?"

"I want to know what's going on."

"It's simple, Hank. I need some time, that's all."

"Why do you stay with him?"

This was the first time either of them spoke directly about her husband. "We've been married a long time. I need time to work it out. It's complicated."

"Are you're afraid of him?"

"I'm not afraid of him." Yeah, it wasn't the first lie she'd told and she hoped it was convincing.

"Maybe I can help." Hank took her hand, holding it almost timidly, like a boy on a high school date. He acted like he wanted to say more. She wanted him to say he might love her and he wanted a chance to find out. If he would say that, maybe she'd say it back to him.

But he didn't speak.

Ruby let the sun beat down on them for long enough to feel a hint of sweat start under her shirt. Damn him. She shook off Hank's hand, stood up from the bench, and said, "I don't think you can help. Goodbye, Hank."

***

Ruby stopped in the women's restroom to cool down after her brisk walk back from the park. As soon as she finished splashing her face with cold water, Tally walked in. Ruby nodded, but didn't bother to speak.

Tally hesitated a moment before looking in the other stalls to be sure they were alone. Ruby dried her face with a paper towel and waited. Fred had warned her along time ago that Tally referred to Ruby as "a little speed bump" in her way to being the first woman partner. Well, Tally could have it. Ruby could care less about making partner.

"I want you to know something," Tally said.

"Fine. So tell me."

"I'm having an affair with Gardner."

Ruby crumpled the towel in her hand and tossed it in the waste basket. "Good. Gardner does so hate to be left out of the loop."

Ruby left Tally standing by the sink and hurried down the hall. In a way, Tally's confession made things simpler. Ruby could work it. And, it wasn't like she cared who Gardner was screwing if it kept him off her.

Still, she had to pretend like it mattered, this Tally thing. Put him off guard somehow. She turned the corner in the hallway and pushed open Gardner's door. She hesitated a second, making herself look more upset than she felt, before marching inside his office. He looked up from a pile of papers on his desk. "Do you ever knock?"

"Do you?"

He shoved the papers into a pile and slid them into a drawer and locked it.

"It's been about the perfect day," Ruby said to Gardner. "I wanted to share it with you."

"I hear the traces of sarcasm."

"Oh, yeah, you think?"

"What happened?"

"You want the high points or the long version?"

"Let's have the high points. Save the details until after dinner."

"I suppose the true high point is a toss up. Might it be—" Ruby paused, pursing her lips, checking Gardner's face. "Your girlfriend's confession to me in the lady's room."

Gardner remained immobile.

"Of course, I'd have had to have been brain dead not to have already known. But it's one thing to ignore it when it's some fuzzy little thing out in the distance and another to ignore it when the girlfriend rubs my nose in it."

"It's over. It's been over."

"Yeah, well maybe you better tell Tally. She seems to think it's an active file."

"I will. I'll tell her now. I'll make sure she understands." He stood up behind his desk.

Ruby continued sitting as Gardner passed by her and paused on his way to the door. When he looked at her, she sat eyes downcast, shoulders rounded, head bent, making herself mimic sadness. Let the bastard feel guilty.

"I'm sorry. But you know it didn't mean anything." He rested his hand on her shoulder and it took all her energy not to fling it off. Instead, she made a slight sniffling noise, careful not to overplay the moment.

"It's not like you're in a position to cast the first stone." His fingers pinched her skin before he lifted his hand from her.

"Please just go. End it with her." Saying it like it mattered, like she cared.

Once Gardner was out of sight and hearing, Ruby jumped up and locked his door. If she knew her husband at all, he'd have one more go at it with Tally before he broke it off. That would give her time to explore his office. Carefully, she systematically began searching his office, starting with the locked drawer.

***

Gardner knocked before he stepped into Tally's office, keeping his expression neutral. Tally had already slipped into her jogging shorts and was preparing for a run. She smiled at him, one foot on the edge of a bookcase for balance as she reached one arm over her head and stretched. Gardner watched, admiring the tautness of her body, the muscles in her legs, the way her knit top pulled against her breasts. What he had to say to her could wait a few minutes.

"Business or pleasure?" Tally asked, slowly switching sides, posturing in what he figured she meant as a seductive manner.

"It was business, but maybe I'll change my mind."

"Maybe? Don't sound so hesitant, it's not flattering."

Without waiting for a response, Tally went behind her desk, pulled out a small purse, cupped a wrapped condom in her hand and returned to the front of her desk. Gardner had not moved from his perch by the door, but he studied her, waiting, knowing her routine. She liked to think she was in charge. He had some news for her.

"Lock the door," she said, and he did, biding his time.

Tally pulled off her cropped top and threw it on the couch. The sports bra underneath it strained to its limit, unflatteringly flattening her breasts. She slipped off her jogging shorts and stood in panties and bra. Leaning backwards until the desk supported her at her hips, Tally posed for him.

"Don't just look," she said, sounding a tad petulant.

Gardner moved up to her and, tugging roughly, pulled off her bra. He reached over to kiss one breast and twisted the nipple of the other between his fingers. Pinching hard, he made her gasp and she pulled back suddenly. He let go and looked at the red imprint his fingers had made on her skin.

"Don't be so rough."

"Rough? You stupid slut. You don't know rough."

With one hand, he unzipped his pants. Without undressing and with such speed and force that he caught Tally off guard, he backed her over the desk, his body pressing heavy over hers. After a brief struggle, he managed to pull her panties down. Gardner used his legs and feet like weapons to keep her pinned against the desk.

Tally still clutched the condom she'd gotten from the purse in her desk. She tried to give it to him, but he knocked it from her hand. His face and lips pressed against her, silencing any cries of protest or pain as he pried her legs apart with his knees and hands.

He shoved her further back on the desk and slammed into her before she could act, loving the power. Tally struggled to push him off, but he was too strong. Gardner rammed into her so hard he crushed her against the top of the desk. Something plastic cracked, breaking under her.

When he was done, Gardner pulled out and turned away from Tally as he zipped his pants. When he turned back to her, she was grabbing up clothes and trying to cover herself. She didn't look at him.

"By the way, I didn't appreciate you telling my wife about us. This is just to let you know we're through and I will personally see to it you never make partner in this firm, or any other firm in this town. Since you have no future here, and I guarantee that, you may wish to leave. Two weeks notice isn't necessary."

"You don't mean that."

He wanted to laugh in her face, but he let her talk. Plead, really.

"I care about you, really. You know that. You've got to know that much." Tally finally looked at him, tilting her head so her hair fell over her face.

He didn't say anything and he guessed she took that as encouragement.

"I'm the best associate this firm has."

Gardner liked that little squeak of desperation in her voice.

"I'm the only associate still making you guys money. All the partners know that. They won't let you throw me out. I'll make an excellent partner. But it's you, Gardner, really, I do care about you. That's why I had to tell Ruby. She doesn't want you. I do."

"Sure, and I can buy a real Rolex for a twenty from the guy on the corner."

"Please. I did you a favor in telling Ruby. We're so much alike, you and me, we could be such a great team. We could run this firm. There's so much potential here. Like you've told me, get rid of the deadwood and we'll make a fortune."

Gardner took a step closer to her. "Let me repeat myself as you seemed not to understand. We, you and I, are through. Absolutely. You will make partner over my dead body. In fact, you will remain here as an associate over my dead body."

Tally stood facing him, half-naked, her face flushed and damp. What he'd said must have finally registered with her. "Over your dead body? Damn you."

Gardner watched her stomach and sides heave as Tally fought for control. "Over your dead body," she yelled. "I'll add that to my Christmas wish list, your fucking dead body under my Christmas tree."

***

Ruby couldn't find what she was looking for anywhere in Gardner's office.

"Damn, damn, damn," she said, spinning around as she heard him coming down the hallway. She'd searched Gardner's office, their house, the garage, had called around at storage units and had tried to finagle information out of the banks in case he had a safety deposit box. The banks, and most of the storage units, had stonewalled her, saying that they couldn't give out that kind of information. She'd hadn't found the damn tape. But soon she'd have to take the chance that those carefully organized print-outs and phone memos would cancel out what he'd hidden somewhere.

Gardner opened the door just seconds after she unlocked it. She asked, "All done?"

***

The next morning Gardner left home for the office before Ruby did, as was usually the case. After his car drove off, she packed two suitcases and a small overnighter. She had plenty of cash reserves now, as well as funds transferred late yesterday from some joint accounts to her own, private one. She wore a pair of black jeans, a close-fitting white silk T-shirt, and a pair of dangling earrings she'd favored when younger. Gardner hated the earrings and had thrown them away, but she'd rescued them from the trash. Just green glass and silver, but she liked them.

Once the packing was done, Ruby unlocked the door that opened out from the master bedroom onto the screened porch. She looked out at the fuchsia bougainvilleas pressing against the screen and at the deep pool. The porch had been her favorite part of the house.

She dragged the chaise lounge over to the pool and shoved it in.

Returning to the bedroom, she slipped on sandals and went out to load the car with her luggage. Yesterday at lunch, she'd rented a small furnished apartment on Dolphin Key, delighted it was tacky enough to revolt Gardner and directly across the street from one of the few undeveloped spaces on the beach.

She was half-way to the law firm before she remembered she left the door from the porch into the bedroom standing open. Deciding it hardly mattered, she kept driving.

Entering through the firm's back door, Ruby grabbed an empty box from the mail room. She didn't figure there would be that much to pack and she hoped to be done quickly, but she ran into Nancy in the hallway.

"Packing?"

"Yeah, leaving."

"Bye." Nancy made a little wave with her hand.

Ruby went to her office and caught her secretary riffling through some papers on her desk and didn't even ask what was up.

"Do this for me. Please, type up a list of all my active files, all the necessary information and take the list to Nathaniel. Maybe a second copy to Fred. Can you do that?"

"Yes. I'll have it done by lunch. Should I give a copy of the list to Gardner?"

"No."

Without speaking further, the woman left for her cubbyhole down the hall. Ruby packed and when she finished, she carried the box down the stairs and out to her car. She slipped into the driver's seat and closed the door, but then just sat.

After a moment, she got out and returned to the firm, again slipping in the back, and walked down the corridor to Nathaniel's office. His secretary said he was in a conference with a client and another lawyer. Ruby picked up a note pad off the woman's desk. "Sorry. I'm gone.

Be in touch. Ruby." She wrote quickly, then handed the small pad back to the woman. "Be sure he gets that."

When Ruby came out of the secretary's cubbyhole, she saw Nancy and Gardner coming around the corner, Nancy holding some print-outs and Gardner with a cup of coffee in one hand.

"What's going on here? Why are you dressed like that?" He stepped closer to her.

"I'm leaving. Quitting this firm."

Gardner started laughing. "Rue, hon, you've got your holidays mixed up. Thanksgiving's coming up, not April Fool's."

"I'm not mixed up. I've never been more sure in my life."

Off to the side, Nancy stood her ground, holding the print-outs at her side and listening. Not wanting a scene in front of her, Ruby turned the other way, leading Gardner away from Nancy and toward the library. Once there she ducked into the room, now empty of its former law clerks. Gardner followed, took a sip of his coffee and put it down on the table. "What's all this about?"

"I know what you've been doing. You and Nancy."

"You figured it all out by yourself, Rue?"

"Yes. And so help me, if you cause Billy or me any trouble, I'll explain it all in careful and documented detail to the state attorney and The Florida Bar."

"No, you won't. You don't have that kind of gumption, even if you had the documentation."

"Yes I do. And I'm leaving you. As of right now. We're done."

Gardner grabbed at her arm and Ruby jumped back from him, tensing for the next parry. "Get out of my way."

Gardner launched himself at Ruby, snatching her hair as she tried to dodge and pull away. With a tight, two-fisted hold on her hair, he dragged her a few inches toward the table where a collection of supplies lay scattered about. He grabbed a pair of scissors. As Ruby cried out and thrashed to get away from Gardner's now one-handed hold, he cut at her hair in violent swipes. She kicked and punched at him, grunting with the struggle, but Gardner was too strong for her.

When he flipped her face down against the table, rubbing her face into the debris, choking her, she stopped fighting against him and fought to breathe. Above her, a woman screamed at Gardner to stop and somebody pulled him off her.

At first, Ruby just concentrated on breathing. Then, she pushed herself off the table and turned around to face them all. Glaring about her, she saw Nancy scowl at Gardner before turning away. Tally pressed against the bookshelves, silent, watching and not moving. Fred and Nathaniel held Gardner back. It took both of them to keep him off her.

Son of a bitch, I'll have to kill him for this. Just like Billy said. The only way out.

Kill or be killed. How many times had Billy told her that was the law of the jungle. If you showed mercy or you hesitated on the trigger, they would kill you and they would eat you. Plain and simple.

She snatched up the scissors in her right hand and aimed for him. Then stopped. Gasping for air, she let go of the scissors. And she made herself take the few steps necessary to stand up right, straight and tall, in front of Gardner, who was trying to affect a sneer.

"You sick fuck. You're done blackmailing me, you hear. You're done with me. So help me if you ever touch me again, I'll see you burn in Hell." Ruby spoke softly. Her words were spaced between sharp inhales of air into her lungs.

Gardner broke loose from the two men holding him and lunged toward her. Before he could hurt her again, Nathaniel spun around at him and jabbed him in the jaw, hard. Gardner fell back against Fred, who grabbed Gardner and held him.

Ruby wanted to hit him, or spit in his face, or pick up the scissors again and ram them into his stomach. She also wanted to end the show and hated it that Tally and Nancy were watching this. Yet somehow, she couldn't move.

As Ruby stood frozen, Tally reached out to her. "Come on, let's get out of here. Let's get some ice on your eye."

Tally's voice cut Ruby loose and she backed out of the room. Once in the hallway, she refused to look at anyone and held her head up and retreated down the corridor and out the back door, walking fast, but not running.

"Don't let them see you running when you're running away, babe," Billy had told her once.

"Wear that black-eye like a badge," he'd also said. And she knew from the way it was throbbing, her eye would swell and darken.

Billy was still inside her head, talking, while she tried to unlock her car. Of all the men, it was Fred who jogged up, took her keys and opened the door for her.

"I'll be all right," she told him and made herself look him in the eyes.

"Sure you will. I know that. But do me a favor? Let me drive you to my house, let Danni mother you some?"

Ruby thought about Danni, Fred's wife, for a half second. She liked the woman. A lot. She mixed a hell of a martini and laughed at all the men in the law firm. Even Fred, who she clearly adored.

But Ruby wanted to be alone and shook her head at Fred.

"Let us do that little bit for you," Fred said. "You shouldn't be driving right now."

Ruby was not sure later how Fred finally convinced her to go home with him, but Fred drove her in her car to his house, with Dave following behind. With a court hearing to attend, Fred left Ruby to Danni and to Dave and drove off in Danni's car.

In no time at all, Ruby surrender to the attention and stopped thinking. Made her mind blank. Waited.

Dave paced in the living room while Danni hovered over Ruby, with wet face cloths and ice packs, until finally Danni insisted Ruby needed to rest in bed. Dave drifted into the bedroom with them, even as Ruby repeated that she was all right. Over Ruby's protests, Danni packed her onto the bed on top of a fluffy blue cover.

"Sit," Danni said to Dave and pointed to a chair. "I'm going to make us all some drinks. We could use that, couldn't we?" And without letting them answer, she spun off into the other room.

Ruby sunk down into the bed and stared at Dave, wondering what this ghost man might say or do. This man who had almost dissolved at his wife's death.

But Dave just sat and looked first at Ruby, then at the floor.

Ruby ran her fingers through her hair, pulling out clumps Gardner had cut, but which had tangled with the rest. The discarded ice pack lay on the nightstand. The black eye was impressive. She'd seen that much in the bathroom mirror. A thin cut curled down her cheek on the right side and her chin had a raised, red lump across the center.

"Damn," she said and rolled a clump of hair into a lump and put it by the nightstand.

"Don't worry, you'll bring back the shag, be a trend setter," Dave said.

Ruby was surprised he'd spoken and pushed herself up into a sitting position. "I don't need to be in bed. I'm not hurt."

"Danni's a mother hen type, indulge her, all right?"

"Dave, thank you. You're sweet to come over, but I'm fine. You can go on back to work." He was a decent man, but he had his own problems and he wasn't strong enough to help her.

"I didn't know Gardner was that bad. To you. I'm sorry."

"Don't apologize. He wasn't always. And looking out after me wasn't your job anyway."

Danni brought in a tray with drinks. "I know it's early still and they're strong. I figured we needed them that way."

They drank, not speaking at first.

"Well, damn," Danni said. "Call the police. That's assault. Don't you take that."

"No," Ruby said. "Let it be. It's all right."

"It's not all right," Danni said. "Don't you let him get away with that."

"Gardner won't get away with it. Now let it be, please." Ruby made her voice sound like she meant it and she did. After that, the three of them sat together in the bedroom for an hour, drinking their strong drinks, then another. Finally, Danni agreed that Ruby didn't need to be in bed and they wandered back into the living room. Later, they ate a pieced together lunch on the deck and tried to talk about other things. After lunch, Ruby assured Dave she was fine. This time he agreed to go. She walked him out.

"There's something ugly going on at the firm, Dave. You watch yourself, all right?"

Dave nodded, his expression grim. "I never thought I'd live to see lawyers acting like they do now."

"Nathaniel says it's the eighties, that the times have made us all greedy cheats. All that Wall Street cheating going on and the recession. No moral compass."

"Maybe. I remember when a lawyers' word in Desoto Cove was good, any lawyer's word. We all knew each other. A handshake was binding. Lawyers like Gardner would never have prospered in a good firm." Dave gazed up at the sun and squinted against its glare. "I never thought I'd feel so obsolete so quick or get so old so soon."

Ruby didn't know what to say, so she didn't say anything.

"I apologize." He lowered his head inch by inch until he looked her in the face. "You're the one in trouble and I'm feeling sorry for myself."

"It's allowed, Dave, really. You've been through a lot. And I'm not in trouble, not anymore."

He nodded, looking like he might ask a question, but Ruby didn't want any questions about her or Gardner. "Besides, being a lawyer wasn't what I thought it would be either," she said.

"Well, I guess we all start out thinking we'll be Atticus Finch, saving the world one down-trodden person at a time."

"Yeah, lofty ideals of helping people. Thing is, I was talking with Gardner once about getting into some other kind of law, maybe Legal Services or environmental work, and I brought up Atticus. Know what he said?"

"Something spiritually uplifting, I'm sure."

Ruby snickered. "Right. He said Atticus lost his case and his client got killed."

"So much for the *To Kill a Mockingbird* theory of the practice of law."

"Yeah, well, Gardner might have been technically correct about Atticus, but he'd missed the point."

"Typical lawyer, then, I'd say."

Ruby thought about Nathaniel then, what Gardner might do to him if he didn't have her to vent his rage on. Wondered if Gardner could pull it off, drive Nathaniel out of his own firm, punish Nathaniel because of those times she'd been with him as his lover. Against her will, she remembered for the briefest of seconds how they had been physically as lovers. Quick, furtive, not at all satisfying. She'd only been with Nathaniel out of some misplaced respect and curiosity, never out of any burning desire. Or maybe because she wanted his love, his help, his approval, and thought that was what she'd had to do to earn his favor. Now she could see that was wrong, that Nathaniel's friendship came without a *quid pro quo* attached.

If she had it to do over again, she'd have kept saying *no*. But if she had it to do over again, that would be way down the list of things she would not have done.

Still, Nathaniel was her friend. Her best friend. Maybe the only one worth having that she still could claim.

"Dave, Nathaniel needs you. Gardner is out to destroy him, me too now, I guess. But if you help Nathaniel, you can stop him. Nathaniel may be the power in this firm, but you're its soul. That's why Gardner hates you, because you kept your moral compass. Because everybody respected you. Pull yourself together. Please. It would kill Nathaniel to lose this firm."

It was a pretty speech. About the best she could do at the moment. But what she'd said was true. She hoped Dave hadn't registered the past tense on respect.

Dave sighed and looked away. When he turned back to her, he wore such a harrowing look on his face that she took his hand. "Oh, Dave, I'm sorry."

"No, you are perfectly correct. Absolutely. I will help Nathaniel. We're a team. Nathaniel deserves better than this from me."

Ruby felt solemn though a bit tipsy and squinted in the strong light, staring at Dave. A long strand of his straight, fine hair hung in his face. Ruby pushed the hair back with her fingers, tucking it behind an ear. What a sweet, gentle face this man had. Smart and kind, but maybe not tough. Well, Nathaniel was tough enough for all of them.

"Get back in there, okay?" She gave Dave a gentle shove.

"Okay. You'll be safe here. I'm sure Fred will be home as soon as he's done with his hearing. Please call me if you need anything. If you just want to talk."

"I'm fine. If you can believe it, I feel better than I have in years."

Dave pulled Ruby into a hug, but let her go almost at once. "Don't worry. I'll figure something out. There's a way to stop Gardner and I'll find it."

Chapter Eight: Billy and Gardner

Billy Dittwilder, two days out of Union Correctional in Starke, rode the Trolley from downtown Desoto Cove to St. Anne's Circle, the famous shopping enclave of the rich and touristy. He had a map and a scribbled address. From the Circle, he made the short walk to Ruby and Gardner's house in no time at all.

Studying the neighboring homes, Billy got a sense of the place before he ambled around their house, trying the doors. The thing about locks was that there was usually a way through or around them. He studied the doors and nodded to himself. These were good deadbolts, no question, but once he got the right tools, he'd be able to get in. He didn't want to risk it in broad open daylight. But didn't hurt to look before he came back at night.

In the backyard, he saw a chaise lounge floating in the pool inside the screened porch. He half laughed, half snorted, at the floating lounge until he saw a door from the porch into the house was standing wide open. Breaking into the porch was easy. Even a kid could slide open the latch on a screened door like that.

The opened door led into the master bedroom. For a moment, Billy stood in the doorway looking at the big room with its unmade king-size bed and expensive furniture. He took in every detail of lushness, of comfort and space. So, this was how they lived. *Damn them both to hell and back.* Sleeping in a bedroom that looked straight out of a magazine, while he was over in Starke making weapons out of stolen kitchenware.

The room was a mess with clothes thrown around in odd piles. He went to Ruby's jewelry box first, studied the empty pill bottles, and riffled through the jewelry itself.

Yeah, damn, there it was. The ruby pendant he'd given Ruby right before he shipped off to Vietnam. She made a point of wearing it when she visited him in prison, but he'd been wondering for over a decade if she still wore it all the time.

Or just when she saw him.

Well, now he had an answer to that.

Two-faced bitch. He dropped the pendant back in the box. If she didn't want it, he didn't want it either.

Billy tossed himself on their bed, rolled around on it, and rubbed his head on their pillows, like he was a cat marking its territory. Then he stood up, shook himself, and drifted about the room a bit.

Done with the bedroom, Billy went into the den, pausing to fix himself a drink of straight vodka from the bar. When he finished the drink, he slung the last drops out over the pearl gray carpet and put the glass right back where he'd found it. To hell with fingerprints. *This time they'll never catch me.* He had a plan. He'd had a long time to work it out.

Billy wandered into the kitchen and opened drawers, looking, planning. The third drawer had keys on a ring. He took the key ring and tried each one on the back door until he found the one that opened it. Taking just that key, he carefully returned the others to the drawer.

***

Hank lay on his weight lifter's bench in his shed, finishing up a set and lowering the weights slowly, exhaling with the effort. He put the weights in their stand over his chest and took a minute to wipe the sweat off his face. It was November at night and still 80 degrees.

Autumn in Desoto Cove was nothing more than a barely perceptible lessening of the heat, a small drop in the humidity. No red and gold leaves. No cold mornings to make Hank feel that altogether common sweet sadness at the change of seasons. He had to pay careful attention to even notice the transition. Sometimes the only signs were traces of color coming into the hard, green oranges on the trees in his backyard and a steady influx of Michigan and Canadian cars, clogging U.S. 41, an early seasonal harbinger of the winter flood of snowbirds turning off I-75 at the three Cove exits, straining the patience of the year-round residents.

It would be dead winter before it felt like fall to him. By then the town would be so choked with the snowbirds that some locals avoided the restaurants and traveled mostly in their necessary circles, sitting with a siege-victim mentality in their homes while the roads were stalled with people from the cold climates who seemed not to know how to drive in the South.

One more set, he told himself, though without a spotter he had already pushed himself past the point of safety. He didn't like what he was thinking about this Gardner fellow. After seeing Ruby at Desoto Park, he'd done a bit of digging. Didn't like it at all.

Chapter Nine: The Dead Man in the Bedroom

Ruby pulled into the driveway, not knowing what else to do. Two marked police cars, an ambulance, and a black Chevrolet were parked in front of her and Gardner's house. As her head and heart both pounded, Ruby wished she hadn't had that extra swig out of Danni's Absolut bottle before coming home to pick up a few things. Friday afternoon and Gardner was supposed to be at the office. No one should be at the house.

When she got out of her car, a uniformed police officer started walking toward her and stopped half-way down the walk way. Ruby stopped too.

"You Mrs. Randolph?"

"Yes."

"Please wait here a minute," he said.

"What for? It's my house. You can't, you—"

"Just stay put, okay? Right there." The cop hurried away and Ruby stood, dread spreading through her.

A moment later, a tall, graying man, slumping slightly and walking as if he might be in pain, came out the door. He hastily took off some white rubber gloves and shoved them into his pocket, frowning as he moved toward her. Ruby stood mute, a numbness that had begun in her face began to work its way down her body.

"Mrs. Randolph, I'm Hank Rider, detective, Desoto Cove P.D." Hank reached into a pocket on the inside of his jacket, pulled out his badge and held it up, one handedly.

Ruby ignored the badge. She couldn't believe he was staring into her face with no obvious sign of recognition. Pretending before the other police officers that he didn't know her. He did not offer Ruby his hand as he took in her bruised face, his own expression grim.

"Damn you." She said it so quietly that the other officers couldn't hear her, but Hank heard. Anger flooded her with strength again. She pushed past him. Though she knew he could have stopped her, he merely turned and followed her into the house.

Hearing people speaking and moving about in the main bedroom, Ruby ran toward it, Hank right behind her. She pushed at the bedroom door, but before she could open it, Hank took her arm with one hand and with the other held the door partly shut. She could feel a kind of a tremble in his hand as it tightened around her arm.

"Come back to the living room with me."

"What's going on?" Her voice was soft and her anger suddenly gone. Unable not to, she felt herself reduced to a small child again in the hallway of the emergency room, a man in a white jacket coming toward her, his footsteps in suspended motion, her mother crying behind the approaching man. Ruby fought down the gall rising at the back of her mouth. Even before he was killed, her father used to teach her brother and her: "Never show them your weakness." Get in control, she commanded herself. Breathe. Get through this.

"I'm sorry to inform you, Mrs. Randolph, but I have bad news about your husband. Would you come back to the living room with me, sit down, and let me tell you about it."

"I want to see him."

"No, ma'am, I don't think you do."

Ruby wrenched his hand off her arm, shook herself, and opened the door. She saw at once that the police had been there for some time. Someone had wrapped a sheet about Gardner, possibly for decency, or probably to preserve any trace evidence of fibers or hair or such. Who ever had draped him had let the edges of the cloth fall over his face. His hands, though, were placed over the sheet and already bagged. A large circle of blood stained the fabric and a mass of red and pale yellow liquid spread out on the floor under him. The room smelled of urine and the sickening smell of something worse.

Beyond her attempt at control, Ruby made a sudden, sharp but inarticulate cry. Another detective put a hand, still wearing the standard issue white gloves, out in front of her in the classic pose for stop. "We're investigating, ma'am, you can't touch anything. Please. The medical examiner's wagon is on its way. You best leave now. You'll have a chance to identify him later."

Ruby ignored him and stepped around the body till she stood at the top of Gardner's head, where she knelt on her knees. But when she started to lift the sheet off Gardner's face, the other detective reached to stop her. "Please, ma'am, you shouldn't touch anything."

Ruby looked back at Hank and saw him waving his hand quietly, signaling the other man to back off. Ruby lifted the sheet.

The face under the sheet didn't look like Gardner. It was flat, pale, weak jawed, with cheeks somehow collapsing into themselves. Vacant. For a moment, Ruby saw the animated Gardner's face flash over this dead thing, obscuring the putty mask on the floor.

Gardner's face, lively, alive, talking. Kinetic, ringing with energy even in sleep. That undercurrent of rage humming in him, keeping him on the move. Alive, his eyes had held everyone, engaged them, tricked them, bullied them. But now though his eyes were open, they were empty and blank. His lips were twisted as if in pain, but even behind the grimace, he looked dull, weak, already cold. Utterly gone.

Ruby rocked forwards on her knees, dropping her head till it was nearly resting her on her thighs as she knelt on the floor. As she leaned downward, the ends of the long, open-weave sweater vest she wore draped outward on the floor, blotting up Gardner's blood. The wet, red stain crept up in the cotton fibers of her vest. Ruby was suddenly hot. Without really thinking, she slipped the vest off and it fell into the circle of blood, soaking up even more.

Still kneeling by Gardner, she put her index finger in the center of his forehead. Then she traced her finger down his nose, down his upper lip, and rested it on his full bottom lip. Inhaling sharply, she said, "Damn you, Gardner. Now what?"

Chapter Ten: Interrogation

In a shabby room at the police station, Ruby ran her fingers through the condensation on a cold can of some sort of soda. When she tried to drink from the can, she gagged. The other detective sat across from her. Neither spoke. Outside the door she could hear Nathaniel and Hank speaking in muffled tones. Had she the energy, she might have been able to pick up some words and make sense of the discussion, but she didn't bother to try. She wanted to put her head down and sleep. She tried to drink again but couldn't seem to swallow. Sputtering, she reached for the tissues on the table to wipe her mouth.

"Could I get you something else, ma'am, perhaps some plain water?"

"You asked me that before, didn't you? Someone did."

"Yes'm, it was me, but you didn't answer."

"No," she said, shaking her head. "This is fine. I'm sorry, what was your name again?"

"Luther Downs. Detective."

"Detective Downs, Luther." She repeated it in a flat voice. Earlier, this man had gotten her to agree to something that sounded like an atomic test, but wasn't. Neutron something. Just a few swabs of her hands to test for any barium and antimony, traces of elements which might tell them if she'd recently fired a gun. Before that, Hank read Ruby her rights, though both he and Luther repeated that she was not being charged. But she heard the word "yet" hanging in the air. Reading her rights was just a careful precaution on their part, technically perhaps not necessary, but not a bad idea when they wanted to test her hands for traces of gun powder. She'd learned that much from Gardner's criminal defense practice.

Even as the technician was swabbing her hands, Ruby knew she should have refused, should have called a lawyer, but she was functioning in a mental fog so thick she'd been honestly unable to remember the most common facts that Hank or Luther asked her. They questioned her about her darkened eye, cut cheek, and swollen chin. She couldn't remember if she'd answered them or not. Might as well have if she hadn't because they were going to learn, and quickly, that the dead man had been beating his wife the day before he got shot.

She knew what that would look like.

Ruby rubbed her temples. Earlier Luther had brought her some aspirin when she asked. Then they left her alone for a while. She couldn't say if it was for just a minute, or an hour, before both detectives came back into the room, reminded her of her right to remain silent, but encouraged her to answer more questions. She tried to, at first. But when Hank moved past her black eye and started asking her the types of things he'd never bothered to ask her before, when it might have made some difference, she woke her up from her fog. She shut up and called Nathaniel.

Now Ruby sat here with this other detective. Waiting. She figured he was just making small talk when he told her he'd been a policeman for twenty-three years, the first ten in Tampa, the last thirteen in Desoto Cove. She half listened, wanting to finish the interview, go, and sleep. But she wasn't going to be able to sleep, not for a while yet. She'd have to make arrangements, call people. There'd have to be a funeral. She'd never arranged a funeral and had no idea how to go about it.

"I don't know what kind of service he'd want." Ruby felt a new kind of panic rising in her. "We don't have a plot. We never discussed this. I don't know what to do."

"First, if you've got a minister, you call him," Luther said. "No minister, you call one of the better funeral homes and they take care of everything for you. Find you a plot, even handle the obit with the newspaper. You want, I got the names of a couple of them that are real decent."

Ruby looked at the man then, really looked. He had clear blue eyes in a wide face and a thick wave of dirty blond hair, going pale with sun and time, and a thick moustache that looked all but white. There was something familiar about him and she leaned forward for a better look. The nose had been broken, but still sat comfortably on Luther's face like that was the way it was supposed to be. He looked intelligent and maybe kind.

Yeah, something definitely familiar. Way back, probably only briefly. Maybe Tampa. She almost asked him how she might know him, but Hank and Nathaniel entered the room.

"We'd like to ask you some more questions," Hank said.

"I'm advising Mrs. Randolph not to speak further at this time," Nathaniel responded, moving to physically block Hank from where Ruby sat.

The men kept talking. She heard the sounds, but couldn't seem to make out words, that fog descending into her brain again, clouding over the edges, softening the blows the words seemed to make in the air around her. Hank and Nathaniel argued, but she didn't care why that might be. Loud voices bit at her, like the mosquitoes at dusk that no amount of Malathion spray could keep out of the city. Ruby sat still, not looking at either Hank or Nathaniel. Finally, she'd had enough. She picked up the canned drink and poured it out on the table, making Luther jump up as the cold liquid ran off the edge toward his lap. The two men stopped arguing. The haze inside her head cleared again as she watched the puddle of spilled drink spread on the floor.

While Luther mopped up the mess, she turned to Hank. "Am I under arrest?"

"No."

"Then I can go, can't I." She didn't say it as a question.

"We thought it would be in everyone's best interest if you answer a few more questions," Luther said.

"Look, boys," Nathaniel said, "None of your usual interrogation tricks will work with her. She understands you have no authority over her and she has an absolute right not to answer any questions."

Damn, already talking like I'm guilty.

Nathaniel turned to her. "Ruby, I've called Peter Golder. He's in a depo, but his secretary was going to speak to him and I expect he'll be here shortly. Until then, you keep quiet." In what sounded like an afterthought, he added, "I'm sorry about Gardner. Are you all right?"

Ruby nodded toward Nathaniel. Then she stood up, paced a moment and came to rest by a table with a coffee machine. "Look, Nathaniel, we're both attorneys. You didn't need to call Peter."

"But we're not criminal defense attorneys."

"No, Gardner was the firm's only crim lawyer." Making a kind of a half laugh, she said, "So where is he when you really need him, eh?"

Nathaniel stepped toward her as if to physically restrain her, but she dodged away and turned to the window. Using her thumb nail she flicked at some gelled brown goo on the glass. "I guess you don't have to worry about making good impressions here, do you?" She glanced back at Hank as she spoke.

"You're still in shock. Please be quiet," Nathaniel said.

"Am I being glib? I'm sorry. I guess that's what we trial attorneys do in exigent circumstances."

"Ruby, sit down and shut up," Nathaniel said.

"No, I want to know what happened to Gardner, then I'll tell them what I know. After that I'm going home. Please leave, Nathaniel. And, you, Luther, thank you but please leave me with Detective Rider."

"No," Nathaniel said, "I'm not leaving you till Peter gets here."

"My partner and I would both like to interview you," Hank said.

She glared at them. "Well then, damn you too. Damn you all."

Ruby walked toward the door and when Hank moved to stop her, she shoved off his hand. "Either arrest me or get out of my way." At that, Hank stood back, Luther did not speak or move, and Ruby crossed through the door and left.

Outside, Ruby remembered she had no car because Luther had driven her to the police station. She was only a few blocks from the law firm, but she couldn't imagine walking there. Instead she thought of Desoto Park, many blocks away. She thought of the bay and the breeze and the snack bar where she could get a beer. A pay phone to call somebody. She set out for Desoto Park.

***

Hank found her, slumped on a bench at the tip of the park, looking out over Desoto Cove Bay, an empty beer can on the ground near her. He sat down beside her and stared straight ahead, not speaking. In the bay, a covey of boats, anchored and rolling in the current, stood in relief against a backdrop of high rise buildings along the bay's curved shore. The sun's bright rays ricocheted off the water like hot shards and Hank squinted against the late afternoon brightness. A few gulls squawked over head. An elderly man ambled by on the sidewalk, tugging at an even older looking dog with white, milky eyes.

"We used to talk about buying a sailboat, maybe even living on it, sailing around the Caribbean," she said.

"Why didn't you?"

"Work. Time. Money. The usual stuff."

He'd had the same fantasy of living on a sailboat. He guessed they all did, living here on the water, watching the rich folks come and go in their yachts and sailboats, with the rest of them stuck with their little skiffs, if that, and the wear and tear of every day's earning a living.

Hank reached out toward her, touching her wrist with his fingers. When she didn't pull away, he rested his hand on top of hers. "I'm sorry."

"I didn't kill him."

"I hope that's true."

"Tell me what you can, please?" Ruby stared out at the bay as if she were afraid to look at him.

"Somebody called 9-1-1 from your home address. About one this afternoon. Didn't say a word. Left the phone off the hook. When the operator couldn't get anybody to answer, she called a patrol car to go by. The officer found the front door standing wide open and went in, found the body. Called the ambulance and for backup. Secured the scene." Hank hesitated, then decided against telling her that the body was so fresh that the officer checked for a pulse and tried CPR on him.

"He was shot in the chest. No defensive wounds to his hands. Somebody just walked right up to him and shot him. Up close." Hank paused, knowing he shouldn't be telling a suspect this kind of information, but unable to find the line between what Ruby was to him and just someone he might have to arrest later. "If it's any comfort, I doubt he suffered."

But he would have. The agony of the shot, the bullet piercing him, tearing through flesh and muscle and lung tissue, his frantic struggles at trying to breathe, the terror he surely felt on top of the pain, the sheer panic in those moments when the brain still worked, but the heart and lungs no longer did. He and Luther had seen where Gardner had flailed his arms about him while on the floor. Almost like angel-wings in the snow, only Gardner made his marks in his own blood. His knees bent up, closing in on the fetal position, the marks in the carpet where his feet had twitched about.

The man had suffered.

But Hank was glad that much had been hidden from Ruby during the time the detectives and the techs had with the body. She had arrived late enough to have missed the real horror of the scene.

Unless, of course, she had shot him and watched it all live and in person. Standing over the man while he crumpled in agony, writhing and grabbing at nothing but more minutes of torture.

Hank made himself shut his mind to that image. Checking carefully for Ruby's reaction, he repeated the lie. "I don't think he suffered."

"I suppose that's something. He was a baby about pain."

Hank squeezed her hand before he let go of it, glad he'd lied after all and at least for a moment, believing her. That she hadn't killed Gardner.

"You should come back to the station. We shouldn't do this here."

"Ask what you want to."

"Do you own a handgun?"

"Yes. A .38."

"Where do you keep it?"

"In the nightstand by the bed. Isn't that where everybody keeps theirs?"

"Where were you during the lunch hour?"

97

Ruby shook her head. She looked confused for a second. "Around noon? At Danni and Fred Ambruski's house, I guess. I stayed with them last night."

"Was anyone with you? During the lunch hour, I mean."

"No."

"The gun's not in the nightstand anymore. Did you move it? Or know if Gardner moved it?"

"I haven't touched it in months."

"All right." He glanced at his watch. "We should go back."

"No. I want to sit out here for a while."

"Fine. Tell me why you didn't have a security system, a big house like that?

"You'd have to ask Gardner to be sure. He made those types of decisions. I guess he felt the locks and the gun made it safe enough. Those are state of the art deadbolts and all the windows had locks. Everything was insured."

Hank nodded. "Then tell me, who else had a key to your house?"

"A key?"

"Yes. There was no sign of forced entry. You said yourself you had state of the art deadbolts. The evidence techs might find something we missed to show a break-in, but I doubt it. Looks like somebody just walked in. So, I need to know who had a key."

"Me. And Gardner."

"That's it?"

"Yeah."

"You sure nobody else had a key? Pest control, repair man, housekeeper, anything like that? Even just for a day, or an hour, where they could have copied it. Valet parking? Anyone?"

"No."

"It helps you a lot if somebody else had a key." Hank spoke with a deliberate calmness. "Either somebody walked into that house with a key, or Gardner let them in and then took them to the bedroom. No signs of struggle anywhere. Anybody else who had a key, that helps you. An old boyfriend?"

Ruby cut her eyes up toward him, then looked back out at the anchored boats. "No, I told you. Nobody else." She paused, then repeated, "Nobody else had a key."

But the hesitancy in her answer registered with Hank. "Who else had a key?"

"Nobody, I told you. Nobody."

Hank leaned toward Ruby and took both of her hands in his. "Look, you've got to tell me the truth here. Okay? Don't try to protect anyone. Tell me the truth."

"I told you, nobody else had a key."

This time she didn't hesitate, she didn't blink or look away. Nothing gave her away. Nothing except that little pause a moment before, hardly noticeable, except maybe to a cop or a lawyer or someone used to watching people lie.

"You're lying," Hank dropped her hands. "Who else had a key?"

Ruby said nothing.

"You need to come back to the station. This is an official police investigation and it is not proper for us to be out here like this." His voice was clipped, formal.

"No. If you have your car, I'd appreciate a ride home."

"You can't stay there until we're done with the crime scene. I can take you somewhere else."

"Your house?"

"No."

"Then, never mind, just go."

Hank stood up. He stared straight ahead, willing himself not to glance back at Ruby as he walked off.

He couldn't help it. He was a cop. Already the doubt was creeping back in.

***

From a pay phone at the snack bar, Ruby called Dave. She wanted to be with Nathaniel now, but his wife wouldn't allow her in their home and anyway Nathaniel was probably still at the police department waiting for Golder. Dave, she knew, would pick her up and do what he could to help her. And if he had questions, she could easily put him off.

Waiting, Ruby remembered shoving the chaise lounge into the pool. Hank said there was no sign of struggle, so she could only suppose Gardner pulled it out and set it right. He'd probably cleaned up the mess she'd left in the bedroom too. That was how he'd been, everything in its place. Especially her.

Chapter Eleven: In a Bar, Luther and Hank

Luther waved the bartender over again. Hank finished straightening out a paper clip, then jabbed at a piece of loose popcorn on the bar. He punched too hard and the kernel skidded away from him onto the floor. Using the paperclip as a spear, Hank stabbed the butt of a cigarette from an ashtray, shredding it into splinters of paper, filter and curls of burnt tobacco.

"I reckon it's dead now," Luther said.

Hank said nothing, but began picking up the torn shreds and putting them back in the ashtray.

"Look, Hank, why don't you come on home with me. I'm not sure what Nora is gonna have for supper, but you know there'll be enough. And those wild kids of mine'll be glad to see you."

"No, thanks, I'm just going to sit here a bit longer."

"Well, now, least ways that's something different," Luther said.

Hank ignored his partner's sarcasm and mutely bent the clip back into some semblance of its former shape before tossing it into the ashtray.

Luther glanced around. "Why do you like this place? I feel like everybody's looking at us like our Sears suits ain't good enough."

"Nobody's looking at us. That's why I like it. No cops. Nobody knows me so I'm invisible. I hate talking work after work."

"Well, all right, bud, but I got to violate that rule. For a minute, anyway."

"Yeah, I've been waiting."

"A real red ball, this one. Prominent attorney, killed in his own house, good neighborhood, broad open daylight. It's only been three days and already had the mayor and two city commissioners jabbering at us on the phone. Not to mention the chief. Like we need him sticking his finger in our eyes. No weapon, no real evidence," Luther said. "What do you think the good widow's doing right now?"

"Calculating the estate taxes, probably." Hank quaffed back his drink and signaled the bartender for another one.

"Well, now, like I told you, I don't think she killed him."

Hank sat still, wanting to believe Luther's instinct. He'd known the man to be right more often than wrong, working on this gut sense, a cop's intuition. And, after all, he'd been ready to believe Ruby when she told him she hadn't killed her husband. Until she lied to him. Told him nobody else had a key to the house. Maybe, probably, that key didn't matter. Just as likely Gardner opened the door to his killer.

But Ruby had lied to him. And that made him start to doubt her. So, Hank sat there, hoping Luther could convince him not to suspect Ruby.

"Look, all we got on her is motive and I'm not so sure of that," Luther said. "Be a lot easier to divorce him, than kill him. Besides, women don't shoot that neatly. There'd've been bullets everywhere."

"This one could shoot straight. And she doesn't have an alibi. And I already told you, I could tell she was lying about somebody else having a key. And there was a life insurance policy." As soon as he said it, Hank realized his mistake. About the shooting straight. The liquor making him stupid. *Either shut up, or stop drinking. Better yet, go home.*

Luther spun around on his bar stool and leaned over toward Hank. "Yeah, how do you know that? That she could shoot straight, I mean?"

Hank shrugged. "She said she did some target practice. Right after Gardner got her the gun."

"Yeah?" Luther was watching Hank now, close, too closely. Hank didn't like the feeling it gave him. He also hated lying to Luther.

"Okay, but so what about not having an alibi. Neither do you or I and we didn't kill the son of a bitch. And I doubt a $250,000 life insurance policy means much to a woman in her situation," Luther said. "You saw that house. I ain't no divorce lawyer, but you know how it goes. She'd take half of everything, plus the house, maybe more. That black eye probably ups the settlement. I'll dig around in their finances some more, but I don't see this as an economic killing."

"Maybe. Something else, though. You saw how calm she was."

"Yeah, she wasn't exactly prostrate with grief. But we both saw her bummed up face. Heard about him smashing her into a table. She was leaving him, sure. And she wasn't exactly calm, not really. Sandbagged, more like it. You think on it. If she'd done it and wanted us to think she was crazy with grief, wouldn't she have put on a show? Besides, I saw that look of surprise when she lifted the sheet. Maybe she didn't carry on the way you wanted her to, but I think we're gonna find somebody else did her this favor. What I can tell so far, that husband of hers was worse than a jerk."

"She had a reason," Hank said, but more to himself than to Luther. "You heard what that other lady lawyer told us about their fight." Continuing his inner debate out loud, hoping Luther could talk him out of what he might believe.

"And I also heard what the rest of the office said. Not about her, but about him. He didn't exactly have a fan club. Nobody's real specific about the whys and the wherefores, but the gist of it's clear. I figure it'll be a pretty short funeral."

"All right. Let's just see what the lab and the fingerprint guys bring us. And let's talk to everybody again. See what they've remembered since the first interviews. Let's get more specifics on why the other lawyers didn't care for the man. And I want Mrs. Randolph in the office again tomorrow for sure."

"I don't suppose it's likely that her gun'll ever turn up." Luther pulled out his wallet. "You know, funny thing about the widow. I could swear I know her from somewhere. Let's see if we can get her background folder from The Florida Bar. Those people do a better job than the FBI." He put down some money, swallowed the last of the drink. "Partner, if I remember right we took my boat out last time. So why don't we take out that funny little boat of yours into the Intercoastal this weekend and see if we can catch us some snook."

"You know there's no snook left around here."

"Sure, sure, but fishing for snook sounds better than just sitting in a little boat, watching all the big boats sail by, and drinking beer and gettin sunburnt. Nora don't understand that, but she understands fishing. We can stop over at Walt's Market on the way home, buy her some nice grouper."

"Sure. Ask little Lutter to come along. Damn if I don't like that kid of yours."

"Fine, fine. Yep, Lutter's a chip, ain't he? Can keep up a running conversation longer'n his own mom. We got a date then. G'night."

Chapter Twelve: Luther and Tally and the Books

On Luther's fourth visit to the law firm, he still couldn't explain why the place gave him the willies. His new-age daughter would have called it bad karma, that is if she were talking to him and not locked in her bedroom in a teenage funk.

A lawyer he couldn't quite put a name to, but recognized from the interviews the other day, walked through and nodded with a scowl. Well, he was a cop investigating a murder of one of their own. He guessed he gave them the creeps, too.

Cooling his heels in the reception area, he flipped through some old magazines. Back at his office, he had what seemed like a zillion forms and reports to finish and he'd been sitting on his butt for nearly half an hour in the damn lobby. The receptionist refused to meet his eyes.

Finally, Luther stood up and walked across the reception area, opened the wide wood door to the corridor he remembered went to Tally's office, and walked straight toward it. The receptionist did nothing to stop him. However, once he reached Tally's office, she was standing at her secretary's desk, obviously waiting for him.

"Well, I reckon I wasn't really invisible to your receptionist. She sure thought to warn you."

Tally smiled with her wide, red lips and ushered him into her office. When she gestured to a chair, he took it, opening his notebook and patting his pocket for a pen. She handed him a gold-plated Cross pen. Luther made a mental note to be sure to give it back, though he figured she had a drawer full. Her jacket hung carefully over the back of her desk chair and her skirt was several inches above her knees. Her complexion was dark, not tanned so much as naturally dark, with chocolate eyes heavy with black lashes. Her hair was also a dark chocolate color, shoulder length and cut in a loose, fluffy style. She wore a white blouse, which opened down to the tops of a fully rounded set of breasts.

When she sat behind her desk, Luther wrote down the time and date and her name—Tally Renore—on top on the page of the notebook and set it on the desk facing him.

Leaning over the desk toward him, she looked at it and said, "ReNoir. Capital N, then o-i-r. It's French, you see."

"Sorry. Figures you can read upside down."

"ReNoir. Like the artist. You do know the artist, don't you?"

Still scribbling in his notebook, Luther muttered, "Yeah, me and him went fishing last weekend." When he looked up, her breasts were pushed under his nose as she continued leaning across the desk toward him, breasts full and close enough to smother him. She licked her lips with the tip of her tongue. For a moment, he felt a warm energy gathering in his groin area. He pushed himself physically back from her, finally able to breathe normal. "I reckon it's just automatic with you, isn't it? Do it with every man comes in here?"

"What's that, Detective Downs?"

"The seduction thing."

"Oh, you underestimate yourself, Detective. May I call you Luther?"

"I'd rather you didn't, Ms. ReNoir like the artist. I think we should keep this formal." He gave her his best "ah shucks, ma'am" smile.

Tally mimicked a pout as if making fun of him before she grinned back. Then, as if she heard an invisible bell signifying the next round, she changed to all business. "What can I tell you I haven't already told you?"

"Well, interesting what you didn't tell me yesterday, or the times before that. That you and the deceased were having an affair."

"People in this office talk about me. I'm a bit too colorful for their cowboy tastes so they make things up. You must not believe it all."

"Then it'd be your story you weren't having a relationship with the deceased?"

"Please, don't call him that. His name was Gardner. Give him that much, will you? A name, not just some problem you have to solve."

"Fine, did you have a relationship with Gardner Randolph?"

"Of course I had a relationship with Gardner. We worked together, we saw each other nearly every day for years. We had a certain closeness, a friendship, but not what people here think. It wasn't like that."

"You're saying you were not messing around with him?"

"Define messing around, please, Luther."

"Detective Downs, if you will. Were you having sex with Gardner Randolph?"

"No. And I must say I'd like to know who told you I was."

Luther knew she was lying not just because of the people who flat out told him about her and Gardner, but because of the subtle signs of nervousness in her. A slight rise in her voice, a tiny shift in her posture, a minute narrowing of her eyes. *She's lying for sure.*

"Did you have a key to his house, by chance?" Luther figured she'd lie about that too, but he had to ask.

"No. Gardner wasn't a trusting type of man. Even *if* we were having an affair, he wouldn't have given me a key to his house."

"Sure you never had a key, working together like you say y'all did?"

"Yes, I'm sure I never had a key." Tally stood up behind her desk, pulled her shoulders and arms back so that her bosom practically jumped out at Luther. "Search me. Go ahead. You won't need a warrant. See if you find a key on me."

Luther felt himself blush and wanted to curse. Or take a cold shower.

"Don't reckon that'd be necessary. Know anybody else who might have a key to the Randolph house?"

"Perhaps Ruby gave somebody a key."

"Like who?"

"Since you like to talk about affairs, I'll tell you who was having one, if we must roll around in office gossip. Ruby, the sainted wife. She'd picked up some guy at a bar some time back. I never saw him myself. But Jacob Stanley did, told me all about him. Jacob said he was a tall guy, dark hair, some gray." Tally half giggled. "Jacob said the man looked tough, like he could beat the tar out of Gardner. Maybe that was the attraction? That he was a thug. Or, maybe the very cool widow just had cheap taste in men."

"Mrs. Randolph?"

"Yes. Nobody mentioned that, did they? After what Jacob told me, I went into Bull Feathers and asked the bartender about the man. Bartender didn't want to say anything at first. Seems the guy was a regular there."

Luther wondered what she gave, or offered, the bartender for information before he asked the obvious. "What's the guy's name?"

"Bartender said he thought it was Hank."

Luther stopped writing and looked down at the notebook. His heart kicked and his pulse picked up. Lots of men drank at Bull Feathers. But mostly lawyers, accountants, the silk tie boys from the offices downtown. Not cops. That's why Hank liked it, no shop talk. Yeah, lots of men drank there, maybe even another man named Hank. Luther tapped the Cross pen on his leg, stalling before he finally made himself look up. "Anything else you remember? Or know?"

"I don't think Gardner ever saw him and maybe didn't even know about him. At least he never hinted to me about any affair. But from what Jacob said, the guy drove a pickup with a tool box in the bed. I'd say the cool Mrs. Randolph was sliding back into her redneck roots. And that she didn't particularly care who knew about this guy, meeting him in a place like Bull Feathers."

Luther folded up the notebook and stood up. Halfway through the office door, he turned and said, "Thank you."

***

Ruby perched at the edge of the couch in Golder's office and watched as Nathaniel came in. Golder sat primly at his desk, well dressed for just an office day, with his red power tie and white-on-white shirt.

"Sit, please," Golder said.

Nathaniel did, but without speaking to either of them. When Ruby called his name, he nodded toward her.

"I know what Gardner was up to," she said.

"If I'm going to defend her, I told Ruby she has to tell me everything. She won't do it unless you say so. That's where we're at," Golder said.

"Tell him," Nathaniel said, head up, eyes straight in front of him.

"Gardner and Nancy, at least I figure Nancy's in on it, they were embezzling some of the checks and Nancy's doing something with the books to cover. It's like some kind of shell game, I mean with the firm income."

Nathaniel barely nodded.

"At first, they took just enough of the money now and then to create cash flow problems. To panic everybody. Like right before the partnership meeting in July. After Gardner shook everybody up in

July, the money flowed back in. Everything looked okay for a time, but then with the big Christmas meeting coming up, he started manipulating the money. Panicked everybody all over again. He tried to convince the junior partners he was the only one who could save the firm. That way, they'd vote his way." Ruby glanced at Nathaniel before turning back to Golder.

"See, he blamed Nathaniel and Dave for mismanagement, for not bringing in enough money. That is Dave, I mean. Nathaniel for mismanagement."

Golder stopped taking notes and looked up. "How do you know this?"

"I put it together from things I heard and saw. It was obvious if anybody studied on it. I never found the second set of books, but I do have some print-outs showing how the time billed was more than the money in. I called around and some of my clients swore they'd paid me, but the checks came to the firm, not directly to me. Those payments never showed up in our books. Certainly not credited to me as they should have been. There must be another bank account somewhere, maybe in some version of the firm's name, that he and Nancy used. They would have had to deposit the checks somewhere or else the clients would have called when their checks didn't clear."

"Actually, it was a lot more complex than that," Nathaniel said.

"So you knew?" Golder asked.

"Of course I knew. Like Ruby said, if you looked at any of the accounting sheets, the right ones, it was obvious."

"Damn it, Nathaniel," Ruby said, "why didn't you call the state attorney, call the police. It was embezzling. A crime."

"Like I said, it was more complex than that. You know what the publicity from a major partner embezzling would do to this firm? What the fall-out of an arrest would have been?"

110

"But it wasn't the client's money he was taking. It was the firm's."

"You think people reading the newspapers would have make that distinction? Besides, we couldn't have stood up to an investigation," Nathaniel said. "For one thing, we put up the clients' accounts receivable as security for our loans. You know that violates the Florida legal ethics' code. Another thing, the way we handle the stock valuations and transfers to the partners would never survive an IRS audit. And, we took money out of the employees' profit sharing in violation of federal regulations to invest in Jacob's brother's office complex."

Which everyone knew had gone belly-up, with the half-built offices standing stark and ruined at the corner of the Tamiami Trail and West Cove Avenue, with a for sale sign garnering no takers.

"And, what do you think those twenty-hour days and double billings on our time sheets would have looked like, anybody snooping in our books? Cheating our clients, that's what it would have looked like. There's more, but you get the idea."

Ruby rose from the chair, walked over and looked out Golder's window at the traffic on U.S. 301. "So Gardner was just the chief crook in a gang of crooks?"

"Like I told you before, it's the eighties, Ruby. We're not thieves. We're astute businessmen, maximizing our cash flow and investment potentials. Taking our lead from Wall Street."

Nathaniel's voice was bitter, which didn't surprise Ruby. But he'd done it himself, made his own bed. And that made her bitter in return.

"So astute you put up your personal assets to keep the firm going," Ruby said, still staring out the window with her back to him.

"We were fine, rolling in the deals and the money until the recession and the downtown building boom collapsed. Gardner used that to launch his own campaign of creative bookkeeping."

With one hand, Ruby lifted her heavy hair off her neck, conscious of a certain heat in the room. She rocked back on her heels, then turned to face him. "You knew what he was doing and you didn't do anything to stop him."

"I contemplated my options."

"Damn you. I thought you could do anything. Fix everything."

"Then beneath that carefully cultivated cynicism, you were naive after all, weren't you?"

***

After a phone call from a corner Seven-Eleven, Luther traced Hank to the Randolph house. The door was unlocked and he stepped over the yellow crime tape and went straight to the bedroom where Hank was standing at the edge of a prominent blood stain on the carpet. Hank rubbed his eyes with the backs of his hands. When he took his hands away, his eyes were raw looking.

"What?" Hank asked.

"When'd you plan on telling me you were screwing our lead suspect?"

Hank stood there a moment while Luther waited, then he walked around the edge of the bloodstain, eyes down.

"What'd we miss? Right now we got nothing we can take to the state attorney. No forced entry. No sign of fighting. Not a pillow, a vase, a picture or a chair out of place. No torn off buttons on his clothes. No visible hair, skin or blood under the victim's nails, no witnesses. No weapon."

"What'd we miss, you want to know? One of the big things we missed was you being up front with me. What'd you figure, it wasn't important you and the dear widow woman, or you figured I wasn't cop enough to find out?" As Luther spoke, his anger seemed to simultaneously refuel and dissipate. Luther wanted to hit his partner, but he wanted to excuse him too.

Hank squatted down by the stain and traced the brown outline of it with his finger. "I'm sorry, Luther."

"Sorry, bud, sorry? You think maybe this makes you look like you might be involved in this some way? I mean, how'd the chief look at this? You can't work this case anymore. Not with me."

"The only thing you need to know," Hank said, standing up, "is that I saw Ruby handle a .38 like a pro. And her husband had something on her that made her afraid of him. The rest doesn't matter." Hank went into the bathroom and rinsed his hands, while Luther stood watching him from the bedroom.

When Hank came out, Luther said, "All right, I ain't over being mad, but let's total up the score."

"I told you the score. We got nothing."

"Fingerprint matches still being worked on. Damn if I know what's taking so long." Luther figured the LPE techs were still checking the latent lifts from the house against the elimination prints he and Hank pulled together. "I've been calling and nagging, but you know how it goes. Still, you never know what'll turn up with the prints."

"Ted Bundy's prints. You wait."

"Yeah, it's not a dunker, but we'll still put it down. Maybe something'll show with the labs," Luther said.

"You know lab never solves a murder. It's luck, instinct, reading the street. And the fact most killers are stupid or do stupid things. We got a killer here who's not stupid. So, our best chance is gone."

"You so down on the lab work, how come you busted your butt for days getting together fingerprints for the LPE to compare to our latent lifts? You badgered a dozen folk into giving us prints, making them think it was just elimination prints, including that wiggly lawyer,

Jacob, the one who about stroked when you asked to take his prints. And then collecting up everything you could think of for them to compare to our latents. Even down to prints from the POs off their parolees."

"Hunches and drudge-work. Ninety percent of what we do. You know that." Hank rubbed his eyes again.

"That doesn't rule out the stupid mistake. Even a smart guy can do stupid. Just today, right before telling me about you and Ruby, only she didn't exactly know that's what she was telling, that Tally lady lawyer—you know the one—lied through her teeth about not sleeping with the dear departed. Up to then, I never thought of her as a suspect, but now, I'd say we oughtta take another look at her."

"She's all show. That's my read on her. Wouldn't have the guts to pull the trigger."

"All right then, what's your theory?"

"We got a bullet dug out of a wall after passing through the body. Logic says that if there's a .38 in the nightstand and the husband is shot by a .38 and that .38 turns up missing, the gun in the nightstand is probably our murder weapon," Hank said, as if Luther hadn't already worked all this through in his own head. "Lab's got the bullet for safe-keeping if we ever get the Randolph gun to make a match."

"Yeah, I'm with you, bud. So, who knew about the gun in the nightstand?"

"The same person who can enter the house without breaking in and walk right up to the guy in the bedroom without him making a move."

"Well, I reckon that'd be Mrs. Randolph, wouldn't it?"

"That's what I've been thinking."

"You know this gal, is she a killer?"

"Anybody's a killer given the right circumstances. You know that."

"Nope, not so, said so yourself no more'n two minutes ago. You said that other lady lawyer wasn't a killer."

"Under the right circumstances, maybe she would be. Who knows? But I don't see a motive that'd make her one now."

"How about if the dead guy stiffed her on something? I got me a list of folks who said she and Randolph were getting it on regular. And she's lying about it. There's something there that don't smell right. Mail room gal, mail room's right across from Tally's office, said Tally cursed him out a blue streak not long before his murder."

"So she got mad at him. She's not exactly on an exclusive list there. I don't see a motive yet. Besides, why are you so set on letting Mrs. Randolph off the hook?"

"Could be 'cause you don't usually take up with killers for girlfriends. And that sixth sense, my cop sense, tells me she ain't the one."

"What if my cop sense says she is?"

"Well, Hank, I reckon you ain't real clear headed on this one."

"I told you, it wasn't important. We stopped seeing each other a while back. It's over."

"Yeah? That's why we were at this for a few days before you slipped up while drinking and mentioned you'd heard Mrs. Randolph was handy with a .38, and now you're telling me you know that for a personal fact. Bud, you gotta make up your mind if you want to hang her or help her. Then let me know which way the wind's blowing."

***

Make up his mind. Hank shook his head as if that would clear his thinking. Could Ruby have killed her husband? Did he still care about her? Those were just the first of twenty questions. Hank didn't want to play that game with himself. He had work to do. More checking.

One of the recent parolees had caught his eye. A man named Billy Dittwilder, let out of Union Correctional two days before the murder, heading to Desoto Cove according to what he told the prison and the parole board. Only he never got to Desoto Cove, or he never checked in with his PO. So, the PO asked for help finding him, sent a report. In flipping through the report on Dittwilder, Hank had stopped when he saw the man's hometown was in Louisiana. City's name practically screamed out at him. Bogalusa. Washington County. Hard to forget a name like Bogalusa. Same hometown as Ruby's. Maybe, he told himself, that wasn't much, not in a world where people probably left Louisiana for the promised land in Florida on a daily basis. But then, it made for a mighty interesting coincidence. And that meant he was damn sure going to get the experts to compare this Dittwilder's prints against the latents from the Randolph house.

Damn, what in the hell had Ruby been involved in?

He wished for a second he didn't have to know. But he was a cop, and a good one, and he'd have to find out, whatever the dirty mess was.

Chapter Thirteen: Late Night Revival and Morning

Hank looked out the window to see who'd knocked on his door. Ruby stood there, her face turned away from the porch light. He glanced at a clock. Past midnight. He'd been smoking one of the rare cigarettes he permitted himself these days and trying his best to make his mind blank. But no matter how he tried, he couldn't stop thinking of Ruby earlier that day at the funeral, protected by a flank of Dave and Fred. Dried eyed, all of them. More wary than sad. Going through the right steps, but not caring a damn about the dead guy in the casket.

Fact was, nobody in the small crowd appeared the least bit grieved. Not a good legacy. Hank hoped somebody would cry at his funeral.

Ruby knocked again. He drew down deep on the cigarette before he dropped it into an empty beer can. For a moment, he pretended he wouldn't answer the door. But he did.

"Thank you for coming to the funeral," Ruby said, still with that wary quality about her. "I saw you and Luther, but I'm sorry I didn't get to speak to you."

"Why are you here?"

"Why was I ever here?"

"Do you want to reduce it to that?"

"No, I don't, but you do."

Hank stood back from the open door and Ruby came in, went straight to the bedroom and began undressing without looking at him. He followed, stopping only long enough to pick up a whiskey bottle from the kitchen.

Once undressed and in bed, he realized how tired he was, profoundly, through and through, but he sipped his whiskey, watched her sip hers, and waited, letting her take the lead.

It might be nice to actually sleep for a change, not just lie there in the bed, listening to the night noises coming in his opened window. But having Ruby in his bed wasn't going to help him sleep. He was about to ask her to dress and leave, when she spoke to him.

"Hold me. Please."

And like that, he was done waiting. He rolled over on top of her, smothering her with his warm body, ready to plunge into her. But she trembled beneath him, shivering as if she were cold. Or afraid. He rolled off her, pulled her head to his chest and wrapped his arms around her. She cried softly as she burrowed into him.

Just like that, his sudden lust gave way to something else.

Compassion.

***

There was no clock in the room when Ruby woke up. She got out of bed and peeked through the curtains. The sun was up, bright and clear.

She was surprised she'd slept at all and wondered where Hank was. She hadn't meant to spend the night and hoped it was all right.

But more than that, she thought of him cradling her most of the night. The hallowed world where the touching was flesh, but the giving was spirit. His caressing had been something beyond sex, a measure of tenderness and physical connection which she'd never felt before. That was what it was supposed to be. That feeling, that gentleness, that pleasure.

Without pain or violence or fear or coercion or threat. Without a *quid pro quo*, real or imagined.

But, rather, pure gift.

Maybe last night was the first time she'd ever really *made love*. She wondered if she and Hank could find that place again. With the morning's demands and a small, nagging headache, Ruby didn't feel too optimistic.

After slipping on her T-shirt from the night before, she drifted down the hallway, listening for Hank. In the kitchen, she found a percolator and filled it with water and coffee and plugged it in. Then she wandered back into Hank's room and ran her hand over the bed. In the crumpled center of the twisted sheets, she could still feel the warmth of them in the cloth. For a moment, fatigue overcame her and she wanted to crawl into his bed and go back to sleep with the smell of him on the pillow under her face. Instead she went into the bathroom. When she was done, she washed her hands and face and rinsed her mouth and went back out into the hallway. The coffee was ready, but Hank still wasn't in the house.

He had a shower outside in his shed so he could clean up after fishing or lifting weights and she went there. Standing outside of the cubicle that held the shower, she imagined hot water pouring over Hank's body.

When she pulled back the shower door, stepped in, and pulled off her T-shirt, Hank turned toward her. But his expression was as blank as the clean sides of the shower stall.

In the harsh overhead light, Ruby saw the small maze of lines and crinkles around his eyes and mouth where the sun had damaged his face. She wondered how old he was.

But his body was straight and thin and hard, his stomach flat and his arms and legs muscled. She took the soap from his hands.

Afterwards, they sat in plastic lawn chairs on his back porch, drinking strong coffee. They hadn't yet said anything basic politeness hadn't required.

But all their communication couldn't be through their bodies. There had to be words.

Ruby said his name out loud. Hank shifted his weight and turned toward her with a quizzical look on his face.

"Look, we are so damned impersonal, so superficial. I know, I mean, I think we meant to be." Ruby stopped. What was she trying to do? Already what they'd had last night was fading.

She almost wanted to laugh at herself, at what she'd wanted. What? Make this sexual thing into something more? *Now?* When the man thought she'd shot her own husband?

"I don't call what we've discussed the last few days so superficial," Hank said in a tone that told her he knew they'd lost that rare connection too. "In fact, there are a few things I'd like to go over with you. Again."

"Damn it, that's your work. It's not the same. And I've told you and told you, I'm not talking to you about the case without Golder."

"What do you want to talk about then? Spring time in the Rockies?"

"Ever been married," she asked, ignoring his sarcasm, figuring he had a right to it.

"Twice."

"Kids?"

"Didn't stay married long enough for that."

Now Ruby did laugh. "Doesn't take more than, what? Fifteen minutes?" Or, all night.

"I had very careful wives."

Ruby sipped her coffee, studied the tree branches hanging over Hank's head, and then looked him in the eyes. "My parents are dead. My father died when I was young. I have a brother. We used to be good friends. He's got a house full of kids I don't know and when this is all over and settled, I'm going back to Louisiana and get to know them. See if my brother and I can still sit out on the porch and talk all night and never run out of things to say."

"Good."

"What about you? Do you have family? I mean, besides the two ex-wives?"

"A mom. In South Carolina."

"Your father?"

"He died a few months ago."

"Oh. I'm sorry."

"Don't be. I'm not. I hope the old bastard is screaming in Hell right now." Hank snapped the words out and his dark eyes narrowed.

"Okay, so trading childhood stories and otherwise baring our souls right now is probably not a good idea. Still, this is more than just sex between us, you know," she said, unable to look at him. Hoping she was right.

Hank stood up, walked to the edge of the porch and slung the last swallow of his coffee out on the azaleas. He walked back into the house. When she came in to get her purse, he caught her eyes.

"I know that much," he said. But he let her dig her car keys out of her purse and leave.

Chapter Fourteen: The State attorney and the Key

Luther eyed Hank, slouched in the other chair, as they waited for the state attorney to finish preaching at them about stuff they already knew. Hank looked angry already and this dandied-up state attorney was just pissing him off more. Still, Luther wanted to get them through this meeting without anybody yelling. After all, they were on the same side.

"So let me translate," Luther said to Jonathan Belt, a man in a good suit, Italian shoes and designer tie, expensive blow-dry cut, and heavy gold ring. "Chief says we put this case down soon or Hank and me'll be working bad checks. We're still waiting for any matches on prints."

"Exactly what do you have?" the state attorney asked.

Hank rose out his chair and Luther braced himself to jump in between the two men if he needed to. But Hank just walked over to the window and looked out at the oleander trees, good bloomers, nice foliage, pretty flowers, so poisonous even the smoke from burning them could harm a healthy man standing close enough to inhale.

When Hank didn't speak, Luther nodded at Belt. "All right, this is what we can show so far. Mind you, so far."

Hank eased back toward Belt, standing over him and glaring. "First thing is motive."

"Usually Hank and me, we don't care so much about motive," Luther said, hoping Hank would sit down. "We care about physical evidence. And witnesses. Only, we don't have witnesses. Or physical evidence, not that proves anything, that is. Means we're stuck with motive. Deceased was blackmailing his wife about something. We don't know what yet. But three witnesses, two lawyers and the law firm's bookkeeper, heard them fighting the day before he got shot and it was pretty clear about the blackmail. She told him he was done with blackmailing her and more or less threatened him. He smashed her face into a table by way of come-back."

Belt looked up at Hank. "Sit down, will you."

Hank kept standing.

Luther jumped back into his spiel, keeping his eyes on Hank. "There was a life insurance policy, quarter mil. Doesn't seem likely that'd be a real motive, but maybe. I snooped around best I could in their money situation and they seemed comfortable enough. Not super-rich by St. Anne Circle standards, but I'd take it. Looks like, and I can't be sure yet, that most of their money was in their big house on the water. Lot of equity in the house. Some stocks in joint title, some mutual funds in his name, and he had a whopper of a 401K plan. But she had a pretty big 401K plan herself at the firm, and some stocks she'd moved over into her name couple of days before his murder. You might want to play with the life insurance as motive to a jury, but Hank and me, we don't figure it was really in play here."

"Okay, motive. What about means and opportunity." Belt sounded bored. "Alibi?"

"Well, interesting enough on the alibi. She tells us that she's staying over at Fred and Danni Ambruski's house. That she's there all by herself during the noon hour on the day her husband's killed. Mr. Randolph was shot some time right after noon, best guess from the medical report, and considering the time he left his office, would be between 12:30 and 1. Wife says she's parked at the Ambruski house all morning till she came over to her house to pick up some clothes later that afternoon. Then she says, oh, no, opps, I forgot. I went to the store. And, get this, conveniently, in the other direction from the house, north of there a pretty good ways, so she couldn't have been in her house at the time her husband was shot. Only she doesn't have any receipt."

"Find anybody to either back up her story or dispute it?" Belt asked, as if Luther wasn't just getting to that part.

"Nobody at the store remembered seeing her, which seems like they would, I mean, given her black eye and all. No cameras at the place. So, we ask everybody in the Ambruski neighborhood, did you see her come and go? See her car? Nobody remembers nothing. Perfectly typical. Till Hank here thinks to round up the maids and the yard men and the pest control people in the Ambruski's neighborhood that day. And sure shooting enough, teenage guy, lawn boy working two houses down, remembers seeing her car drive off that day, round noon. Says it was going south, like to St. Anne, not like north to the store like Ruby said. Reason he remembers is he wants one of those sporty little 280Z's and she was driving one, so he watched it, then he was hungry and checked his watch. Since it was a little before noon, he went to lunch," Luther said.

"Be a good witness?" Belt asked.

"Yeah, seems a straight up kid."

"What you're telling is that she lied one way or the other about being at the Ambruski house about the time of the murder. What else?"

"Mrs. Randolph admits to me right during the initial interview that she owns a .38. Kept it in the bedroom in the nightstand. Get this, her husband gave it to her for when he was out of town, traveling. And, yes, she admits she can shoot it," Hank said.

"That's it?" Belt asked. "You got to have more than that."

"Hank and I spent half our lives go'n through this dead guy's files. Subpoenaed the ones from his office and the ones from his house. Mrs. Randolph put up quite a fuss, rather her hired mouth did, but we got them. All the trouble they put up to try and stop us makes me think there's something in there they don't want us to know. But we didn't find any smoking guns so to speak."

"What else? I'm still not hearing anything I can take to a jury."

"Means and opportunity. No breaking and entering. No forced entry at all. Somebody just walked in, walked right up to the poor guy and popped him. In the bedroom," Luther said.

"Either the murderer had a key or Gardner let her, or him, in and went with the murderer to the bedroom," Hank said. "Bedroom sure suggests a woman. No signs of struggle. No defensive wounds."

"Yes, I saw the ME's report, read your notes," Belt said. "I also saw the part where the neutron activation test on the wife just came back negative. No traces of gunpowder on her hands."

"It'd been a few hours. So what? The negative doesn't prove anything, only the positive," Hank said. "Yeah, you're the guy with the law degree, but I see motive, a lie, access to the probable murder weapon, plus access to the house and the victim."

Luther eased around to study his partner. Man sure went hot and cold on this woman. One day wanting to hang her for it, next day, looking around for somebody else to put down for the crime. Thing was, Hank was usually sure of himself, not at all indecisive or fickle.

That made Luther wonder what was going on to make Hank bounce around like this.

"Damned if I'll go to a jury with only that," Belt said. "You've got to get me more."

"Come on, Jonathan, work with us here," Luther said, more worried about Hank now than concerned with Belt, but knowing he had to say something at least half way conciliatory.

"You work with me. You boys got a couple of loose ends. Why'd Gardner go home at noon that day? Was that his habit?"

"No. His regular secretary says he didn't usually go home for lunch. She doesn't know why he went home that day. Seems she was out at some lunch party for the girls that day. Somebody's birthday and they were all at Marina Jack's. But the substitute receptionist thinks she remembered Gardner getting a phone call from a man after 11 or maybe 11:30. She's suppose to screen the calls, let the attorneys know who it is and all, but she said the lines were all ringing at once so she just put it straight into Gardner's office after answering it. Girl remembers the guy on the line was rude, maybe angry. But then, she says, maybe that was one of the other calls. I get the idea she was kinda pissed she was the only girl in the office not drinking wine, peeling shrimp, at Marina Jack's that day."

"Not a very good witness, I'd say." Belt shifted in his chair, glaring first at Luther, then at Hank. "And how does that help if we don't know who called Gardner?"

"Well, we ain't betting the family farm on anything that woman said, but we're working on getting and going through the list of incoming calls from the phone company."

"All right," Belt said. "We arrest her, then we negotiate from an advantage. Maybe plead down to second. Maybe manslaughter. He ever knock her around before? I mean, was it just that time, or was there a pattern? Maybe we can trick her into an admission if we pretend we're looking at self-defense. You know, the old battered woman syndrome stuff. I say bring her in again."

Hank shook his head. "You all go right ahead, but I'm telling you it's a waste of time. She's smart, she's has self-control, and she knows we don't have anything on her. No way we're tricking her into any admissions or confessions. Unlike most dickheads we pull in off the street, this one understands what it means to have a right to remain silent."

"Then what do you suggest?" Belt wasn't even trying to hide his contempt.

Hank shrugged.

"Was she a battered wife?" Luther asked, looking directly at Hank.

Hank shrugged again.

"Set it up. I'll sit in," Belt said. "Now, you two get, let me do my job."

Outside after leaving Belt's office, the sun hitting both of them in the eyes so bright and hard it hurt, Hank said, "I'd quit this for a living if there was something else I could do."

"Hey, bud, we all say that, but we don't mean it."

Hank made a guttural noise, not quite a word.

***

They were all there this time. Belt in his prosecutor's dark gray and Golder in his defense attorney steel gray, Luther and Hank in their off-the-racks, Ruby in her jeans.

126

Golder and Belt were already huffing and puffing with each other.

"Well, well, well. Deja vu all over again, ain't it?" Luther said.

Golder had urged Ruby to refuse to go to police headquarters. But she insisted that giving the appearance of full cooperation, with its implication of nothing to hide, would stand her better in the long run than pointedly refusing to grant another interview.

But the truth had been simpler than that. She wanted to see Hank and try to gage what he was thinking and feeling, where he was landing on his theory of her guilt or innocence.

"If there's nothing new, maybe we should wind this up right now before we waste everybody's time." Golder's eyes swept the room with the pained expression of a spoiled child thwarted in some indulgence.

Hank ignored Golder and paced in front of Ruby. "Who else had a key to your house? No forced entry. Whoever shot Mr. Randolph must have had a key."

"I told you, nobody but Gardner and me." Ruby shifted her weight uncomfortably in the hard chair and pulled her hair off her face with one hand. Small, uneven clumps of it escaped and hung in her face.

"Think about it again. Carefully. Who had a key? Even for one hour, a day?"

"Nobody, I told you," Ruby said, a frayed sound in her voice. No warm up this time, just Hank jumping in right at her. The way he looked at her shook her up.

Luther tilted forward in his chair, studying her eyes. "Would Gardner have given anyone a key?"

"Not that I know about. He wasn't trusting."

"Did you ever lose your keys?" Luther scooted closer, invading her personal space until she wanted to push him away.

"Enough with the damn keys. Nobody else had any keys to the house. Now get out of my face."

Luther slid back, but before he could speak, Belt cut in. "Mrs. Randolph, we have witnesses who claim you accused your husband of blackmailing you in some way. Yet you continue to deny this."

"What's the question?" Golder asked.

"Was he blackmailing you?"

"You don't have to answer that," Golder said.

"We went over that, remember?" This time Ruby had the right tone, bored and vaguely irritated, a woman vexed with the repetition but with nothing serious to hide. "I don't know what else to tell you. Like I said, I don't know what I said that day in the office. I was angry. Gardner was angry. It was a fight, all right? We were both out of control. I don't know what I said or what I meant."

"Why were you angry with Mr. Randolph?" Belt asked.

"We'd been angry with each for a long time. It was a bad marriage. Look, I've been over this and over this. A marriage goes bad. You get mad. It's not like you can say 'I'm angry because he didn't take the garbage out.' It's all complex. And ordinary. You say things you don't mean and don't remember." Now she played some of that bored tone into a kind of melancholia, mixed with a hint of world-weariness, altogether the right attitude of a recent and regretful widow. She and Golder had worked on that approach for quite some time.

"Was your husband having an affair?" Luther asked.

Ruby remained silent. She and Golder had argued about this too. Golder thought they should offer up Tally as a spurned lover and possible suspect. Ruby might not like the woman much, but she didn't want to drag her into this mess.

"I'm tired," she said. "Very tired."

"Yes, we all are," Luther replied.

"Then we should leave, right now," Golder said, rising in his chair.

"Please. One minute," Luther said. "Answer the question. Was your husband having an affair?"

Ruby studied Luther. Some faint glimmer in his expression told her he already knew the answer. After all, he was a good cop and it wouldn't have been that hard for him to have learned about Tally and Gardner.

"Yes. That is, I think so. Thought so, I mean. I believe he had broken it off, but I don't really know."

"Who?"

"I'm very uncomfortable with this," Ruby said.

"Why? You want to protect your husband's lover?" Luther gazed at her as if urging her to finish.

"Tally ReNoir. Another attorney in our office. Tally told me herself they were having an affair." Ruby looked at Luther as if to ask, *is that what you wanted?*

Luther nodded. "Is it possible he gave her a key?"

"No. I mean, I don't think so. It wouldn't have been like him to. I told you, he wasn't trusting."

"And you," Belt said, "were you also having an affair?"

Ruby cut her eyes from Luther to Belt without ever looking at Hank. "I told you, it wasn't a good marriage. But at the time of his murder, I was not having an affair."

Belt jotted something in his notepad and then opened his mouth to ask another question when Hank spun around in front of Ruby. "Why'd you lie about being at Danni and Fred Ambruski's house at noon the day your husband was killed?"

"I *was* at their house. I didn't lie."

"We have a witness who saw you driving away around noon, heading south," Hank said. "Gave a great description of your car."

Golder rested his hand on Ruby's shoulder. "This is enough. Stop."

Ruby shook her head. "Look, I was at their house. I did go out earlier to get some hair gel, barrettes, stuff like that, to see what I could do with my hair after Gardner whacked chunks out of it. Danni didn't have anything like that. I told you all this."

"Yeah, but you told us that later on, changing your first story, like maybe you thought you needed an alibi," Luther said.

"Look, how many times do I have to say this. I was confused the first time I told you I was alone at Fred and Danni's at noon. I went out. I came back to their house, everybody was gone. I ate lunch. I did what I could with my hair. Then I went to my house to get some things." Ruby shut her eyes for a minute, trying to rest them. But it didn't help.

"And you were there." Ruby opened her eyes and gazed at Hank.

For a half second, she saw something in his expression that made her all but flinch and she turned away. Luther leaned in toward her again and Ruby suspected that he knew about them, that he'd seen or sensed something in the way she had just looked at Hank.

"Okay, then tell me where you went, exactly what you bought, and whether you have any receipts, or anything that can establish where you went. And when," Luther said. "Maybe the boy was wrong in his timing. Maybe you're wrong in yours. If you have a receipt, that might narrow it down."

"Receipt? Damnit, don't you understand? The day before my husband threw me down on a table in front of half the people I worked with and started chopping off my hair. I wasn't thinking, I wasn't keeping track of time, of receipts." What she didn't say was the night before Gardner had been shot she'd taken some Percocet, with a Valium chaser, and the next morning she'd taken a Valium, washed it down with Danni's Absolut. "I was lucky I could even drive, let alone keep a damn receipt."

"You should calm down," Belt said.

"Why don't you go to hell?" Flinging back her chair, Ruby stood up and glared around the room. "Most of the time, Gardner was a real asshole. But he didn't deserve to be shot. Somebody killed him and you're all sitting around with your thumbs up your ass asking me about receipts. You make me sick." She turned to Golder. "Come on. Let's get out of here."

***

"Well, well, that went good, bud, don't you think?" Luther asked, once Ruby and Golder were well out of sight.

"Yeah, actually it did. She's losing her cool, so we're getting somewhere with her now. She's not so confident," Hank said.

"Why'd she look at you like that?" Belt said, turning to Hank. "When she said she went to her house and you were there."

"Oh, he's her father figure, you know. The gray hair, the strong chin, it's a game we work a lot in interrogations with young women." Luther grinned at Hank and Belt in turn.

"She's not so young," Belt said. "And fatherly wasn't how she was looking at you."

"Yeah, well, who knows what secrets lurk in the hearts of poor *young* widow women," Luther said. "What I want to know is what you think about her as a suspect?"

"You have anybody else? I have a lot of pressure from the top to see somebody in the jail house soon on this. High profile. Newspaper's on my back." Belt kept staring at Hank. "What's with you and Mrs. Randolph?"

"Right, yeah, *you* got pressure to see an arrest," Luther said, quickly. "Like we don't have a half dozen folk sticking their fingers in our eyes on this. I repeat, what do you think of her as a suspect?"

"I don't know. Who else have we got?"

"Maybe that Tally woman," Luther said. "She's not being straight with us, but we don't have anything on her except that she was screwing the dead guy and lying about it. They had some kinda fight before he's killed. I'm still sniffing around it."

"I know Tally," Belt said, pausing so long Luther turned to study him. "She's not a murderer."

"You *know* her, huh?" Luther picked up on something in Belt's voice when he'd spoken and looked at Belt with a hint of a leer. Belt turned away, his face red.

When he looked back, his anger couldn't be missed. "I want to talk with that boy says he saw Mrs. Randolph leaving the Ambruski's house around noon. Make sure he's certain she was heading south toward her home, not north toward the store. If he sticks, and if she can't come up with a better story than going to the drugstore, I say arrest her." With that, Belt rose and left the room.

After Belt stomped off, Hank thanked Luther for sidetracking Belt.

"Yeah, it wouldn't do to have Belt sniffing around you and Ruby too close, now would it? And if you're still seeing your girlfriend, tell her to get a grip. You're so big on her being a cool liar, but, bud, she was hanging out today."

"I'm not still seeing her," Hank said.

But Luther was already studying on something else. Ruby said Gardner wouldn't have given Tally a key, that he wasn't a trusting man. Yeah, that's what Tally said too, exactly the same words, the same phrase. Luther wondered briefly if the two women had coached each other, maybe had a couple of secrets between them. Then he remembered how Tally ratted on Ruby with such an air of satisfaction. *Naw, they'd never be able to work together, keep a secret.*

Or would they?

Chapter Fifteen: At the Gulf

Dave sat next to Ruby on a musty, flowered sofa at her rental apartment as she shuffled through some computer printouts. "It's not all there," he said. "The second set of books is missing, but there's enough here to prove what was going on. Do you understand them?"

"I already know the big picture." Ruby handed the papers back. "But I don't really want to know any more of the details. Not now."

"Just as well. I'm fuzzy on some of the details. Nancy's got the computer programs all rigged with passwords and such that I've only retrieved part of the materials. But I'll work it out, get the rest. It's the second set of books I need and to find out where the money is. They had to deposit it somewhere. I'm working the banks best I can, using lawyerly threats and such." Dave gave a weak smile at that, then shook his head. "But they need subpoenas, that is unless I just find a weak link in the chain at the right bank."

"I'm surprised the police haven't already gotten wind of this."

"I'm not. Everyone's trying to protect the firm or protect themselves. There's been a kind of tacit understanding among the attorneys not to talk about this. The secretaries are following the lead of their attorneys. Besides, I don't think any of them actually know anything but rumors. I'm sure the police have some idea the firm is in trouble because we couldn't keep that kind of gossip away from them."

"Nancy might know where the money is."

"I'll leave that to the detectives to ask. I'm taking these reports to the police. I've gone round and round with this, but it's got to be done. First, I'm meeting with Golder and Fred. I want to know Golder's spin on how this impacts you. Fred needs to do what he can to protect the firm. Might be a few days before we go to the police, Fred and me.

We're not going until we've finished with the computerized bookkeeping reports. But we are taking all this to the police."

"Dave, if this goes public, the firm's dead. That's why I asked Golder to hold up with my suspicions about Gardner embezzling. Of course, that was before there was any real evidence of it." Ruby glanced at the papers in Dave's hands and wondered if Nathaniel would be able to protect himself.

"The firm's already dead. I'm not letting you get arrested over Gardner when this will show the police that any one of the partners had a motive to kill him. Bringing the firm to the edge of bankruptcy and getting all those people fired just to run Nathaniel and me out. I could have killed him myself."

Ruby tensed at the sudden vehemence in Dave's voice. "Did you?"

Dave folded up the computer print-outs and returned them to the briefcase on the coffee table in Ruby's beach rental. "No, but the truth is I'm flattered you thought to ask. I wish I had."

***

After Dave left, Ruby slipped on a pair of cut-offs and walked across the street to the beach. Shabby as her apartment was, the Dolphin Key address meant it was expensive. Its location across from an open, undeveloped stretch of beach was its redeeming quality. To people like Ruby who'd lived in Florida a number of years, it was too cold to swim, but a few hardy northern visitors splashed about in the gulf. Ruby waded at the edge of the beach, barely getting her feet wet as the sun slipped lower in the western sky. Two dolphins arced out of the water, moving parallel with the horizon. A black lab ran splashing into the waves after a frisbee. Singularly and in small groups, middle-aged men trying to jog their way out of heart attacks ran by. Old couples drifted by, stopping occasionally to pick up broken shells.

Ruby turned her face to the orange glow on the horizon. Against her will she remembered walking the beaches at sunset with Gardner, holding hands and feeling good right after they first moved to Desoto Cove from Tampa.

They had both loved Desoto Cove. Ruby remembered one night when they had been out dancing and afterwards walked on Turtle Beach to cool down after the hot bar and loud band. Well past midnight they saw a sea turtle come out of the Gulf of Mexico and dig a nest to lay her eggs. When they approached her for a better look, she hissed. They'd backed off, but stood and watched, transfixed. After the turtle swam back out to sea, they collapsed into a nearby beach cabana. The sex that night had been exceptional, even with that tension that was always between them.

There had been times when they worked together like a real couple, if not happy exactly, then at least in a kind of sync, with a forward momentum. Ruby could remember her sense of oddly comfortable complacency in those early days. She'd ignored the fact they weren't happy as well as the hints of warning at the beginning of their relationship, content to be coddled, pampered and told precisely what to do. But as her confidence and skills grew and she wanted his guidance less, Gardner's need to control every facet of her life increased. He was jealous of Nathaniel as her mentor at the firm even before she and Nathaniel became lovers. After finding out about her affair with Nathaniel, Gardner was unrelenting in his attempts to command every moment of her life, even to the point of force. Finally, there was little more than an open battle of wills between them, a struggle with a lingering shadow of violence.

Gardner built a rock-solid safety harbor for her during their first years together. Then he eroded it, stone by stone, every time he lunged at her, cornered her, pushed her into some act she did not want to take. But from what little remained, or what little she remembered of that safety harbor, Ruby felt some kind of positive emotion—gratitude, if not love, perhaps. She was amazed that she grieved for Gardner and in some unfathomable way missed him.

Or missed the notion of who she had once thought he was.

***

Later that night, staring at a TV screen without really listening, Ruby jumped up from the old couch. Pausing only long enough to run some cold water over her face and finish the Vodka Gimlet she was nursing, Ruby got in her car and drove inland, down the back roads into an older Desoto Cove neighborhood. She'd been to Nancy's house before with Gardner on some strange, late night response to her phone call, and Ruby was sure she could find the house again.

Nancy's car was in the carport and a light was visible in a back window when Ruby knocked on the door. After a long moment, a light in the living room came on and Nancy opened the door.

"What do you want?" Nancy asked.

"To warn you."

"Warn me? You think you know something I don't know?"

"May I come in?"

"No. Say what you have to say."

"You need to take any steps you can to protect yourself. Dave's going to the police with Gardner's embezzling. He's got some computer print-outs. Thinks he can show what went on. You'll be implicated."

"He's a fool to put the whole firm at risk like that."

"There's not much firm left. You've got a couple of days before he goes to the police."

"Why are you telling me this?"

"I don't want anyone, even you, going to jail because of something Gardner made them do."

"And?"

"Let me in."

This time Nancy stood back and Ruby stepped in. The living room looked normal, but Ruby pushed past Nancy and went in the direction of the light she'd seen when she first drove up. Nancy followed.

In Nancy's bedroom, two closed suitcases were already leaning against the wall and a third was all but full.

"I see you're finally taking a vacation," Ruby said. "About time."

"Yes. Overdue. Now what do you really want?"

"I want to know where Gardner kept the second books, or his copy. I don't care about the account books, or the money, but there's something else he had that I want and I can't find it. I figure it might be in the same place as the account books. Did he keep them in a safe deposit box? A storage unit? Or what?"

"He never told me where. Just that I shouldn't worry, the books weren't at his home or his office."

"That's all you know?"

"Yes."

"Are you sure? You must have some idea—some hint—of where he hid things."

"Gardner was my co-conspirator, not my confidant."

The two women stared at each other without speaking. Nancy seemed to be telling the truth and she was right that Gardner wasn't likely to trust her with personal information. It'd been a long shot at best. Ruby headed back toward the front door.

"Enjoy that vacation," Ruby said as she opened the door to leave. She turned back for a moment. "I guess you're taking the money."

Nancy shut the door.

***

Ruby was making a sandwich the next day when Luther and Hank knocked on her door. She let them in without speaking.

"I'd have called," Luther said.

"Yeah, I know, no phone. And the manager won't take messages. I've been meaning to get a phone put in." She looked down at Luther's hands, full of official papers. "So Belt made up his mind?"

"Yeah. After he talked with the kid who says he saw you leaving Fred's at the right time, heading out in the direction of your house." Luther paused. "I'm sorry. I shouldn't be explaining this to you." Luther stopped talking and Hank stood behind him, silent, looking over his shoulder at the grungy rental, unable to look Ruby in the eyes.

"You better call Golder. We'll stop at the first pay phone," Luther said.

"Let me get a few things. Finish my lunch. If you want a sandwich, you can make them yourselves."

Luther nodded. "Don't take too long."

Ruby figured this wasn't exactly standard police procedure and wondered why Luther acted like he was on her side.

And that Hank wasn't. Not anymore.

But she'd have plenty of time for thinking. She took one more bite of the sandwich and put it down. She went into the bathroom and came out a few minutes later, carrying a large purse, which she dropped on the couch in front of Luther. "In case you want to search it, make sure I'm not carrying."

As Luther looked through her purse, Hank approached her, his expression stern.

"I'm sorry you have to do this, Hank," she said.

Hank pulled out a set of handcuffs. "It's regulations."

Ruby felt the warm animal heat off his body as Hank stepped up close to her to snap on the handcuffs.

Chapter Sixteen: Luther and Ruby

Ruby crouched on the bench in the cell, knees drawn up with her arms around them, head tucked down. She heard the footsteps approach, the cell door unlocked and opened, but she did not look up.

"Mrs. Randolph," Luther said, "I'd like a minute with you. Off the record."

"I learned a long time ago there is no such thing as off the record." Ruby sat without lifting her head, her voice muffled.

"This is. Off the record. I'd get in trouble for talking to you without your lawyer. But I gotta take my chances right now since Golder will get you out of here soon, smooth as that arraignment went for you."

"So don't plan on a long conversation." Ruby finally straightened up and untangled her long legs.

"Yes, ma'am."

"Now we're all through buttering each other up, what do you want?"

Luther glanced around the cell before letting his eyes rest on Ruby. "I tell you, you're a piece of work."

"I said we were done buttering each other up, okay."

"Yeah. All right. What I want to know is what you're leaving out. What I mean, and I mean this off the record, is you're hiding something. Fact is, I get the feeling you're hiding a big pot full of something. And that whole big ole law firm's hiding something too. And maybe if you can bring yourself to trust me enough to tell me, I might can help you."

"Why?"

"Why should you trust me? 'Cause you got need of another friend right now. I'm not saying you haven't got friends. Seems you've got a loyal following, but I am saying you need a friend who can actually help find who killed your husband."

"I meant why do you want to help me?"

"Well, it's partly 'cause you need help. And it's partly I got the feeling you didn't kill your husband. And maybe it's mostly I want to solve this murder and I need your help to do that."

Ruby stretched, stood up and walked over to the cell door. She tested it to see if it was locked. "Am I so dangerous they have to lock you in with me?"

"Normal procedure. No need to take offense."

Ruby pulled on the door again before turning back to Luther. "I don't know who killed Gardner."

"All right, I accept that. But there's stuff you do know. Like what was going on at that law firm that it's falling to pieces and everybody seems to somehow or other blame Gardner? It's not what anybody says, not specifically, you know, but it's damn sure a feeling I get."

Ruby wondered if Nancy was gone yet. Probably. She looked back at Luther, taking in the sleepy blue eyes, the sandy fringe of the long eyelashes, the thick droop of the mustache over his lips, the wary expression. Luther had the worn look of a man waiting for the other shoe to drop.

"I used to live in Tampa," Ruby said. "You were a cop there for a while?"

"Yes, ma'am."

"I was just part of the crap that collects around the edges of a college campus, back then, in 71, 72."

"Crap?"

"Yes, the garbage people, trash, you know, the dope dealers, the guys looking to grab the young coeds their first time away from home, the cons, the drop outs. The people who feed off the students."

"Yeah, got it. I've worked that beat."

"I got in some trouble. Gardner got me out of it, cleaned me up some, sent me to college, and married me. I was grateful. Some, maybe most of the last few years I've spent hating him, but I never stopped being grateful. Does that make any sense?"

"Sure. I think I can understand that."

Nothing like some time in a cell to make a body contemplative. She wondered why she was beginning to trust Luther. Why she wanted him on her side.

"I didn't kill him. That's all I can tell you."

"So, it's Gardner you're protecting?"

Ruby walked from the door toward Luther, watching his face. "It doesn't make any sense to protect him now, does it?"

"Maybe not, but sounds like that's what you're doing."

Ruby shook her head.

"Who are you protecting? What else aren't you telling me? I mean, giving up the girlfriend was like pulling teeth out of you and I can't figure why you'd want to protect her. The big story out there, the one you ain't telling, must be pretty good."

"Look, I get the feeling you're a decent guy. But I'm dead tired and I can't help you. I want you to leave now."

Luther ambled to the cell door and motioned a guard down to unlock the door. While the guard walked toward the cell, Luther turned back to Ruby. "We didn't have this little talk, you understand?"

"Doesn't the guard know?"

"He's an old friend and he won't mention it. Will you?"

"No."

"One last thing. Watch your self-control. Especially around Hank. Don't be giving him any more of those looks."

Ruby stared at Luther almost blankly. "I'm not sure I understand," she said, making her voice utterly without emotion.

"Good, good, that's it, you got it now."

"I don't know what you mean."

"Look, I know about you and Hank. But I admire the poker face you got on you right now. Keep it on, okay, where Hank's concerned?"

Ruby held his eyes for a moment. He was trying to protect Hank, she realized. That's what this was about. She walked toward the cell door and offered him her hand. He shook it as she smiled tentatively at him. "I doubt we'll have anymore of our little tete-a-tetes for a while. I'll have my act together by trial," she said.

"Yes, ma'am, I'm sure you will."

The guard unlocked the door and Luther stepped out. Taking one last shot, he asked, "Just give me a hint where I should start looking, okay?"

"I don't know, really."

"Then tell me who had the extra key? Who are you protecting?"

"Nobody."

The guard re-locked the door and walked off. Luther lowered his voice and leaned back toward the locked cell door.

"It wasn't Hank, was it? Hank didn't have an extra key?"

"No," Ruby said, meeting his eyes, hoping he believed her.

"Thank you." Luther nodded at her, then walked off.

But Luther knew she'd lied before. Maybe he thought she'd given Hank a key so he could shoot Gardner.

***

Ruby squinted in the sunlight as Golder walked her to his car to drive her home after he'd bailed her out. "You've got to find that receipt," he said. "My investigator has interviewed the cashier who was on duty at the front around noon and she doesn't remember you. There're no surveillance tapes or any other documentation. There's nothing to show you were at that store around 12:30 or so. Lunch hour like that, there was lots of traffic in the store. You didn't make any kind of impression on anybody working there. Yet it seems like you might have, black eye and all. Belt will make it look like you lied about going to the store to cover up lying about being at the Ambruski's house, unless you find the receipt."

"Look, I've told you, I doubt I kept it. I mean, why would I keep a receipt for a little junk from a drugstore? Probably thrown out in the sack." Ruby shook her head.

"You know what the half-life of Valium is? You ought to think about that."

142

"Look, I told you, I'm hazy about that night and day because I'd had a few drinks that afternoon with Danni and then I took some Percocet, little Valium to sleep, and I was still upset the next day, so I had some vodka to steady myself before I went over there. After that, the shock, all right? I just don't remember everything in detail."

"Sure, and a jury will love that. I use it all the time to great success. The so-full-of-drugs-and-booze I can't remember defense."

"It'll never get to a jury." Ruby stopped listening to Golder. What she was thinking about was just getting away from the jail to someplace clean and taking a long, hot shower. She planned to stay under the shower until all the hot water was gone. Even then, Ruby doubted she would feel clean.

***

Hank looked up from his desk as the most junior of the detectives, Rufus Wilson, paused in front of him. "What?" Hank liked the young man, though he found him largely inept and somewhat goofy.

Luther, who was grumpily working a phone list at the next desk, put down the receiver and glanced at Wilson. "You got something for us?"

Wilson, dressed in off-the-rack suit pants and a perma-press shirt yellowing in the pits, nodded. "Detectives, those fingerprint reports you've been hounding everybody for are here. I personally went up to get them, soon as they called. You guys were out." He handed an envelope to Luther. "You might want to look at these now that you're back."

"Guess you've already done just that," Hank said, feeling territorial.

"Yep. Right interesting. You all have a nice day now." Wilson grinned and stepped away.

Luther opened the envelope, turning pages and reading, then returning to the first page and reading it again. Hank resisted the urge to snatch the papers out of Luther's hands.

"Yep, right interesting. Here we got something new. Something that adds a mighty interesting turn of events. And you said lab work never adds anything much. Listen to this." Luther jabbed a finger at a line on a page. "Fingerprints all over the damn house belonging to an ex-con, name of Billy Dittwilder. Just out of UCI two days before the murder. Matched up with prints you sent them from the parole board. I remember you thinking something was mighty interesting about his file."

"Hunches and drudge-work." Hank tapped a finger on his keyboard and tried to act casual. *Yeah, here it comes.*

"And who says there ain't no God?" Luther winked at Hank. "What'd you want to bet that ole Billy might just be, say, an old client of the recently departed Mr. Randolph?"

"You know that, do you?"

"No, but we will. Stay tuned." Luther flipped through a few more pages. "Wilson's aiming for being a good boy. He's already attached the basic info from the parole office. Just paints the big picture. Fifteen years in Union Correctional. Picked up in Tampa in 1972. PO wanted us to try and find him because he never checked in. I reckon we'll sure do our best to find him now."

"What'd he do time for?" Pretending, for reasons Hank wasn't completely sure of, that he didn't already know this.

"Drugs. Intent to sell. Resisting arrest with violence. Assault. Arson. Multiple attempted escapes. One killing inside the joint that went down as self-defense but ruined any shot at parole. Another time, beating crap out of an inmate."

"Nice guy."

"Yeah, had a previous in Louisiana for B & E. No jail time there. Washington County, mean anything to you?"

Hank grunted.

"Hey, wait. Didn't those Florida Bar files on Ruby show she came from Louisiana? I don't remember the county. I'll look it up in a minute." Luther raised his eyebrows as he studied Hank.

"Don't bother. She's from Washington County too."

Luther stood outwardly impassive for a moment, but Hank could sense the anger in him.

"Go ahead, Luther. Say it."

"That's why you were so interested in Dittwilder's file, wasn't it? Why you followed up on his prints? Don't you think, maybe, you should have shared the Washington County connection with me?"

"Just a hunch, not even that."

"You owe me better'n that, bud."

"Yes."

"All right." Luther let it go to Hank's relief, then turned back to the report. "Just the basics. Here, you look." Luther handed the paperwork over to Hank.

"You remember anything about any Dittwilder in all those files that Randolph had?" Luther asked. "Any file, or notes, anything on a Billy Dittwilder?"

Hank shook his head.

"Nope, me neither. Let me go get Wilson back, see if he did when he was helping us. He'll be hanging out with the coffee machine this time of day."

A few minutes later, Hank leaned against his desk, cradling the phone to his ear, as he watched Luther and Wilson come back in, talking. They stopped in front of Hank and he whispered he was on hold.

"Kept everything, that Randolph guy did, that's what they say about him. If there's a connection, it's in one of those boxes of paper," Luther said. Wilson nodded in agreement. "Trouble is, we looked at so much crap, we might have forgotten."

"Damn." Hank slammed the phone down. "Cut off."

Luther and Wilson cut their eyes at each other as Hank picked up the phone from where it'd bounced and put it back where it belonged. He told them he'd left a message with the secretary of the only person who was at UCI that day who could possibly, so the secretary assured him, release the files on Dittwilder. He'd been waiting for her to confirm someone would call him back as soon as possible about getting those files to him right away. He guessed being cut off was his answer.

"Well, shoot," Wilson said. "Let's get at those files of Mr. Randolph."

Together they all went to the storage area where boxes of Gardner's neatly labeled files were stacked, taking up so much room that other detectives had been grumbling, stepping and kicking over the boxes any time they came into the area. "Let's find the D's in the stuff from his work files," Luther said, even as Hank was already sliding boxes out of the way to get at the box with the D's.

After Wilson lifted the box off the floor to a table to study it better, the men went through the files twice. No Dittwilder.

"Way he kept everything, you know if this guy had been a client, there'd be a damn file," Luther said.

"You always were best at stating the obvious," Hank said.

"Well, bud, somebody's gotta, because what's obvious to you and me might not be so plain to the rest of the world. Like say to Wilson here, who don't have the benefit of our years of experience, being just a young pup, you see."

"Report with the fingerprints said he'd served fifteen years for trafficking in narcotics and other assorted stuff, so it'd be an old file. Maybe it's in the home stuff," Wilson said.

They turned and looked at the other boxes. "Damn," Luther said. "Wilson, go get that Jerry fellow in here looking too. Even he can recognize the words Billy Dittwilder. Hank and me got better stuff to do right now."

"Maybe he had a storage unit someplace else. Get that new woman detective on the phone calling all the storage units in town," Hank added. "Between us, let's get it done."

But Hank had the sense he was moving through wet cement as it hardened around him. If he could have figured out a way to cut and run, he would have.

***

An hour later, with no Dittwilder file among Gardner's belongings, Luther was back on the phone, calling up to Tampa and to UCI for the files and further information on Billy Dittwilder. Luther was putting

146

the personal touch on the phone calls, reminding everyone he used to be on the Tampa PD, because the first hour's worth of calls had netted nothing but assurances that somebody would call them back sometime, and, yes, just as soon as they could. He wanted the information straight and fast. Hank was working another phone at his desk and apparently having no better luck.

Luther was tapping his fingers to the oldies playing through the phone when Tally approached him. Nothing slinky or seductive today. She had on a white blouse, buttoned up to her collar bone, and a pair of tailored navy pants.

"Detective Downs," she said, "I need to talk to you. But not here. Please, it's important."

"All right. Let's go into one of the interview rooms." He stretched the phone over to Hank's other hand, saying, "On hold, records, girl's name is Susie, don't growl, she's a sweetheart." Then he took Tally to an interview room, motioned for her to sit, offered her coffee, and waited.

Tally didn't want to sit or to sip coffee. What she wanted to do was a little bit of cleaning house. Luther settled back to listen.

"This is not easy for me," she said.

He nodded, encouragingly, he hoped.

"I'm leaving the law firm. In fact, I'm leaving town. Soon as I can arrange everything. But I want to be up front with you. I lied to you the other day. I was sleeping with Gardner Randolph. But he broke it off. We had a fight. But I didn't kill him. I lied because I was afraid. Being involved in a murder case isn't good on a resume." She said it all in one fast rush, then inhaled long and hard.

Luther felt a tinge of embarrassment for her. She didn't know she was humiliating herself just an hour after she'd dropped off his list of suspects. "Why are you telling me this now?"

"Because one of the guiding principles every trial lawyer knows is that bad facts sound better coming from you, rather than from your opponent."

"I'm not sure I understand."

147

"Because Jacob Stanley overheard us fighting the night Gardner broke it off with me. I was very angry and very hurt and…well, I…I more or less threatened to kill him, Gardner, I mean. Now Jacob is threatening to tell you if I don't, shall we say, cooperate with him, if you know what I mean. But I don't blackmail. So, I'm telling you the truth."

"See, honesty *is* the best policy," Luther said, amused by her earnest performance. Yet he had no doubt this time she was telling the plain, unadorned truth—especially since the mail room clerk had already told him about the affair, the fight, and Tally's threat.

"I appreciate your interest," Luther said, matching his voice to her serious tone. "And thank you for coming in. And *do* leave a forwarding address with the detective's division."

"I can go then?"

"Yes."

"You should look into Jacob, too. He does a great deal of cocaine. Or at least that's what I've heard, I don't know it from first-hand experience. A man his age, doing coke, it might have pushed him over. I don't know." Tally pushed a strand of her dark hair behind an ear with a movement that seemed to be part caress and started for the door.

Luther enjoyed watching her walk and kept his seat till she was out of his sight. *What an odd thing, this detective work.* Yesterday he and Hank were massaging a few circumstantial facts against the widow, basically on the fundamental principle that when one spouse is killed, the other spouse is the best suspect. And now they had an ex-con with some connection to the dead man. Better yet, an ex-con helpful enough to leave his fingerprints in the bedroom and on the back door. And maybe a coked-up lawyer. And Tally, admitting her own motive and her lie.

Thing was, he didn't want or need Tally as a suspect anymore, or the nervous little coke-head with his ridiculous hair because he was pleased with just the ex-con. The moment Luther saw the fingerprint report, he considered the crime solved. Billy Dittwilder did it. Now it was just a matter of dotting the i's and crossing the t's before it was all official. And finding the ex-con.

Even Hank ought to lighten up now. Luther started humming as he went back to the office he shared with Hank and the other detectives.

When Luther came back into the office, Hank looked up, his left hand still holding Luther's phone, his right hand awkwardly jotting notes on a slip of paper that kept sliding out from under his pen as he tried to write. Before he asked, Hank told him.

"Susie transferred me to a guy named Buttercup or something, who's trying to see if the Dittwilder files are around in storage. Says he remembers you, you guys were buddies or something. Dittwilder was his case, according to the case jacket. Figures he might need to call back, but he's trying real fast, right now, to get a girl in records to see if the whole file is still around. UCI's pulling their papers together for us."

Luther took his phone, put it to his ear, hearing the familiar sound of oldies on hold, and thought, yeah, Butterfield. He smiled, remembering a jovial, big fellow, a decade older than him, somebody he used to go fishing with when Nora let him. "Butterfield, like the band, okay?" he corrected Hank, who was already doing something else.

When Luther got off the phone ten minutes and three calls later, he said, "When it rains it pours. I'm driving up to Tampa right now to get the paper files. Butterfield, old guy who worked the Dittwilder case, doesn't exactly remember the file. But like you said, he sure remembers me. Gave up on the girl in records. Says he'll go fish out the official file himself and wait for me. Meanwhile, I got my call-back and the state attorney's office up there has some of the prosecution file still in storage. Somebody'll dig it out for me. I'll swing by there too. And who says there ain't no God?"

"Before you go, tell me about the visitor."

"Aw, just a paranoid admission, I lied, I'm sorry, I didn't do it. Don't worry. I got a feeling about this Dittwilder guy. You were right, Tally's not our killer. Fill you in on the dirty details when I get back."

While he was gathering up his jacket, the woman detective who had been diligently calling every rental storage unit, big and small, in Desoto Cove, and stressing the power of the local police to guarantee cooperation, came up to them. From the eager look on her face, Luther knew she had something.

"Okay, don't hold back, now," Luther said. "What'd you find out?"

"Storage unit place off Tuttle has a unit rented to a Gardner Randolph. I got the address and the phone number. Had to threaten to use police powers and such though."

"Thank you, we appreciate it," Luther said, smiling at her as she walked off.

"Go on to Tampa," Hank said. "I'll work it at this end. Probably need a subpoena, though it won't hurt to try otherwise."

"Local news updates at Six," Luther said, grinning. "Bud, this one's going down."

***

Hank glared at the boxes in the unit. *Damn, it'll take forever to look through all this.* "I'm kind of sorry we got that subpoena." He was also sorry about what Luther had learned two days before in Tampa, but had kept that to himself. He wasn't used to keeping stuff from Luther and had to watch that he didn't slip up, say the wrong thing, give something away.

"Yeah, old Golder, he sure huffed and puffed and he obstructed," Luther said, squatting on the concrete floor of Gardner Randolph's rented storage unit, "but here we are."

One of Golder's young associates was standing outside the door, charged with the tasks of watching, listening and noting anything the detectives found and took. "Easy billing at the regular hourly rate. Beats the law library," the associate said.

"I'll take this side," Hank said. He dreaded what today's search might turn up about Billy and Ruby. He hated what he and Luther already knew, or thought they did.

Working with a few facts and some imagination, Hank and Luther figured Ruby and Billy came down to Tampa together from Louisiana.

When Billy got in trouble, Ruby must have met Gardner while he was representing Billy. With no transcript from Billy's trial and no one in the state attorney's office who'd been there fifteen years ago, they didn't know if Ruby had testified. But the police files indicated she'd been questioned repeatedly, but never arrested. Reading the photocopies of poorly microfilmed files had been difficult and frustrating and seemed mostly to open the door for more questions than answers.

The prison records showed Ruby had visited Billy at UCI on a regular basis during his first six months, then there was a long gap with no visits. But four years ago she'd started back visiting Billy, often monthly, with the last visit in August of this year. Hank couldn't help but notice that Ruby stopped those jail visits to Billy right after she met him.

Perhaps the more puzzling thing, though, was that Gardner had visited Billy on a Saturday one week before Billy's release. But after a long and fruitless drive yesterday to Starke and their interviews with guards and other prisoners, neither Hank nor Luther heard any explanation for Gardner's visit. A guard named Jimmy, who Hank figured most have weighted 300 pounds, claimed to remember the two men were angry with each other.

That was where they were when they finally got the court order allowing them into this storage unit. Now, Hank fought the urge to eat a handful of Tums, dully kicked out a box, and squatted down to look through it.

Next to him, Luther grunted as he crouched down between a wooden crate and a row of cardboard boxes. "What do you reckon the good widow is trying to hide that every time we go to look at a file of her late husband's she has a hissy fit?"

Hank ignored the question and kept digging through paper, but he wondered the same thing.

A while later, Hank held up a black spiral notebook with computer printouts neatly hole-punched and placed inside the three-ring binder. "Now what?"

Luther moved to look over his shoulder at the print-outs.

In the first column, some kind of identification abbreviations were listed in a long vertical line. In the second column, numbers apparently representing amounts of money, or printed like amounts of money but without dollar signs, were listed coinciding with the abbreviations. In the third column, something that might be bank account numbers appeared. Hank and Luther studied it, turning the pages. In the back of the book, unlabeled columns of numbers were set out in small, tidy columns. Golder's young guard dog walked over and looked down.

"All right, we're taking this back to the office with us," Hank said. "So mark it down." The associate jotted down a note on his legal pad.

"Source, amount, location," Hank said. "That'd be my guess about the first pages. Rest of it looks like some kind of bookkeeping stuff."

"Yeah. Reckon he was a bookie on top of everything else?"

"Looks like client identification numbers to me, that first column," Belt's associate said.

Hank put the binder down and each man bent back to his search. The floor was hard, cold concrete and Hank's knees protested. With his back to Luther, he pawed through some files, then he slowed down to study one. After reading a typed page, he rocked back on his haunches, and stared ahead, his lips tightly drawn in his tired face.

Luther was looking through several boxes of record albums. "Man had good taste, got every last one of the Stones' LPs. Sure like to take these home. As the last man in the city to still have a turn-table."

Hank kept staring ahead at nothing.

"I gotta go take a leak," Luther said, standing and stretching.

"I wouldn't mind a break," the associate said.

"Yeah, yeah, I'll go outside so you don't have to worry about us stealing the man's record collection," Hank said.

After the three men were outside the storage unit, Hank pulled the door shut and put his hand over the padlock and pushed at it. Then they walked off.

But once Luther was safely down the hallway and the associate was out of sight lighting up, Hank eased back to the unit.

He stared at the padlock he'd only pretended to lock. Then he gave up and ate four Tums. And opened the padlock and walked back inside the storage unit.

Once back inside the unit, he squatted down by the last boxed he'd searched, reached into an unlabeled file and took out a sheet of paper with typing on both sides. There was a cassette tape in an envelope with it. Hank folded up the paper, slipped it and the tape inside the back pocket of his pants, smoothed it down, and stepped back out of the unit. This time he did lock the padlock.

When the associate came back, Hank was standing by a drink machine, sipping on a soda. Luther was chatting with the woman who ran the office. They went back to the unit and the associate used the key to open the unit to them.

***

Ruby got out of bed, but didn't flip on the lights as she made her way, barefoot, into the kitchen. After glancing at the clock and moaning when she saw it was 2:20 in the morning, she ran tap water into a glass and drank a few sips before she poured the rest out. She reached for the vodka, her eyes able to find it in the half-light of the moon and the street lights.

After she finished drinking a two-finger shot, she stood staring out the kitchen window. And saw a car. A dark Chevy. Like the unmarked police car Hank sometimes drove when he wasn't using his pickup.

"Damn." She wished she had a gun so she could shoot through the window, scare the bastard for spying on her.

Without thinking, Ruby slammed out the only door to her apartment and aimed herself right at the car. Yeah, it was Hank all right, watching her, sitting there in the front seat. She stomped up to the car door and snatched it open.

Hank stared at her but didn't speak. She reached in and grabbed the coffee cup from his hand. She meant to throw it on him, scald him with it if the coffee was still hot.

But Ruby glanced at Hank's face and then his empty hand, taking careful note of his thick, long fingers that had just a second before held the coffee cup. A quiver started up through her. As angry as she was, just looking at his fingers made her want them on her. She threw the coffee out on the ground. The vodka made her dizzy and under her foot a sharp stone cut into her bare heel. She wasn't wearing anything but an old T-shirt and she crawled on top of him, one leg on each side of his hips, her face toward him, her back to the front windshield of the car. In the narrow, cramped space, she jammed against his body.

Before he could react, Ruby had his zipper down and her hands found him soft, pliable under her touch. A few deft strokes with her fingers and he was as hard as if they'd been slow dancing nude for an hour. She climbed on, slammed herself down, dry and tight without the juice of desire. She hoped she rubbed him raw. That's what it felt like she was doing to herself.

Hank reached up and cupped her breasts, still clothed in the T-shirt, and he flicked at her nipples with his thumbs until they hardened. He put both his hands behind her head and pulled her mouth toward his. As soon as his tongue was inside her lips, the ragged pain gave way to a raw, wet pleasure. She moaned and paced herself, rocking first side to side, then gyrating slowly, carefully in a circle.

When they were done and her breathing was coming back to normal, she struggled in the narrow space to pull off him. "You might as well come on inside. Get comfortable. I'm not going out anymore tonight."

Ruby crawled out of the car. Without looking back, she headed to her apartment, afraid for a minute Hank wasn't going to follow her. But by the time she reached her door, he was crossing the sand and gravel of the yard while she waited for him. Then they went inside together. She wondered if they might find that tenderness again between them, that sweetness from the only night she'd spent with him. Or if there was too much anger now between them. Too much doubt and blame and knowledge.

Chapter Seventeen: Reunion

Luther grimaced in the stale air. This was like a bad habit. A tiresome one.

Ruby sat in a hard-backed chair in the interrogation room of the police department, with Golder sitting in watch beside her. Hank stood with his back to her and Luther walked around the table until he was standing across from her. They'd been at it for an hour. Going over the old stuff. Why'd you lie about where you were? What did you mean by using the word blackmail during the fight the day before he was killed? Was your husband blackmailing you? Did you kill him?

Ruby either answered the same as before or sat still and moot when Golder recited "On advice of her attorney, Mrs. Randolph will not answer that."

Luther was waiting until she was exhausted and Golder disinterested by the repetition before he sprung the new questions about Billy Dittwilder. Yet he had to act before Golder ended the session. He also suspected his efforts would be pointless, that he wasn't going to trick Ruby or Golder into saying anything that would hurt her. Unless just the surprise of it all shocked some utterances from her. He'd been surprised she even agreed to this session after indicating that night in her cell she would refuse any further questions. Perhaps, Ruby had regained her confidence. She'd certainly lied convincingly about not having a recent affair.

Trouble was, nobody was letting their guard down. Hank was edgy, angry, harsh when he questioned her, and how much of that was a calculated act, and how much was Hank truly seething at this woman, Luther didn't know.

But when Hank finished butting Ruby with his questions, Luther had tried out his "shucks, ma'am" country boy routine. That didn't work any better than Hank's frontal attack.

Luther paused, wondering whether to go on with the dog and pony show or get to the chase, ask about that con up in Starke, the one from the same hometown, the one who left prints in the bedroom.

Making up his mind, Luther leaned closer to Ruby, and in a half-whispered, conspiratorial tone, he asked the question of the day. "Mrs. Randolph, do you know a Billy Dittwilder?"

Ruby and Golder both glared at Luther. Ruby lost her bored, petulant poker face. Golder reached over and put his hand on her arm.

"Shut up," Golder told her.

"Do you know a Billy Dittwilder?" Hank repeated, his anger clear in the way he spoke.

Golder looked at Ruby, then turned to Hank and Luther. "I'd like a minute alone with my client, if you please."

Standing outside the interrogation room, Hank and Luther loitered in the hallway, waiting for Golder. The look Hank gave him told Luther to keep quiet and he did. After about twenty minutes, Golder waved them back in.

"My client will prepare a statement about her relationship with Mr. Dittwilder and we will be back in touch. And now, since she is out on bail, I am unaware of any legal way you can hold her against her will. So, if you will excuse us."

Luther studied Hank as Golder led Ruby off, trying once more to read his partner's hard, stone face. He used to trust this man without question, without reserve, had trusted this man with his back for years on the street.

Now Luther wasn't so sure he could read Hank anymore. Or trust him. And he'd be damned if he had any notion what to do about it.

***

Hank wasn't ready to give up, but he knew that in a city like Desoto Cove, with its urban sprawl geography and layers of diverse population, it was hard to find one man. Especially when that man was staying away from the obvious places.

"Nothing. Not a damn thing. No sign of him," Hank said, coming back into the station and sinking into a chair in front of Luther at his desk.

"You didn't really expect to find old Billy boy, did you? I mean at that hotel address he gave the prison officials? Come on. That'd be too easy," Luther said. "Anything else?"

"No. Wilson and me looked about, showed his picture at most of the cheap dives up and down the Tamiami Trail, but we need to get the uniforms in on it. I'm still bugging the chief to okay surveillance on Ruby. If Dittwilder's gonna surface, I say he'll surface with her. Meanwhile, if we get the uniforms out there, looking and asking, maybe we'll flush him out. But keep it low key. Out of the press. I don't want him knowing what's up and taking off, running. What about here?"

"Oh, hell, now everybody's coming out of the woodwork volunteering to be suspects," Luther said. "This one even called to make an appointment."

"What do you have?" Hank sat, sinking further in the chair and wiping his face off with his sleeve. Most of the day, he'd been out with Wilson trying to find Billy Dittwilder, a task they'd been at without any luck ever since they read the prison file on Billy. Hank felt sticky and dirty.

"Remember Dave Thompson? The chubby lawyer, the one who talked like he was some kinda college professor? We wrote him off early as any kind of suspect. Nice guy, seemed a cut above the rest of the crew down at the law firm. Well, he called while you were out beating the bushes. Called to make an appointment. Said he had, and I quote, 'relevant materials' to share on the Randolph case."

"So you make him an appointment?" Hank asked.

"Yeah, I told him to get his butt right over here. Right then. And he did. He'll come back too. I told him you and me was partners, and we'd have to do this all together. Said he would, but he gave me what he wanted to. Here, look at these." Luther pulled some computer print-outs from of a file on top of his desk.

Hank flipped through them, puzzled. He turned a few pages, went back to the front, checked a figure and flipped back to the middle. Then he went slowly page by page. Luther got up and poured them each a cup of coffee, sat down again.

"Now we know what that second set of books we got from the storage unit was all about," Hank said. "Randolph was embezzling money from his own firm."

"Yep. Dave was a little fuzzy on just when he figured this out. But thought he'd better come on in. Had another attorney with him, Fred Ambruski, remember him? The chain smoker, answered every question in the initial interview with a grunt."

"Sure, I remember him. Wondered how he could be an attorney if he couldn't talk."

"Well, he didn't talk today either. But Dave sure did. He was spilling his guts so fast I had to slow him down just to make sense of it. Dave says to me, all earnest like, that he and Fred were trying to figure it out and they had to break some kind of code or password or something the bookkeeper had on the computers. That's why there was this delay, see? They were trying to get the whole story, he says, all nice like, to help us out, and that's why they didn't march their butts in here and tell us right off when they first figured out their dead partner'd been stealing from the firm."

Luther reached for his coffee cup, swallowed, frowned, and put the cup down. "But since they couldn't get the password to get into the bookkeeping stuff on the computer, it took them a bit longer to try and get us what he calls the 'whole truth.'"

"So why didn't they ask the bookkeeper for the password?"

"Damn, Hank, wake up, will you? The bookkeeper had to be in on it. You paying attention? Dave says they decided to come in today because the bookkeeper erased the entire bookkeeping files in the computers going back a whole year and then she disappeared. Left her furniture in a rental house, but cleaned out her personal stuff."

"Like she cleaned out the files, eh?"

"Yep. Must have been some serious night work go'n on at that firm. Anyway, they've been looking for her, hired their own investigator, some guy who did their workers' comp surveillance. Also hired some computer geek to try and retrieve the missing files, but boys, it's all she wrote. Files and bookkeeper."

"Don't those big firms have back-up tapes or disks or something? Off the computers. I mean, don't they have paper?"

"Yeah, but the paper's gone too. And what Dave said about the back-up disks is every night they back up all the files on the computers, bookkeeping and everything else. And they store the disks off-site in case the building burns down or something. Naturally then, Dave and Fred hotfooted it over to the where the disks are. Again, he's real fuzzy on just when all this took place, but it must have been real recent. Anyway, it took them a long time to work through the disks, but the thing is, the bookkeeping disks since last winter are all blank."

"Blank?"

"Yeah, like, you know, nothing on them. Seems like it was the managing partner's obligation to look out for the disks," Luther said. "They rotate among the partners and every year one of them is the managing partner. He's got to do a lot of extra stuff like ordering pencils and things. Being responsible for seeing the right folks are securing the back-up disks is one of his jobs. You want to take a guess who the managing partner was last year?"

"Yeah, let me. I guess Mr. Gardner Randolph," Hank said.

"Bingo."

"So the firm's financial records are all gone. The bookkeeper is in the wind. We've got the second set of books, but even if we figure out which bank the money was in, as a betting man, I'd bet that the bookkeeper cleaned out those accounts."

"Well, I reckon," Luther said, leaning back in his chair.

"Why're you looking so pleased? This means any one of the attorneys at that firm had a reason to kill Randolph. He destroyed that law firm."

"Yeah, sure, but also, let's think about that bookkeeper, that Nancy woman. She's embezzling with Gardner in some scheme. Knows where the checks are going, she's probably a signatory on the account. He gets shot and she's cool, waits till we arrest Ruby, thinks nobody's watching her real close, packs her bags, makes a run for it, no doubt, taking all that money they'd embezzled."

"So, she's a suspect now too?"

"Yep. I'm putting out the paperwork to get a warrant for her arrest on embezzling, and if we ever get her back, I'd say we ought to bear down on her about shooting the man that was standing between her and that money."

Hank was nodding now, seeing where Luther was going. "Sure, she comes knocking on his front door, he lets her in. She's a woman, they go to the bedroom together, she shoots him. Figures the timing is good because everyone will suspect Ruby after their brawl the day before. Cool enough to hang around a bit and not take the money and run the next day."

"Yep, I'm thinking we might've overlooked her in the suspect round-up, sure," Luther said. "But this info from Dave opens a whole bunch of new folks on the suspect list, don't it?"

"Plus, it explains why everybody apparently hated the man."

"Yeah. Randolph pretty much did that place in. No question about that. That firm's screwed big time. Dave makes a pretty good suspect himself. And the big guy, Nathaniel. You know, the founding partner. I gather that law firm was like Nathaniel's baby."

Hank sat still, quiet, and digested the new information. Wondered if it made any real difference. He wasn't a hundred percent sure he understood what Gardner had done, exactly. Not because he wasn't smart, but because half his brain kept going back to Ruby. Too hung up trying to figure her out to figure out much of anything else. "Take me through that embezzling again," he said.

"Look, here's how Dave explained it to me," Luther said. "Seems like Randolph's whole plan wasn't to really steal the money, but to seize control of the firm by manipulating the money so he could run Nathaniel and our new best friend, Ole Dave, out. Seems like Randolph made that pretty clear to Nathaniel as far back as July. Had them a big lawyer meeting. Mid-year," Luther said.

"Idea was, he'd dry up the money and blame Nathaniel and Dave, get the other partners to vote with him and against them and then he'd loosen up the money again once he got his way. Did you see the pattern on those print-outs? Money dries up before the big July meeting. So, they fire a bunch of the staff at that meeting. Cut back on overhead. Randolph talks them all to voting his way, except Nathaniel and Dave and that other guy, one who only grunts and smokes. After July, that firm is pretty much run by Randolph. While he's running things, money flows back in. He claims the credit, you know, tells everybody it's 'cause he's managing the firm so much better than Nathaniel had."

As Luther talked, Hank started flipping back through the firm's financial papers on his lap. Gardner Randolph's plans had been simple and complex, genius and stupid, all at the same time.

"Coming up this fall, everybody thinking on the big Christmas meeting, Nathaniel and Dave still aren't going along with leaving, and so the money dries up again. Dave says that Randolph drew up an analysis that blamed it all on Nathaniel and Dave, showing neither of them had brought in clients, or earned enough money, yet both were responsible for spending a big chunk of the overhead. Dave says the figures were mostly bogus, but he couldn't make anybody believe him about that. Says at first he and Nathaniel didn't even know that Randolph had that bogus report and was showing it around to the other partners. Didn't learn about it till somebody showed it to Mr. Grunt and Smoke and he took the bogus report to Nathaniel and Dave."

"When did that happen?" Hank leaned toward Luther, waiting for the answer.

"Yeah, that was about my favorite question too. Seems Nathaniel and Dave got that fake report a couple of days before Randolph got killed. I got the exact date in my notes." Luther reached over on his desk and picked up a notebook, pushed it over toward Hank.

"Anyway, while that bogus report was circulating, and before Nathaniel and Dave knew about it, all the attorneys got freaked out.

162

Went without their paychecks a few weeks even. That Randolph character was trying to convince them that it was all Dave's and Nathaniel's fault. Seems like everybody agrees Randolph's powers of persuasion were pretty darn strong even when the money was flowing. And Dave admits he'd had been way off for a year and everybody knew that, so it was easy for the Randolph character to blame him."

"Even Belt mentioned Randolph could about talk anybody into anything," Hank said, wondering what the man had talked Ruby into over the years. "Did the other partners know? I mean that Randolph was taking some of the money?"

"Dave says not."

"But?"

"But you got to figure some of them were at least beginning to suspect. I mean, they're lawyers, so they ain't stupid. And that's probably one of the things Ruby was hiding from us."

"Why would she hide what Randolph was doing?"

"Beats me, but she must've known. By the time he turned up dead, I figure most of the partners at least had some idea." Luther grinned again. "And that ain't all."

"Damn, it's enough though."

"Oh, no, I'm saving the good stuff for last. There was a life insurance policy on Gardner Randolph for $500,000 and the law firm was the beneficiary."

"Half mill?"

"Yes, sir. Something they called 'key man' insurance. Seems all the partners had the same policy on themselves. Firm bought it. Somebody might just have figured he'd kill two birds, you know, stop the embezzling and get a quick influx of cash."

"Insurance company paid off?"

163

"Day before yesterday. Seems the company was holding up because of the murder. What's his name, the grunt guy, Fred, was threatening the company with a lawsuit and when Ruby was formally charged, he badgered the company into paying the check over to the firm. You know, company doesn't have to pay proceeds to a person that kills an insured, but Dave says Fred convinced them that since *the firm* was the beneficiary and *the firm* can't kill anybody, that provision wouldn't help them no matter what. Besides, the charges against Ruby are well known now and she wasn't a partner. So, the insurance company paid up. That money is sitting in an account right now. Only the four named partners can draw on this account."

"All four of them have to sign together, or just any one of them?"

"Any one of them," Luther said. "The paranoia levels ought to be way high right now 'cause just one of them could decide the bookkeeper had the right idea. Take the money and run."

"I want to see them all in here again," Hank said. "Especially Dave and that tall guy, Nathaniel."

"Yep, I figured as much. Already got a call in to Belt. I reckon he might want to re-think his charges against Mrs. Randolph."

"Why?" Hank asked, not sure where Luther was going with this. "The best bet is still her and her old boyfriend."

"Maybe the boyfriend. I don't know, maybe she encouraged him. Gave him a key. But the other thing keeps coming back to me, like one of those damn little voices won't shut up, is the key thing and the other lover."

"What do you mean?"

"Well, what if that old lover she up and admitted to having way back when was one of the partners? What if she gave him a key a long time ago? What if he kept it? And what if he just let himself in one sunny Friday and killed the troublesome Mr. Randolph?"

164

"Yeah, could be, but I don't know, it doesn't feel right," Hank said. "We can ask Nathaniel and Dave if they had something going with Ruby. The rest of the partners too."

"Can't see Dave with her, or that is, can't see her with him. You know, he's one of those chubby, nice guys and they don't get much extra-curricular sex. I reckon Nathaniel and Fred would be about old enough to be her father. Jacob's too squirrely. So, I don't see her with any of the big four. Do you?"

"Nope."

"Then, let's go back to this basic idea. Ruby had a lover. The lover had a key. And maybe Ruby gives him a motive. Lover doesn't have to be a partner at the firm."

Hank saw where Luther was going with this line of reasoning. He figured it meant Luther thought Hank made a good suspect himself.

Hank patted his pocket like he thought there were cigarettes there, his face tense, unhappy.

"You still can't make up your mind, can you?"

Hank put his hands down and made sure he didn't fidget. "Make up my mind about what?"

"Whether you want to prove her guilty or prove her innocent."

Hank stood up, slowly, carefully. "Sure, we've got to walk all this new info through for Belt and better update the chief. We're gonna run those attorneys through the ringer four ways to Sunday for sure. If for no other reason, just for the fun of it. Payback for holding out on us about the bookkeeping and the insurance. But it's still the ex-con and Ruby I'm looking at."

"Bud, I'm looking at them all," Luther said.

And now, for sure, Hank figured Luther was counting him on the list of possible suspects.

***

Ruby opened the door a crack, looking at Billy's taut face in the shadows. It was 3 A.M. She kept the safety latch on the door.

"I was wondering when you'd show up." Ruby swallowed hard and gripped the door. She'd been in bed, pretending to sleep, and trying not to think about Gardner and Billy. "I didn't know where to find you. So, I waited for you to find me."

"Yeah, I bet you did. You know some cop sits out there half the night in a big ass Chevy, which even a blind guy could tell is an unmarked police car. Some old gray-haired guy." Billy glared at her through the crack between the chained door and the wooden frame, scaring Ruby as she studied his face in the half-darkness.

Ruby took her hands off the door, shifted her weight backwards, but still left the safety latch on. "He's not old."

"Yeah? He looked it to me. But he ain't here now."

"I figured, or you wouldn't be standing out there."

"You inviting me in?"

"Did you kill Gardner?" As she asked, Ruby braced herself against the door.

"The hell you ask." Billy crashed his shoulder against the door hard enough to break the safety latch out of the frame. He shoved past Ruby and walked into the apartment. For a moment, she stood in the doorway and looked out toward the parking lot.

"Forget it. I'd catch you before you got ten yards. Why you in a rat hole like this?"

"I like it. Reminds me of our early years together." Ruby moved out of the doorway and shut the door, but didn't lock it.

"Babe, we never had it this good," he said, walking to the refrigerator.

"No, we didn't, did we? I can't believe you got out two months early and didn't let me know. Why didn't you call and tell me about the early release?"

"Why didn't you call or visit?" Billy slammed the refrigerator door. "No beer. You got any pot?"

"You were so angry with me last time. I didn't know what to do, so I didn't visit. You know me, 'path of least resistance.' No, I don't have any pot. Vodka, that's all."

"Bull. I've never known you not to have something. Pills?" But even as he said it, Billy moved into the bedroom and started pulling open drawers and looking around.

Ruby followed. "When you're done having a good time showing me how tough you are, try the medicine cabinet in the bathroom. I'll go pour us some vodka."

When she came back in the bedroom, Billy was sitting on the bed, scattering pills on the bedspread and running his hands over the colorful capsules. Three empty pill bottles were on the bed covers. "Downers. Some good stuff. Legal and everything." He looked up at Ruby and smiled. "You come up some from copping street mess at the laundromats and bars."

"Yeah, when your husband gets murdered, the doctors will write you a script for some good drugs."

Billy picked up a couple of pills, popped them in his mouth and swallowed them with the vodka Ruby handed him.

"You can't be passing out here, you know. The police are looking for you. You might want to cut that hair and the beard. It's not 1972 anymore."

"No shit."

"Look, I mean it. You can't stay here."

"So who's ass you protecting here? Mine or yours?"

"Wouldn't it have to be yours? I mean, I'm already arrested for murder, aren't I?"

"Shut up and come over here." Billy grinned as he patted the bed beside him.

Ruby stood still, staring at him as Billy watched her. He picked up a couple of pills from the bed cover and got up, moving toward her. She backed up a few steps. He put one finger on her lips.

She licked his finger, tasting the salt on his skin as he held his finger pressed to her opened lips. Then she swallowed the two pills he pushed into her mouth and followed them with the vodka.

"Been a long time, baby," he said, putting his strong hands on either side of her face. Ruby closed her eyes.

Chapter Eighteen: Purged

Ruby woke up slow and confused, dizzy with a hangover. She rolled her eyes to the clock by the bed. 10:57 A.M. "Billy," she called out, sitting up. Nausea surged through her body and she slipped back down in the bed, holding very still and hoping it would pass. It felt like rats were fighting in her belly and that an iron ratchet was eating her head. Lying still was not going to help and she rolled out of the bed, collapsing and gasping on the floor. Half-walking, half-crouching, she struggled to the bathroom, making it no further than the edge of the bathtub.

She was still there, her arms and head hanging limp over the edge, her torso twisted out on the cold tile floor, when she heard somebody come in. "Billy," she whispered, before she shut her eyes against the next round of nausea.

***

Hank found Ruby's front door unlocked and no one answered his knock. On alert, he put a hand on his gun, but didn't draw it as he eased inside the door. When he saw the safety chain had been ripped out of the wooden frame, he pulled his weapon and carefully, but quickly, prowled through the small apartment. When he heard vomiting from the bathroom, he ran in there.

Ruby was curled over the tub, a T-shirt twisted on her upper body, showing her legs and buttocks. As he grabbed up a washcloth and wet it in the sink, she vomited and fell back on the floor. Kneeling beside her, he cupped her head in one hand, and with the other, he cleaned her face with the cold cloth. He got a towel and wet it, then sat down on the bathroom floor and gently straightened out her body and pulled her head into his lap. He laid the cold wet cloth across her forehead. When she was quiet, he reached down and took her pulse. Fast, but not dangerous.

Hank held her like that, stroking her forehead and talking to her in a soft, inarticulate manner until he saw some semblance of color coming back into her face. Her hair was knotted and wet in spots and he noticed a clump of vomit caught in the fringe around her face. He slipped the cloth off her face and cleaned up her hair.

"Let's try to get you back to bed." When she didn't respond, he slipped out from under her body and bent over to pick her up. Hank grunted with the effort as he lifted and carried her limp body to the bed. When he slipped her on top of the sheets, empty pill bottles rolled across the bed. One caught between two pillows and two others bounced off onto the floor. A vodka bottle with only an inch or so left was sitting on the nightstand.

Hank straightened up and stared down at Ruby for a long moment. Sighing, he went back to the bathroom and wet still another clean cloth. Returning, he put the cool cloth on Ruby's forehead. She moaned and opened her eyes a second, then shut them.

He left her in the bedroom and went to the kitchen, slipped off his jacket, hung it over a chair and started a pot of coffee. While the coffee perked, he looked around for anything like ginger ale or Pepto-Bismol. All he could come up with was some crackers, a store brand cola, and some aspirin. He poured a glass of soda and took the crackers and aspirin into the bedroom. He held her head up and helped Ruby sip the cola until she could swallow the aspirin. Leaving the crackers on the side of the bed, he went back to the kitchen, poured a cup of coffee. After sipping the first half of the cup, he simply sat in the kitchen, holding the warm cup but not drinking. Only when he heard Ruby shutting the bathroom door and moments later flushing the toilet, did he move.

By the time Hank returned to the bedroom, Ruby was back in bed, not moving, eyes tightly closed.

"Look at me," Hank said.

He watched Ruby try to push herself up a bit in the bed. She looked straight at Hank.

"Were you trying to kill yourself?"

"No."

"Did somebody else come in here and hurt you?" Hank could not bring himself to ask if Billy Dittwilder had been inside this apartment. He didn't trust his control if she admitted Billy had been with her.

"No."

"Can you eat some of the crackers?"

"No."

Hank glanced at his watch. Nearly two in the afternoon. Earlier, he'd told Luther he was going for lunch and then to cruise some of the cheaper bay side dives on Dolphin Key to show Billy's photo around.

He should get back or call in, Luther being the mother hen type. Ruby appeared to be recovering all right now. But still Hank sat, looking at her. Thinking Billy Dittwilder had probably come in soon after Hank gave up last night and drove home around 2:30 or so in the morning to try and catch a little sleep.

He hadn't slept, instead tossing and fretting over what to do about the tape and the file he'd found in the storage room. He had come here to ask her about it not as a policeman, but as something else. But he wasn't sure what else he was besides a policeman to her now and anyway, he couldn't ask her about the file when she was this hung over from pills and vodka.

Hank shifted uncomfortably in the chair by the bed, anger and jealousy and compassion all fighting it out inside his head. For a second, Ruby opened her eyes and looked back at him. Before he spoke, she closed her eyes.

When she shut her eyes against him, Hank reached over and took a cracker and bit down on the stale saltiness of it. He'd never made it to lunch. Then he started looking around the room with a cop's scrutiny. As he bit down into his third cracker, he noticed something gray on the carpet by the bathroom door. Hank walked over, bent down, and ran his finger through it. Ash. Like from a cigarette.

He went into the bathroom and found a cracked cockle shell thrown into the trash can. With a pencil from his shirt pocket, he fished it out of the trash without touching it. Someone must have flushed the cigarette butts, but a hint of the ash dusted the inside the shell. Someone had used it as an ashtray. Hank carried the shell, balanced on the end of his pencil, with him to the kitchen.

He wrapped it carefully in a plastic sack from a grocery store and put it in the deep pocket of his jacket. He could lift the latents, see if Billy's fingerprints were on it. Tie him to Ruby. Or he could throw it away so no one else could use it against her. Hank didn't know which he would do.

From the bedroom, Ruby called out. "Could you bring me some more cola?"

When he brought her a glass, she drank the soda, put the glass down, ate a cracker, and then another.

"Taking up smoking again or entertaining company? Maybe the same company that broke your door?"

"I'm smoking again. Why are you here?"

"I don't really know."

"You aren't allowed to talk to me without my lawyer." She reached for another cracker.

"Maybe I didn't come here as a cop."

This time she gagged on the dry cracker and collapsed back into the bed. Sweat gathered on her forehead and upper lip. She turned pale again.

"All right. Just rest. I'm going to run out and get some ginger ale and some bananas and peppermint tea. My mom's famous cure-alls. You got any requests?"

From the bed, Ruby barely grunted.

Hank called Luther from the nearest store and told him he got hung up on something, keeping things vague, and glad Luther didn't press him for details. He picked up the few items and returned to Ruby's place. He fed her a banana, bite by bite, and helped her drink some ginger ale. Hank left her long enough to walk through the apartment, carefully studying the place. After he finished his search, he put on hot water for peppermint tea and took it in to her. He ate a banana while she sipped at the tea.

When Ruby gave up on the tea, Hank took the cup away from her. "You're in a lot of trouble here. You know that?"

"Yes," she said, rolling over in bed, her back to him.

When Hank was sure her crying was real, he crawled into bed with her, cupping himself around her curled back, holding her while she sobbed.

***

Ruby could remember now. She hadn't let Billy have sex with her. He'd been in prison so long, he didn't have any control, and all she'd had to do was take off her panties, run them over him, use her hands with the satin-like fabric rubbing against him. And then the drugs kicked in, so Billy didn't get around to trying again. Thank God that did it because other wise she'd have had to fight him and he'd have won.

Curled inside Hank's arms, she wondered if the panties were lying around somewhere, if Hank would notice, study on them. Figure it out. She had cried herself out with Hank holding her and he was still there, next to her. But rather than draw comfort, she worried about what Billy had left behind.

"I need a shower." She crawled out of bed, still woozy, but on the mend. "Maybe I can eat some more."

"You want, I'll go down to the Wildflower, get us some sandwiches."

Ruby agreed quickly because she wanted him out of the apartment so she could flush or clean up any signs of Billy.

As soon as Hank pulled the door shut behind him, Ruby went over everything. Trying to see it the way Hank would—the busted latch, the messed-up bed, the empty pill bottles. The shell Billy had used for an ashtray. Holding her breath against a rising sense of panic, Ruby wondered if Hank had found and taken the ashtray—he did ask her if she'd been smoking again—or if Billy'd had enough sense to take it with him.

Either way, Hank would figure it out. After all, once they found Billy's prints in her house, it didn't take much police work to connect her and Billy. Golder had yelled at her for not telling him up front about Billy. But until the detectives had identified his prints, Ruby held out a faint hope that Hank and Luther would never make the connection between Billy, Gardner, and her.

Well, so much for that.

Ruby found her panties under her pillow and put them in the garbage beneath some damp newspapers. Thank goodness Hank hadn't seen those. Still, he probably knew Billy had busted the latch on the door and been with her during the night.

There wasn't any fixing it, so Ruby showered. By the time she was dressed again, Hank brought food, and they ate, sitting side by side against the headboard in the rented bed. Neither of them spoke.

When Ruby finished eating and felt almost all right, or at least not like she was dying, she reached over and put her hand on the zipper of Hank's pants and pressed her palm down. With her other hand, she pulled his head toward her and kissed him. Though he hardened under her hand, he tightened his lips against her own.

Hank took her hand and shoved her off him.

"I've got to go back to work."

And he got up and left.

As Ruby sat in the bed, it wasn't so much the dismissive quality of Hank's parting words—after all, he did have to go back to work—that chilled her. It was the quick flicker of disgust across Hank's face when he pulled himself away from her.

***

The next morning, Ruby stirred still half-asleep and rolled in the bed. When she touched another warm arm, she whispered, "Hank."

The arm picked up a pillow and slammed it down on her face. Ruby jolted awake, struggled to push off the pillow and sat up to see Billy beside her.

"If you want to smother me, go ahead. I'm not strong enough to stop you. But if you're just showing off again, let me get up and make some coffee."

Billy drew back on the bed, letting Ruby rise. She went to the bathroom and when she came out, heading to the kitchen, Billy rose out of the bed and followed her.

"How'd you get in?"

"I took your spare key with me. Besides, you think that old jalousie door would lock anybody out? Keep me out?"

"If you weren't sick as a dog yesterday, you aren't human," Ruby said, pouring coffee into the percolator, wondering where Hank was.

"I didn't drink the whole damn bottle. You never did learn, did you?"

"What are you going to do if the cops come?"

"Hold you hostage, what else?"

"What do you want?"

"I came back for you. Get your money and let's get. Tonight. Tomorrow. How ever long it takes to get your money. New England, I figure. Maybe Maine. Everybody'll think we went to L.A. I already laid down a false trail. Nobody runs off to Maine, do they?"

"If you didn't kill Gardner, why leave a false trail?"

"You don't get it, huh? 'Cause I meant to kill him." Billy had been leaning against the wall, but after he said that, he took a couple of steps toward Ruby. "Only somebody done me the favor."

Ruby concentrated on the coffee pot, listening to every perking sound it made. Finally, she made herself look up at him. "What do you mean?"

"What do you mean, what do I mean? He was dead when I got there."

Ruby stared at him, studying his eyes and trying to read if there was truth there. When the percolator finished, she poured two cups of coffee, then added generous sugar to each. As she moved to the refrigerator for milk, Billy grabbed her by the arm.

"You hear me? He was dead when I got there."

Ruby slung his arm off. "Yeah, I heard." She poured milk into her coffee and put both cups on the table. With her hand, she gestured toward the chairs and she never took her eyes off Billy as he slunk forward and sat down.

"Did you call 9-1-1?"

"No. I saw the body, made sure you weren't still there. Then I hightailed it out of there. That seemed like a real good idea at the time." He took a few sips of his coffee. "Should've let me know you were gonna off him, save me the trouble of planning it."

"I told you, I didn't kill him."

"Yeah, and bears don't shit in the woods."

"I didn't kill him." This time Ruby's voice had a shrill edge to it.

Billy snorted a low rude kind of laugh. "Yeah, well, what do I care?"

"What plans? What did you mean you made plans?"

"Got to town Thursday and laid low, checking things out. Friday, I made a stinking scene in the bus station. About getting tickets to L.A. Made sure everybody'd remember me. That I was going to L.A. Then I bought me a ticket, one ticket, to L.A. One of those tickets you can use anytime in the next month. I called Gardner. He agreed to meet me at y'all's house. Told him I wanted more money and I'd go on, without seeing you."

"I don't believe you. He wouldn't have met you alone. He was afraid of you."

"Yeah, so I care anymore if you believe me?" But Billy paused, as if he were thinking and finally grinned a little. "Yeah, him agreeing to meet me surprised me too. But he had that gun, or he figured he did. And I'd've come to his office if he didn't agree to meet me. You can bet your ass he didn't want that. But, mostly, I figure he was freaked out over you, thinking we were meeting up, planning something. You leaving him on Thursday, me coming into town same day, then calling him up on Friday. I can see why he thought it. That must've made

177

him paranoid as hell. See, I think he planned to shoot me. Make a self-defense claim."

Ruby put her face deep into her hands and slumped over. Gardner had planned to murder Billy, that much she could see now.

"Course I didn't know at the time that you'd left him. Till I figured it out from his ranting on the phone. He thought you'd left him because I'd got out and you were meeting me. Always was a jealous son-a-bitch. Truth is, I didn't study on why he said he'd meet me at the house at the time. I just went."

Ruby slowly lifted her head out of her hands as Billy talked.

"I got there, the front door was unlocked, so I went on in. Way I figured it when I found him, was you. But it's kinda like we did it together. Like old times." Billy laughed again. "That's why I say, you get your money together and we'll skip out to Maine while the cops try and track us to L.A."

The coffee burned in Ruby's raw stomach and she thought she might be sick again. She hadn't even known Billy was out on Thursday. But Gardner would have believed she ran to Billy as soon as he got out. Maybe even thought she'd sent Billy to kill him. Ruby suddenly appreciated that Gardner had a kind of physical courage that she'd underestimated. To meet Billy alone. Scared as Gardner must have been, he would have had the gun and been waiting for Billy. To murder him.

Ruby's late appreciation for Gardner's courage didn't last long before she jumped to the next point that was knocking around inside her skull. If Billy was telling her the truth, and Ruby knew that was a big if, then who had killed Gardner?

For a fleeting moment, she thought of Luther's question about whether Hank had a key, and the implications of Luther's concerns.

She hadn't given Hank a key, but that didn't mean he couldn't have made a copy or gotten in the house some other way.

"You're lying," Ruby said, not so much because she believed Billy was, but because she profoundly hoped that he was.

"Nope, not this time. Now, let's you and me talk on you getting your money and us getting out of here."

Under Billy's glare, Ruby's face felt as raw as her stomach. "There isn't much money. And I'm not going with you. But you should go."

"No money? Get real, sweetheart. You and that Gardner were lawyers. I saw that house you lived in."

"There's no money because everything except a few stocks and some ready cash was in joint title or his name, and it's tied up in probate. I don't guess you know this, but you can't inherit from somebody you murder. And since I've been arrested for his murder, the whole estate's stalled in probate court."

"Don't talk down to me. I'm the one pulled you out of Louisiana."

"Sure, you and two bus tickets my brother paid for. That was nearly seventeen years ago. We're different people now. I'm telling you, the money's all tied up in probate. House too. I can get you a few hundred, but you need more. Lots more. My life insurance policy on him is tied up also since I've been charged with his murder."

"So how you gonna get me some money?"

Ruby couldn't ignore the burning in her stomach any longer and got up from the table to look for food. There was one banana left on the counter. She peeled it, broke it down the middle and handed one half to Billy. "I got an idea."

"Yeah, I bet you do."

Ruby made sure she didn't flinch, though she felt like doing so. "You scare me, Billy. It didn't used to be like this. You used to love me."

"Ain't the ticket anymore." He smashed his banana half on the table with the heel of his hand and reached into his shirt pocket for a cigarette. "Where's that damn shell I was using for an ashtray?"

Well, that answered one question. Hank had Billy's ashtray and probably his prints. Now Hank could link her and Billy both before and after Gardner's murder.

She was enough of a trial attorney to know how that would play out for a jury. But a jury of her peers wasn't her immediate problem. Getting Billy out of town, and out of her life, was.

"I threw the shell ashtray out so the cops wouldn't think you were coming around here. Of course, the busted door was a nice touch. Least one cop saw that, thinks you're hanging around. Which means you need to stay away from me until you leave town, which you should be doing very soon."

"So? He ain't here now, is he?"

"All right. I think I know how I can get you a lot of money," Ruby said. "Maybe a hundred thousand. I can't guarantee anything but I'll try. Gardner had life insurance that went to the firm. I'm not sure if the company has paid out yet, but if they have, it'll be in the firm's operating account. I might be able to get at it. If I can get that money, I'll give it to you. But then you go."

"I go? And what else?"

"Nothing. Just go."

"And leave you sitting here with murder charges?"

"They don't have any real evidence. It'll never get to trial. They arrested me to try and scare me into a deal. You know about deals, don't you? I fess up to second, or maybe manslaughter, and they don't prosecute for first degree. But it won't work because I know they haven't got enough evidence to get to a jury." Yeah, the ashtray Hank found could be a problem, but no reason to spell that out for Billy

180

when she needed to get him out of town. "You get the money and you go. Alone. Safest thing for you to do."

Billy laughed out loud, surprising Ruby. "Yeah, and me leaving my prints in that big-ass house of yours and then running would sure take the blame off you, huh?"

"Maybe." She looked at him sideways, tilting her head, trying out a coy look, but thinking: yeah, damn, it sure would take the heat off her.

Ruby swept her hair up in her hands, some of the uneven lengths left from Gardner's rampage with the scissors tumbled around her face. "Maybe we could fix it up so it does more than just take *some* of the blame off me."

Billy finished his coffee. "Yeah, I figured you'd get to that. It's like a personal habit, ain't it? Get me the money and I'll go. That's all. No setup this time."

Ruby moved over to the window and glanced out.

"He ain't there, your cop."

"No, I didn't think he would be, or you wouldn't still be here."

Billy stood up, walked over to her, and pulled her away from the window toward the bedroom.

"No," Ruby said. "Not now."

Billy dragged her a few feet toward the narrow hallway leading to the bedroom. When she struggled, he held on to her arms, tightening his grip for a moment, pushing her against the hallway wall. Then he dropped his hands, freeing her. "Yeah, it ain't the same, is it?"

Ruby shook her head and glanced away so he couldn't see her expression. Swallowing hard twice, she collected herself, shutting her mouth against saying what she felt. Finally, she looked at him. "Give me until Friday. Get out of Desoto Cove. Cut your hair, shave. Meet me in Tampa, at the old church park. You remember it? Friday at 3."

"Yeah, I remember."

Ruby reached out, putting her hand on his arm though she did not want to touch him. "Billy, please. Before you go."

"Yeah? What?"

"I've got to know for sure. Are you telling me the truth that you didn't kill Gardner?"

"Drop the act. No, like I said, you beat me to it. Or were you too doped up to remember that?"

"I didn't kill him, Billy."

"Yeah, right, and I'm the pope. This is me you're talking to, okay?"

"I mean it. I was convinced till now you killed him. That is, once I heard you'd gotten out early and that your fingerprints were all over our house."

Billy shook his head. "Nope, I'm telling you." He reached out and put his hands on the top curves of her hips and tried to rock her toward him, but she fought to get away. For a moment, his hands gripped her, hurting, and he pressed closer.

"No." She went limp under his hold, knowing she couldn't fight him off if he was determined.

"To hell with you, you act like that." He dropped his hands, stomped out, slamming the damaged door shut behind him.

Ruby felt weak, shaky, like her legs couldn't support her. She slid down the wall and collapsed on the floor. She felt nauseous again and slid over sideways until her head was lying on the cold floor. She lay there and studied the sand, dirt, and dust scattered across the terrazzo floor, waiting for her heart to stop hammering against her ribs.

***

It wasn't the first time Hank had used his own time and money to stalk a suspect. But it was the first time he'd tailed someone he probably loved. Turned out not to be as hard as it should have been, he thought, staring at the man he'd paid to spy on Ruby when he couldn't.

"She didn't leave the apartment all day," the apartment complex manager said.

"You sure? I mean you couldn't watch her all the time, could you?"

"Look, her car didn't move. See here, my office window looks right out at her door. There ain't but the one door in her place. Nobody came and nobody left. Less they came and went while I was in the john, but what da ya figure the odds on that kinda perfect timing would be?"

Hank reached into his billfold and handed the man some money. "Keep an eye out, okay. You got the picture of the guy I'm looking for. You keep it handy."

Outside, Hank sat in his car for a moment, rubbing his hands over his jaw, not surprised to find a spot he'd missed shaving. He didn't trust the manager, but he couldn't convince the chief to okay surveillance on Ruby. Hank did the best he could, sitting outside after work until he could no longer keep his eyes open. He couldn't bring himself to ask Luther to help because Luther had a wife and three kids and needed to be at home as much as he could. But Hank knew his own private watch was not enough. Billy had already been there, maybe more than that once. And Billy would come back again. Maybe he could ask Wilson to take a shift. After all, Wilson was a single guy, maybe he would help.

Sunset, and he had work to finish back at his office. Still Hank sat in his car, debating whether he should knock on Ruby's door, or leave. If he went back to the PD now, later he could go home, grab a quick bite, and come back in his truck. On the other hand, Hank wanted to see Ruby, make sure she was all right, and try to get her to tell him what was going on. Hank almost got out of his Chevy, but then he stopped, angry as hell. At himself. Mad, disgusted really, that after everything he knew about Ruby he still wanted her. That after Billy had been there, he still wanted her and he didn't know if he could push her away from him next time.

Ruby's hands on him. Her mouth pressing his, edging for an opening. And him, hard as a teenage boy in the backseat of a car, ready, wanting her.

Hank thought about that file he'd hidden and that shell ashtray. He wasn't going to be that kind of man, he told himself. Not that kind of cop, either.

With an effort, he started the car and drove off.

***

Across the street, standing with his back to the gulf, Billy smoked a cigarette and watched the Chevy drive off. He'd gotten a haircut and a shave and wore a plaid pair of shorts and a name-brand polo shirt in a style that shouted aging frat boy. Nice of Gardner to leave him that cash, money that was supposed to pay him back for fifteen years and to bribe him to stay away from Ruby. "Yeah, fucking right," Billy said, looking at the door to her apartment.

Chapter Nineteen: Billy

Hank looked up the next morning as Luther tossed a copy of the *Desoto Cove Herald-Tribune* across the top of his desk toward him.

"Yeah, I saw it."

"Chief phoned before I'd woke up good. Scared Nora, him calling so early. Spare you the details. Likely you'll hear them from him anyways. Chief wants to know who leaked it. I told him nobody in the detective division."

"None of the uniforms know this much. It wasn't a cop," Hank said.

"It's got to be her lawyer, that Golder fella."

"Yeah. I think so too. Only person who benefits from this story is Ruby, so whether Golder freelanced the idea or whether she put him up to it, I don't know. And you notice they leave out the connection between Dittwilder and Ruby."

"I called the reporter. Tried to find out her sources. She did that big First Amendment thing. I couldn't even get her to understand a story like this hurts our chances of catching Dittwilder. I got the idea she didn't exactly care about that. Sort of an 'it ain't my job' attitude," Luther said. "Chief was going to have one of the department lawyers call her, see if he can find out from her how she got the story."

"Sure, that'll help." Hank got up and headed for the coffee machine.

"Such sarcasm so early."

Wilson came in and flashed open the paper. "She's a cute thing," he said. "I mean the reporter wrote this. Shoot, the widow suspect ain't so bad, either. You boys might want to check if any of the uniforms helping you been looking for a date. I mean with the reporter."

"We was figuring you," Luther said. "Single guy and all. Thinking you're trying to get brownie points with that reporter."

"Yeah, right. But what about Hank? Ain't he a hound dog too?"

Hank came back with his coffee and sat down at his desk. "It's none of us and we all damn well know it." He picked up the paper and started reading the story again for the fourth or fifth time.

New developments in the murder of prominent, local attorney Gardner Randolph have led to speculations that charges against the late attorney's widow, Ruby Randolph, might be dropped soon. According to sources within the police department, detectives in that case are now focusing their investigation on a recently released convicted felon by the name of William "Billy" Dittwilder.

Gardner Randolph was Dittwilder's defense attorney some 15 years ago in Tampa, according to official documents. Dittwilder blamed Randolph for his harsh sentence, said Suzanne Boatman, a member of the Pardons and Parole Board who interviewed Dittwilder when he was eligible for parole. "I remember his anger very clearly," Boatman said. "He claimed his attorney 'sold him out.' That anger, and not taking responsibility for his own actions, having no remorse, those were the reasons we denied him parole the year before."

Fingerprints of Dittwilder were found in the Randolph residence, said police sources who spoke only on the basis of anonymity. Union Correctional Institution released Dittwilder two days before the murder as part of an early-release due to overcrowding. The investigating officers have determined that Dittwilder arrived in Desoto Cove the day before Randolph was murdered at his bay front home near St. Anne's Circle. Dittwilder was serving a 20-year-sentence for trafficking in narcotics, arson, assault, resisting arrest with violence, and repeated attempted escapes.

The state attorney, Jonathan Belt, in charge of Ms. Randolph's prosecution declined comment on whether charges against the late attorney's widow would be dropped in light of the new developments. Police officers Luther Downs and Hank Rider, the lead detectives investigating the murder, did not return phone calls. However, a well-placed source in the department explained that the two detectives, as well as select uniformed police officers in the patrol division, have actively been searching for Dittwilder in the Desoto Cove area since the fingerprint reports linked him to the site of the murder.

"I am confident that the improper and grossly premature charges against Ruby Randolph will be dropped any day now," said her attorney, Peter Golder. "The police have never had any evidence against Mrs. Randolph, who has repeatedly proclaimed her innocence."

There was more to the story, but Hank slammed the paper down, unable to reread further. A police mug shot of Dittwilder ran with the story as well as a photograph of Ruby and Gardner taken at the 1986 Barrister's Ball. Gardner was in a tuxedo and Ruby was in an off-the-shoulder evening gown with her hair piled up in an elegant twist that showed off her long neck and sharp cheekbones. Gardner's arm wrapped around Ruby and they both laughed into the camera. A happy, beautiful couple. Hank wondered whether the newspaper already had the photograph of Ruby and Gardner, or whether Golder had supplied the photo along with the news leak.

"Damn Golder." Looking at Wilson, Hank said, "Reason we didn't return phone calls was that reporter left a message with the front desk near midnight and said it wasn't urgent. By the time we got the message, the story'd been printed."

"Well, what'd you expect really? And you got to wonder about that Boatman lady, why she's singing her head off, all nice and chatty." Luther shook his head. "That's sure not the norm for any parole board member I ever met. At least they didn't print the stuff about the phone call."

"Yeah, 'cause they don't have it," Wilson said. "I just confirmed that yesterday and Golder doesn't know it yet. Not even Belt. I found the best evidence, didn't I? I want to be around when you tell Belt."

Hank rolled his eyes over at the younger detective, almost embarrassed for him at being so proud of reading down a list of phone numbers and making a match. But Hank couldn't deny the importance of what Wilson established yesterday, even if it was just through routine legwork. Now they had respectable circumstantial evidence that Dittwilder called Gardner less than an hour before he was shot.

Piecing it all together, the detectives felt confident that Dittwilder went to the local bus station around 11:20 A.M. on the day Randolph was murdered to buy a bus ticket to L.A. How long he'd been in town, they didn't know. But on Friday, at 11:43 A.M., someone fitting Dittwilder's description made a call from the pay phone in the bus station. Phone records showed that call went to the law firm of Vincent, Ambruski, Stanley, and Thompson. It all tied in with the temporary receptionist's recollection that someone rude or angry had called for Gardner Randolph around that time. And, as they already knew, shortly after the phone call Randolph left the law firm and went home, even though going home at lunch was not his habit. Someone there shot him between 12:30 and 1 P.M.

"Once Golder and Belt learn this latest, won't it just be a matter of time before charges against Ms. Randolph are dropped?" Wilson asked.

"I reckon," Luther said.

"What do you think, Hank?" Wilson asked. "I mean, I know we got that stuff the paper didn't get into that links up Dittwilder and Ms. Randolph from way back when, but you think that's enough for any kind of conspiracy to murder charges?"

Hank shrugged without ever glancing at either Wilson or Luther. The shell ashtray that linked Billy to Ruby was stuffed in a drawer in his nightstand.

"All right, Hank, look, Wilson's got a point. We gotta walk through this and see what we got says Dittwilder and Ruby were in this together. Belt will be huffing and puffing in here before long, less I miss my guess."

Hank's phone line lit up and he picked it up. "Hank Rider here." He nodded as if the speaker could see him. "Yeah. Bring him up." He put down the phone. "All right guys, stay put. Got a guy at the front desk, a barber, says he cut Billy Dittwilder's hair yesterday. Recognized him from the newspaper, even if that mug shot was old. Maybe that story in the paper will do us some good after all."

***

Luther closed his eyes to half-mast as he tilted his head at Jonathan Belt. Man, he was tired of the state attorney.

"I'm getting pressure to drop the charges." Belt's voice was plaintive, but his expression as he looked at Hank, Wilson, and Luther was accusatory. "Mrs. Randolph apparently has some well-placed friends who are pressuring our office."

"Yeah, that, and maybe like the fact you are so fond of pointing out that we don't have any *real* evidence against her." Luther never thought Belt should have ordered her arrest in the first place.

Belt ignored him. "Wilson told me all about linking up the phone calls." Belt turned to the younger detective and put on a half-way decent smile. "Good work, Wilson." When he swung back to Luther

189

and Hank, the smile was gone. "You've been canvassing the county looking for Dittwilder, right? Update me on that first of all."

"We got a positive ID from the man at the ticket counter at the bus station on the Friday Mr. Randolph was killed. Ticket agent remembers a guy looked like Dittwilder's photo asking about prices and schedules for a bus to L.A. Says the guy stood out because of his hair. That, and he made himself buds with the ticket agent because he was real pissed off about how long it took to ride a bus to L.A., like it was the agent's fault," Luther said.

"And we have the barber who cut his hair. All that does, really, is tell us to look for a clean shaven, short-haired, tall, skinny white guy pushing forty and that he was in this area as late as yesterday. We got an artist from Ringling Art School to do a drawing of how Dittwilder might look clean shaven. We made some calls to his hometown, but he doesn't have any family left. We're still looking for a photo of him without a beard," Hank added. "Got a call into the high school, thinking his yearbook photo's gotta be beardless, even if it's almost two decades old. I don't think anybody's exactly tripping over themselves to find a 1969 yearbook for us, though."

"So where's he been staying?" Belt asked.

"We've checked about every low rent place in the county and the sheriffs in the next three counties have all put some of their people into looking. Nothing. Maybe he's staying with somebody, or maybe he's just crashing in the great out doors," Hank said.

"Anything further on why Gardner visited him in prison?"

"Nope," Luther said. "After we side-swiped them both springing those Dittwilder questions on her, Golder won't let us near Mrs. Randolph. All we know is that Mr. Randolph visited Dittwilder and a guard thinks he remembers those two growling at each other before the visit was over."

"Okay." Belt stroked his silk tie, his expression thoughtful. "We have a decent circumstantial case beginning to build here. The big question is what do we have that links Dittwilder and Mrs. Randolph both to her husband's murder?"

"Just what we've already put in the report," Luther said. "They knew each other back in Louisiana. They were together when he got arrested. She didn't get arrested and convinced Gardner to defend Dittwilder. Dittwilder goes to jail, Gardner marries the girl. It's a classic love story, don't you think?"

"Any evidence of contact between Dittwilder and Mrs. Randolph since her last visit to him in prison in August?"

"No." Luther fidgeted, more tired of all of this than he could have explained. "If they talked after that, they didn't leave an obvious trace."

"Any chance he's staying with her now?"

"Aw, Belt, you know she ain't that dumb. Besides, Hank and Wilson been keeping a kind of unofficial surveillance on her, plus paying off the manager of her apartment to watch. No way. We got nothing that puts them together since the murder."

"All right, here's the deal. I'm giving you forty-eight hours to get something which suggests that Mrs. Randolph hired or encouraged Dittwilder to kill her husband. Or something that makes her a more likely suspect than him. If you don't find anything, then we'll *nolle prosse* the charges against her. I assume you are already doing everything you can to bring him in?"

"Yeah." Luther made a gesture like he was sticking his finger in his right eye.

"Luther, you said you knew the detective involved in Dittwilder's arrest in Tampa. Why don't you talk to him again?"

"Already did. Called him a few times, matter of fact. He doesn't remember anything. Too many years and other scum bags under the dam. He couldn't find anything special in the reports in the microfilm and he couldn't find his own notes from that far back."

"Give it another try anyway. And re-interview that guard at UCI. I want to know why Mr. Randolph was visiting up there."

"Yeah, Belt, and next closing argument you do, you give me a call so's I can write it out for you."

"I'll be going then," Belt said, ignoring Luther's sarcasm.

Hank and Luther didn't speak until Belt was long gone. Wilson told them goodnight and left the building.

"Look, we might as well go up to Tampa tomorrow anyway," Luther said. "Talk to Butterfield again. Snoop around the old neighborhood, look up their trailer park address. See what shakes out. Maybe get some Tampa uniforms to pass the Dittwilder drawing around. Makes sense he might be staying up there. But I'll be damned if I can see going over to UCI again. We both know damn good and well we got all we're getting that last visit."

"What's Dittwilder doing for money?" Hank asked.

"Stealing it? Maybe Ruby gave him some? Let's go through their bank records for any unusual withdrawals about then. But not tonight. Look, Hank, I gotta go home now. I know you're gonna spend the night camped outside her apartment. So, what I got to say is short and simple."

"Yeah?"

"You make up your mind, bud, you hear? You make up your mind about this gal once and for all."

***

The next day Luther and Hank drove to Tampa, little more than an hour's drive on I-75. Convinced before they began of the unlikelihood of new information, they agreed to split up to speed up the investigation. While Hank went to the state attorney's office, Luther sought out Butterfield, having already talked with him on the phone the day before.

At the Tampa PD, Butterfield handed over some scribbled notes to Luther. "After you called me yesterday, I got to thinking about it again. Still can't say I remember this guy any different than anybody else. You know Andy, my partner from back then, doesn't know squat anymore, can't remember you or me. But anyways, I remembered this box of stuff from when I moved over from vice to homicide, had to clean out my desk and so I mostly just threw stuff in a big box to sort out later. Only, of course I didn't exactly sort it, just shoved it in the garage."

"Yeah, that's about how I move."

"Well, last night, I figure what the hey, ain't nothing on TV and the wife and me get along better these days if we aren't actually in the same room, so I figure it's worth looking for this box. Sure enough, there it is. After about a six pack, I found my notebooks from 1972."

Luther flipped through the rubber-banded collection of notebooks and shook his head. "I can't find this morning's newspaper, let along something from fifteen years back."

"Well, it's mostly just dumb luck, okay. I spent half hour this morning looking for my glasses."

"I hear you, bud," Luther said. "Listen, my partner's downtown at the state attorney's office going over their file again. I'll just sit here and read these and drink this fine coffee, okay?"

"Yeah. Good seeing you again. Come by my desk when you're done."

Luther settled in and started looking through the books in earnest now. After the first third of a cup of coffee, he found the book with some notes about Billy Dittwilder. Routine stuff. Then a notation: "Check girlfriend again. Landlord says girl lives in trailer too." A few notes later, Luther read: "Girlfriend is Ruby Johnson. Good looker, playing dumb. Andy remembers her. Checked his notes—bar fight with some college professor. Same college prof turned up missing. Pull GF in again. Get names of uniforms from bar."

Luther looked at the space above the desk, rolling his eyes up as if trying to see something in the air above him. He had a strange tickle at the back of his throat. Down deep, he didn't want Ruby to be guilty of murder. And though he'd had some moments when it made sense that she'd killed her husband, Luther had never at that gut-level point where it counted believed she had. But something here, a tinge of an old memory, bothered him. Luther finished the rest of the notes, but nothing else of any particular interest jumped out at him, certainly nothing else about Ruby.

After reading through the notebook again and finishing his coffee, Luther wandered over to Butterfield's desk.

"Find anything?"

"Yeah, some stuff about the widow when she was Dittwilder's girlfriend. We're maybe looking at her as an accomplice to Dittwilder. Charges against just her right now, but state attorney's looking to drop them, like I explained last night. Here, read this and see if you remember anything."

Butterfield read through the notes. "Let me see that photo of the girl again," he said. Luther showed him her police mug shot from her recent arrest and the photo out of the paper. "Course she'd've been younger," Butterfield said. "Still, I can't say as I can remember anything."

"I don't remember much about a missing college professor. Looks like Andy might've thought there was a connection. You remember?"

Butterfield shook his head. "Naw. Don't ring any bells. But that's the goofy thing about Andy, you know. He sits up there in that nursing home and he don't remember squat now. But in those days when he was partnering with me that man remembered everything. Missing persons wouldn't even been our case. He must've heard some other cops talking, made a connection. Now how you figure a man with a mind like that ends up like he is?" Butterfield shook his head, while Luther shared his indignation at Andy's fate.

"You can go through the missing persons' files, you want to, Luther, look through 1972. See what you find. I'll walk you over to records, introduce you, use my charm and all."

"Yeah, I think I'd like to do that," Luther said. When he got that tickle in the back of his throat, there wasn't anything he could do but keep digging till he could swallow clean and clear again. Even when he didn't want the answers he had to look for.

***

Hank, Luther, and Butterfield slid into a booth at the Tropicana in Ybor City, Hank surprised he was hungry.

"Best damn Cubans in town," Butterfield said. "Hot crusty bread and cold pork."

"Yeah, I remember," Luther said. "And great Cuban coffee. Save room for the guava tarts too."

Hank glanced at a menu and folded it shut. He moved the glass of water the waitress had put down in front of him to the side and looked straight at Luther, momentarily ignoring Butterfield. "What'd you find?"

"I've proven my favorite theory about cop work. That it's all mostly serendipity."

"Serendipity," Butterfield repeated, stuttering a little with a mouthful of ice water. "Isn't that fancy for a country boy when all you mean is plain dumb luck?"

"Sure, plain dumb luck. But more. With coincidental connections of cosmic capacity. Like that alliteration? Hank here gave me one of those 'improve your vocabulary' calendars. Ain't I learning up good?" Luther and Butterfield grinned at each other.

They were having a good time play-acting like they were hicks and for some reason it pissed Hank off. He knew for a fact Luther had a college degree and was smarter than anybody on the force. "Yeah, yeah, yeah, cut the *Hee-Haw* crap. What'd you find?"

"Lighten up, bud. Didn't find nothing really, just some historical background on the ever-fascinating Mrs. Randolph," Luther said.

When the waitress came up, Hank glowered at her a moment but then they ordered and she left. Without prompting, Luther started talking again.

"Butterfield's notes mentioned a bar fight involving Ruby and some college professor. Something about that maybe seemed vaguely familiar to me. The fight I mean. But then later the professor guy turns up missing—but I didn't know that until just now. Butterfield and me, we didn't remember anything about a missing college professor. So, I went through the missing person files for 1972. Let me tell you, little girl working records was sure tickled pink to dig around to find that file for me."

Butterfield snickered.

"Sure enough, there's the file. Never found the professor. Sister in Kansas filed a missing person's claim. Guy named Harlan LaSalle. Taught biology at South Florida." Luther paused as the waitress set down their café con leches. Drinking the coffee slow, enjoying the feel of the caffeine shifting into high gear in his veins, Hank didn't prompt

Luther to go on even though he wondered how much of it Luther understood.

"Well, let me tell you, the officer who worked the missing persons report did a real fine job," Luther said, a trace of sarcasm in his tone. "Typed up a report before filing that case in the inactive files. Shut down active work on the file 'cause he figured the professor guy left town with no forwarding address on purpose. USF'd fired him, see, and his bank account had been emptied out a few weeks before hand. And in sniffing around, seeing if there was any basis for foul play, the detective found out somebody'd shot this guy's dog about the time he cleaned out the bank account."

Luther paused in his story, sipped at his café con leche. "Story was, and the notes don't say how the officer found it out, that this professor'd been dipping into one of his students and she came up pregnant. Then turns out, the girl's mom worked at USF and the professor'd been dipping into her too. So, the father and husband, respectively speaking, finds all this out and the prevailing thought was he shot the dog. Like a sick warning. Then, theory goes, the now fired professor just left town. Guy who shot the dog, naturally enough, was a kind of suspect, but seems there just wasn't enough to prosecute him or nothing. After that, it was just written up and filed. But the dog lived. Humane Society took him. Detective made a big note of that."

"Double dipping a gal and her mom both, jez." Butterfield shook his head.

"Yeah, there was a couple of photos of this guy in the file. Real good looking. I mean like movie star looks. Reckon that's how he got away with it."

"Okay, it's a pretty good story, but why are you tellin' us all this?" Butterfield asked.

"Ah, this here is the interesting part, proving that it is indeed a small world after all. Seems that a few weeks before this professor up and disappears, he and Ruby had quite the set-to at a local bar. Bartender called the cops when they started shouting at each other and wouldn't stop. By the time the uniforms got there, they were punching and hitting and stuff. Anyway, college professor tries to make nice and the whole thing kinda blows over. Except, course, like I just learned earlier today, when he turns up missing, Ruby is one of the people called in 'cause the investigating officer heard she'd lived with him some time or the other. Must've been a short interview. Just a few notes, time and date stuff. Apparently, it didn't amount to much and there wasn't anything about her that made the detective suspicious. I just thought it was right interesting. Mighty interesting."

"Why?" Hank asked.

"See, I was one of the uniforms. At the bar. Remember, I told you I had the feeling I'd met Ruby before? I remember that fight. That is, when I saw those notes, I remembered. Not just 'cause she was pretty and all, but 'cause she was a sneaky fighter. Professor's making nice to us, being all Mr. Charm and not watching her and she hauls off and gets a good punch in on him. Funny what you remember. But, in the overall scheme of things, it doesn't amount to a hill of beans."

"Nothing that pulls Dittwilder into that picture? Puts him and the professor together? Or the two of them with Ruby?" Hank hoped he sounded nonchalance when he felt anything but.

"Naw. Nothing. File didn't have anything to connect Dittwilder to LaSalle."

Hank sat back in the booth and tried to make his face blank while Luther cut him a curious look.

Chapter Twenty: Evening and the Long Night

Rental car places wanted too much identification these days, Billy learned, so he just bought an old car. Big, faded blue Olds. For $900, it wasn't much and he didn't bother with the paperwork and transfer of title. Dude selling it didn't care about anything but the cash. Car didn't have to last him long and paying more money for something he'd have to abandon somewhere in Florida didn't make any sense.

All in all, getting out of Desoto Cove seemed like a smart move after giving up on Ruby. Hell, he wasn't going to be a rapist, she take that attitude.

Billy drove the car up to Tampa, scouted the old neighborhoods and checked into a hotel across the street from where the trailer park had been. The trailers were gone now and a strip shopping center that featured cheap auto insurance and discount liquor stores had replaced them. The little county park by the church where he and Ruby had hung out in the early seventies was still there, right across the road from where the trailers used to be. An easy walk from Billy's hotel. Ruby must have known about the park since she'd said to meet her there. He wondered if she had visited it recently.

Three days to kill, he thought, looking at himself in the mirror in the hotel room. That was nothing. What'd he been doing all this time but killing time anyway? Only thing he had to figure out was whether he'd make Ruby come with him.

***

Ruby was driving inland from Dolphin Key to Nathaniel's house and passed a beauty saloon with a big "Open" sign on the door even though it was after six P.M. On impulse, she braked the car and turned in. The door was unlocked and she walked inside. "Still open?" she asked a young man with a pudgy face and a long blond pony tail.

"Sure thing." He smiled and patted the back of a salon chair. "You can be my last customer. I promise you I get more creative as the day wears on."

"Are you the owner?" she asked, looking around. The mauve walls matched the man's jumpsuit.

"No, maybe someday. Right now, I'm just the new guy so I get the late shift."

"I'm Ruby and I don't need anything fancy. Just a chin length bob."

"Oh, baby, a head full of hair like you have, we can do better than that. Let me have a look." He motioned her to the chair. "My name is Brock," he said with a small bow.

Brock combed out Ruby's hair and fluffed it about her face, taking in the chopped off chunks that hung in shaggy disarray no matter how carefully he combed. Then he turned away and went into the back. When he came out, he had two martinis on a silver-plated tray.

"The last customer of the day house special. I made them doubles. And don't you even try to tell me you don't drink," he said, offering her the tray.

Ruby took one of the glasses, smiling back at the grin on Brock's face. After the first long swallow, she let out an exaggerated sigh. "I haven't had a martini in years."

"Well, baby, it's just what the doctor ordered. Now, let's see what we can do with this." Brock combed and looked and pulled and tucked at the odd lengths. He paused to take a healthy sip of his drink. Then he leaned so close to Ruby that she could smell the gin and a sweet perfume about him. "Baby, either you live with some mean ass children who play with scissors, or your last hair dresser was on some serious, and I do mean serious, drugs."

Ruby laughed out loud and took a huge swallow of her drink, feeling the warming buzz flow through her body as she relaxed into the chair. Brock had her giggling within minutes, launching off on hairdressers on drugs and winding into a routine about a customer so messed up even her dog was on Valium.

Half an hour later, tipsy and laughing, she paid Brock what he asked and gave him a $50 bill for a tip. "I think you should be a psychiatrist," Ruby said as she offered the tip.

"Oh, baby, I am, I am, you just don't know. You sure look good. I told you I was a genius at haircuts."

Ruby took one more look at her reflection in the beauty shop mirror. Her hair was cut chin length with wispy bangs, but with layers to work in the odd remnants of Gardner's rage. Freed of its weight, her hair curled and softened the sharp angles of her face. Even Ruby could tell she looked wonderful.

Brock tucked a card in her hand. "You get ready to come out as a redhead, you give me a call. Color is my real thing, and baby, with those big green eyes, you'd make a great redhead."

Yeah, a great redhead, like that mattered at all, but she thanked Brock again and slid into her car, liking the martini buzz, thinking another one might be just the thing.

Although it was out of the way, Ruby drove downtown to Bull Feathers before heading to Nathaniel's house. She walked around the bar looking for Hank, conscious of the stares of a few customers.

At the bar, the bartender gave her a once-over with hostile eyes and leaned over the bar toward her as if to whisper a confidence. "Read where you were out on bail," he said. "Didn't think murderers got out on bail, but then being a hot shot lawyer, I guess you have some pull with the big boys."

"Yeah, you're bucking for a big tip."

"Vodka Gimlet, with Absolut Vodka, right?"

"No, let me have a martini. Dry." The bartender moved away without further comment and Ruby turned and watched the door. But Hank did not come.

Leaving the bar after she gulped her drink, Ruby headed toward Nathaniel's house, eyeing the clock in her car. A little spout of headache began to tunnel in between her eyes.

By the time she turned into Nathaniel's driveway, the clock read just after 8:30 P.M. Bit late to just drop in, but she needed to see him now, tonight. Ruby knocked on the door and waited. She'd almost given up when the door finally opened. Lena stood there, not speaking.

"Lena, I'm sorry to bother you this late, but I need to talk to Nathaniel."

For a moment Lena stood unresponsive, then she started to shut the door. Ruby put her hand out and caught the door. "Please. It's important."

Ruby remembered Lena's perfunctory condolences at Gardner's funeral and how pointedly Nathaniel had ignored her in the presence of his wife. "Lena, it's firm business. Just business."

Lena dropped her hands from the door and walked off. Ruby watched. Short and with a graceful roundness to her, with tiny hands and feet and a wide, round mouth, round eyes and delicate nose, Lena was in her sixties and beautiful, with her plumpness in perfect hour glass proportions. Every time Ruby saw Lena and Nathaniel standing together she thought how absurdly matched they appeared to be—a thin giant and a round doll.

Ruby eased into the big house and closed the front door behind her. She listened for sounds that might tell her where Nathaniel was. Hearing nothing, on instinct she headed for a back room that functioned as Nathaniel's private den.

He was there, sitting in semi-darkness and absolute silence. He did not stand up or speak when she called his name.

"Nathaniel," Ruby repeated, louder.

Finally, he turned and studied Ruby before slowly rising from his chair. He switched on a small lamp on a table.

"Come in. Have a seat." He gestured to the couch.

Ruby slumped down where he pointed. To her relief, he sat beside her. "How have you been?"

"Fine. And you?"

"Fine," Ruby said, reaching out her hand to cover one of his.

Nathaniel put his other hand on top of hers, sandwiching it between his two.

She leaned back into the soft cushioning of the couch and let the warmth of his touch flow through her. "If I can just sit here with you long enough, everything will be all right."

When he did not speak, Ruby leaned her head down on his shoulder. But he shifted upright, rose from the sofa, and switched on a second light on the desk.

"Why are you here?" His voice was formal, but not unkind as he stood in front of her. A thin man to begin with, he now had the emaciated look of a man with a serious illness. The skin around his eyes was puckered and his straight, narrow lips looked gray.

"Are you really all right?" Ruby asked him again, knowing he would hear the worry in her voice.

"I'm fine." Nathaniel moved across from her and slid down into a chair, facing her. "Why are you here?"

Ruby inhaled, feeling shaky under his stare. "Okay, business it is, then. I need money."

"I haven't got any."

"No, I don't want your money personally. I want the firm's money. Some of it. Part of Gardner's key man life insurance. You can withdraw it from the firm's operating account."

"How'd you know we received the proceeds and still had some in that account?"

"I guessed." Actually, Fred told her, but Ruby didn't want Nathaniel to know that Fred and she regularly talked.

"Good guess. But you aren't entitled to any of that money."

"Oh, yes, I am." She glared straight into Nathaniel's eyes, daring him to challenge her. "I don't want it all. Just $150,000. And I'll pay it back when Gardner's probate is settled. I'll have money from his life insurance and we've got decent equity in the house. There are some stocks and I'm the beneficiary of his 401K. You'll get the money back."

"If you've got that money coming to you, why do you need the firm's?"

"I need money right now. By Friday," she said. "You know it's going to take time to get Gardner's probate settled. Think of it as a loan."

"What if you never get his money?"

"His money? Try *our* money. I contributed too. And I'll get it. No way these murder charges stick."

"I agree. Golder does too. But even so, it will take some time to settle the estate, sell the house."

"Yes, that's exactly what I'm saying. I can pay you back eventually, but I need some money now. *Right now.*"

"Why do you need the money?" Nathaniel asked, trapping her eyes with his own.

"It's a long story. Trust me, you'll be happier not knowing."

"I don't doubt that's true, but I'm not giving you the money unless I understand what it's for. You know me that well, don't you?" Nathaniel looked like his old self for a moment.

"Yes, I know you." She waited, wishing she had a drink, debating whether to ask for one. "I could use a drink."

"I don't doubt that's true either. Why do you need the money?"

Ruby leaned forward, getting as close to Nathaniel as she could without rising from the couch. "I need the money to give to Billy Dittwilder." Ruby watched Nathaniel's stiff posture as he perched in the chair, his back straight and not touching the soft padding of the back of the chair. He remained poker faced, his best lawyer non-committal face taped carefully over his own while she stared at him.

After what seemed to Ruby an interminable moment, Nathaniel lifted his chin a bit. "Your ex-con. I read the story in the *Herald-Tribune.* Golder did a masterful job in leaking that. I especially liked the photograph of you and Gardner as the perfect couple. I had to look through three boxes of photographs in the County Bar Association office to find that one. I gave it to Golder. He put it to good use."

Ruby clinched her jaws. Golder hadn't mentioned Nathaniel's involvement. Rather, he'd pitched the story as his own idea. "So here I'm thinking Golder is working for me, but maybe he's working for you?"

"There's no conflict of interest, Ruby. Golder keeps me informed. The leak was as much his idea as mine. He's doing a good job of looking out for you, even if you fight him every step."

"So Golder's looking out for me. You used to,"

"Doll, didn't I teach you, in this world you got to look out for yourself?"

"Sure, that's what you said. But you looked out for me anyway. I need you, now."

"Damn you." Nathaniel jumped up, almost kicking the chair to get away from it, and rushed toward the door as if to leave. For a moment Ruby feared he would abandon her. But he stopped, slumping till his back collapsed against the doorway and his face twisted toward Ruby.

She thought he was going to fall and her heart jammed against her ribs. Standing, she moved toward him, but he held out his hand, palm raised toward her in a clear motion to stop.

Ruby concentrated on breathing. "Control," Gardner's voice came back to her, drowning out her heartbeat. "When you walk into a courtroom everyone is watching, waiting for you to screw up. Even your own client expects it. Control is the only way you can beat them." Gardner's voice was so clear Ruby scanned the room in a new panic.

"Get your control back," Gardner said to her, his voice once more startlingly clear. Ruby wondered if she were drunk and hallucinating, or if he were really in the room.

"Shut up," she said to the ghost.

"I didn't say anything," Nathaniel said, pushing himself off the doorway.

"You've been a little shy about coming to call," Ruby said, struggling to get back on solid ground, not to be talking with a dead man while the live man who might help her was standing in front of her.

They stared at each other for a strained moment. "I've missed you, that's all." Ruby realized it was true, that she had missed Nathaniel.

"Why give money to Billy Dittwilder?"

As if Nathaniel wasn't smart enough to see that coming from a mile away. Just making her say it. "So he can get away. Make an escape. I haven't discussed this with Golder and in fairness to him, I won't. But for the right price Billy will run. He's smart in his own way. Pissed off at the world, but smart. He'll get away and with that money he might be able to make a good life for himself somewhere else."

Glad she got through that without sounding drunk, or panicked, Ruby fell back onto the couch and stared down at her lap, noticing a stain on her wrinkled khaki pants. She rubbed a finger across it, then looked back up at Nathaniel.

"But before he goes, I need to find some way of implicating him further. I'm still studying on that, something that seals his guilt in the eyes of the police." Ruby paused, wanting that drink now desperately, but reluctant to point-blank ask for one. "Some way to make him the sole suspect, you know what I mean?" Really, asking if Nathaniel had any ideas how to frame Billy.

"Go on."

"See, it's basic, actually. If Billy is the only suspect and he flees, they drop charges against me. And they don't go looking for anybody else because the perfect suspect is on the road to L.A." She stopped when she said that, waiting to see Nathaniel's reaction, but he was stoic.

"That's the simple version. But without money, he's not going to go away. Here, caught or not, he's dangerous to me."

Nathaniel nodded slightly, his lips stretched into a narrow grimace. "I figured something like that."

"He runs, you know, it makes it a lot easier."

"All right. I'll get the money, $150,000. I'll go first thing in the morning before going to the firm."

"Cash."

"Yes, I understood that."

"I'm sorry, Nathaniel, really. I know the position this puts you in with the firm, but I can't see any other way. I just couldn't figure out anything else. You don't understand about Billy, but I owe him."

She rose and stepped toward him. When she reached around him for a hug, he stiffened at her touch and she dropped her arms.

"I don't have a phone, but I'll call you tomorrow evening from a pay phone somewhere."

When he didn't respond, Ruby walked out of the room and down the hallway toward the front of the house.

As Ruby opened the front door to leave, Lena appeared out of the darkened entryway. "I want to ask you something," she said, her voice high, light, girl-like.

"Yes?"

"Is Nathaniel a lot like your father?"

"That's a sick question."

"It's an appropriate question. Is Nathaniel like your father?"

Ruby thought of her father, a dusty memory of a shadow. He hadn't lived long enough to teach her much of anything except not to cry. It was her mother that taught her how to take a punch.

"No, my father is dead and Nathaniel is still very much alive."

Lena closed the door behind her and Ruby ran to her car, eager to get away.

Ruby drove back to Bull Feathers, looking for Hank. After circling the place, noting a subtle change in the thinned crowds, she sat at the bar and ordered a Vodka Gimlet.

"Give up on the martini already, eh?" the bartender said.

"Just bring it."

After he brought Ruby's drink and she'd paid, he stood in front of her for a moment too long for politeness. "Yeah?" she said.

"He's not here. He doesn't come here anymore. Maybe there's not much point in you coming around here either." Ruby took the drink, rose from the barstool and drifted through the tables, not hiding the fact she was looking. She saw a few lawyers she had a passing acquaintance with but neither she nor they spoke.

Ruby turned away and kept prowling through the bar. Definitely no Hank, but a young man in the corner caught her eye. Somebody else familiar. Badly dressed. A bit sloppy. But young and with a kind of puppy-faced eager look. Ruby stared at him long enough that he ducked his head a second, then looked up at her and grinned.

He's a cop, she remembered with some hazy memory of the face from one of the times in Hank and Luther's office. She studied him long enough to finish her drink before she walked over to him.

He stood up, awkwardly, but politely.

"Is this just an accident or are you cops following me?"

"Please," he said, gesturing for her to sit. Ruby perched on the end of the chair.

"My name is Wilson. Rufus Wilson, but everybody calls me Wilson."

"Rufus?" Ruby grinned a quick, almost flirtatious smile at the younger man. "So, Wilson Rufus Wilson, are you following me?"

"No, ma'am."

Ruby looked at his nearly empty glass. "Order us another round. Then look me in the eyes and tell me you aren't following me." Ruby paused slightly between the words, concentrating on not slurring her speech.

Wilson signaled for a waitress and gave the orders, specifying her drink and brand without her having told him.

"How'd you know I drank Absolut Vodka?"

"I'm a detective. I read your file." He sounded so proud of himself that she impulsively grinned at him again.

The vodka was seeping into her brain, but had not yet relaxed the spasms in the back of her neck and shoulders. She wanted to go dancing. "Do you dance, Wilson?"

"No, ma'am."

"No? Well, then I guess you aren't much help to me tonight."

Her drink came and Ruby drank it, quickly. Neither of them spoke. She stood up to leave. "Thank you, Rufus Wilson for the drink. Now, if you'd like to follow me some more, I'm aiming to find somebody to dance with me, so you'll have to step briskly."

Ruby stopped at the bar. "Give me one more, ... make it a double, on the ... house, and I'll ...preserve your ... reputation by not coming here anymore." She had to stop between a few of the words and think of the next phrase, but she got the sentence out. Within a minute, the bartender set a drink in front of her and didn't speak. She gulped it and left, a slight ringing in her ears, a small chisel cracking at her skull. Outside she fished in her purse until she found a bottle of aspirin and she swallowed a few without water.

From Bull Feathers, she drove slowly down Osprey Avenue until she came to the Short Stop. She fished for change to make a phone call and got out of the car while two teenaged boys gabbed on the only payphone. She waited, went inside and got a package of cigarettes, and waited some more. She wanted to call somebody, find somebody to go out dancing with her. Like old times. But she couldn't think of who to call. And the boys seemed camped out at the phone, so she got back in the car and drove to the VAST parking lot, only a few blocks away.

Ruby had trouble getting the key in the backdoor, afraid at first the lock had been changed. In some part of her mind she thought that the firm should have changed the lock or asked for her key back. Mostly she was glad to get inside the cold, sterile air of the old law firm. For December, the night was muggy and the liquor made her hot. Ruby went to Nathaniel's office and helped herself to his private bar. He still kept the Absolut. She took a slug of the clear liquid down her throat and then lay down on the couch, clutching the bottle. There was a loud buzzing and it took her a second to connect the sound, to realize it was external, not internal.

"Damn." She had forgotten about the alarm system and wouldn't have had the current code to pacify it. Ruby took the bottle of Absolut and, bumping softly against the door facing, left Nathaniel's office.

Ruby wasn't quite sure how she got in her car, but she headed out toward Dolphin Key. On the bridge, there were all these lights blinking, blinding her, not quite registering. Suddenly, she understood the drawbridge was up and she braked, swerving some. She came to rest close to the guard rails but with no harm done.

When the boat passed under the bridge and the crossbar rose, she took a minute to just sit there, then she took another swig from the bottle and eased her foot off the brake. "Go slow, go slow," she repeated to herself. "You'll be fine." She had to work at paying attention to the road and traffic, work at focusing her eyes.

After a drive that seemed to take the rest of the night and left her sticky with sweat, she pulled into the parking lot at the Beach Club, a guaranteed loud dance bar. The back of her throat was itchy and bitter. "Let's rock and roll," she said, stumbling slightly as she crawled out of the car.

***

Ruby woke the next morning lying face up in the sand on the public beach at Dolphin Key, closer to her apartment than from the Beach

Club bar. Her first conscious act was to roll over on her hands and knees dog-style and throw up.

Finished with that task, she managed to pull herself up and walk to the water. Ruby bent over, grimacing at the pain as her brain seemed to collide with her skull with an agonizing thump. She cupped her palms for a handful of gulf water. After rinsing her face, she took a second handful and rinsed out her mouth. She couldn't say which tasted worse, her mouth or the salty water.

Like some rote programming, she scanned her body. No visible wounds, no torn clothing. Good signs. Ruby checked her pockets, not surprised to find neither money nor keys. Her purse was gone too.

Only a little after dawn, no one was at the beach yet and the sky still held a hint of pink. She didn't remember much past ordering a drink at the Beach Club. She had a vague feeling she'd been dancing with someone too young for her. After that, nothing.

For a while, Ruby merely drooped over on the beach and watched the ebb and flow of the tide. She doubted she could walk back to her apartment, though it probably wasn't much more than a mile. Rolling over and going back to sleep was as sensible a plan as any. She eased up from the water's edge, limped to a picnic area, slouched down under the shade of an Australian Pine, and closed her eyes.

When Ruby woke up again, she was hot, sweaty, parched and sore as if she'd been on the losing side of a fist fight. She checked again for bruises. None. Traffic and people noises rose around her. She propped herself in the direction of the road, watching the line of cars feeding into the beach parking lot. There was nothing to do but ask someone for help or drag herself back to the apartment. Ruby stood up and started walking.

***

Hank was waiting for her.

He watched her stagger up to the apartment and jiggle the locked knob. She started prying open the jalousie panels in the door to break into her own apartment without looking around. He figured Ruby hadn't noticed his pickup out in the parking lot when she'd limped in. He crawled out of the cab, slamming the door after him. Wilson had called late last night, admitting he'd lost her at Bull Feathers. While he was in the john. How the boy ever made detective was beyond Hank.

She'd had all night to be with Billy somewhere.

Hank clinched both hands into tight fists but forced himself to keep them at his side as he walked up beside her. Ruby gave no indication she'd seen him, but she must have.

"Where've you been?" As soon as he spoke, he wished he'd used a softer tone.

"I'm not sure," she said, still working on the jalousie panes, not looking up at him when she spoke.

Hank watched her breaking into her own apartment, taking in the look and smell of her, wondering if any of this was his fault, or if he could have stopped it, if he could still stop her from self-destructing.

Finally, Ruby lifted the jalousie panels out enough to tear a hole in the old screen with a broken shell. Reaching through the narrow opening, she unlocked the door from inside. She went immediately into the kitchen and drank two glasses of tap water, then rattled around in a drawer for aspirin and took several.

Following close behind her, Hank grabbed her by both shoulders and shook her, but not hard. She pulled out of his arms and backed up against the wall. She acted dizzy but stayed put, propped against the wall staring at Hank.

"Where were you?" Still with that anger, that tone of demand.

"I don't know. I went to the Beach Club to go dancing. I had a black out. I woke up on the beach. My purse and car keys are gone. I don't know where I've been."

Ruby cringed as he moved toward her again, but he was just trying to make sure she wasn't physically wounded, searching her body for any blood or torn clothing. "Are you hurt?"

"No."

When she relaxed, he realized she'd expected him to hit her, to hurt her somehow, and was relieved when he didn't.

For a fleeting second he wanted to take her into his arms, hold her, quiet her, tell it was all right, or it would be, that he'd help her.

But he thought about the shell ashtray, the empty bottles of pills. Of Billy. With her. In her apartment. The messed up bed. He took a few steps back from her.

"You look like hell. And you stink."

"If you'll make me some coffee, I'll go take a shower." She started taking off her shirt as she spoke and dropped it in the middle of the kitchen. She was bra-less.

Her bare breasts stared up at Hank, pale mounds of flesh that he wanted to touch.

I'm stronger than this.

"No. Make your own damn coffee." Trying not to look at her, Hank turned to leave. But for one moment he glanced back over his shoulder, studied her face, her slender neck and the firmness of her breasts, the curve of her waist into her sloped hips.

"I'm done with you now." He made it to the door before pity rose in him, beating out everything else he'd felt. Once more, he turned back to look at her.

"I'll check the Beach Club for your car. If it's not there, I'll report it stolen along with the purse and keys. Call your credit card holders."

"Yes. Thank you."

"You need to start standing on your own. Maybe think about going to AA as a place to start. You're not going to last long as a drunk." He closed the jalousie panels on the door, tugged the torn screen back in place, and locked the door as he left.

Chapter Twenty-One: Dancing with Ghosts

Under the floor of the house, formless beings began to pull together into shrouded and diaphanous shapes with appendages like arms and legs. One, larger and stronger than the others, rose from the pit of dirt and dust and began digging at the floor, trying to scoop out the wood and escape upward into the room. The other shapes writhed in the dust, flowing above it only to sink back into it. The strong one stopped digging at the flooring and began pounding on it. His shadowy lips formed the shape of words being screamed over and over, yet his screams made no sound. There was only the pounding from beneath the flooring. A second being now, nothing but a skeleton, a body rotted down to its bare bones, rose and began scratching at the floor, then butting its head against it.

The banging finally penetrated Ruby's consciousness and she partially woke up, sweating. Her heart beat too fast and her mouth was dry. For a moment, she didn't know where she was and the dream of the dead things clutched at her head. After slapping at her face as if to drive away gnats, Ruby threw herself out of the bed and stumbled, falling onto the terrazzo floor. The sharp pain when she landed on her hip jarred her fully awake. She pulled herself reluctantly from the floor and shook herself off.

The banging noise continued and Ruby recognized it not as dream, but simply someone knocking. She drank a glass of tepid water sitting on the nightstand by the bed and ambled toward the door. Through the semitransparent glass of the jalousie panes, she recognized one of the young detectives, but struggled to put a name to him. She opened the door, backing off from him as he came in.

"I, um, I've got your car."

Ruby nodded, aimed herself at the kitchen sink and poured a glass of water. She was hungry, groggy, and very thirsty.

The detective followed her from the front door through the small living room into the cramped kitchen with its plastic dinette set. "It was right there at the Beach Club. I mean, your car. Your purse and keys were inside the club. The bartender had them. Looks like you just walked out and left them." He reached out his hand and offered her the purse. "Keys are inside. If you had any money, it's gone now."

"Yeah," she said, taking the purse and putting it down on the counter. "Thanks." She was so hungry her stomach burned. Ignoring the man, she opened the refrigerator, grabbed and unwrapped a chunk of cheese that had hardened and darkened at the edges. She bit into it, chewing and swallowing quickly.

"I, um, I've been thinking, maybe I can take some dance lessons," he said.

"Huh?" Ruby looked up at him, momentarily puzzled that he was even still there.

"You know, last night? You wanted me to go dancing with you. Remember?"

Ruby took another bite of the cheese, ignoring both the detective and the queasy feeling fluttering up in her gut.

The man didn't bother to hide the way he was looking at her and Ruby felt creepy under his stare. She wore a thin cotton T-shirt and the shapes of her breasts were clear under it. The shirt barely skimmed the tops of her thighs.

"What was your name again?"

"Everybody calls me Wilson."

"Well then Wilson, thank you for bringing the car back. But unless I'm supposed to sign some kind of receipt or something, I'd like for you to leave now."

"Yes, ma'am." He blushed as he hurried out of the apartment. Outside, a patrol car waited to take him back to the police department and Ruby watched it leave through her window.

***

After another long shower, Ruby went out to the car and put the key in the ignition. She hesitated, then inhaled deeply and started the car, planning to drive to the house on St. Anne's Key. Her house now, she guessed. Or it would be when the murder charges were dropped and probate was concluded. As she crossed the first bridge, the trip seemed momentarily too long and too hard. But by the time she got on Hernando Causeway, her head was clearing.

Once at her house, Ruby pulled into the driveway and saw the grass needed cutting. The yard already had that abandoned, junky look that comes about quickly with the least neglect in a semi-tropic environment. She figured the neighbors were tracking her to complain. Gardner had taken care of the lawn, not that he cut it himself, but that he handled the lawn maintenance folks. She wondered who he had hired. She'd need to search for a card or a number or something from the people who used to keep it green and short.

After treading through the high grass, Ruby stood at the front door, vaguely surprised that her key worked, though she couldn't think why it shouldn't.

The inside of the house hit her with a jolt with its stale, fetid smell. She hadn't been back since the day Gardner was shot and it didn't seem like anyone had cracked a door or window, or adjusted the air conditioning since then. Despite seeing all the things that were once

216

hers and Gardner's, the place didn't seem like her house at all. She glanced around, feeling like a burglar.

The living room looked the same, except dusty and with some disarray, probably from the detectives. Wandering from the living room, Ruby stepped into the kitchen, a sudden kick of hunger hitting her. She found an unopened box of imported cookies and not much else. Though the cookies were stale, she kept eating them anyway as she drifted around the rest of the house, avoiding the bedroom.

The odor she'd first noticed when she'd stepped inside grew stronger as she walked around in the house. Probably no one had taken out the garbage and it was piled in the garage. On her way to check on that and Gardner's car, which she supposed was still in the garage, Ruby cut through the laundry room. There, the smell stopped her. She looked around and didn't see anything that should cause such a stink, no piles of raw garbage, no dead rat or possum, no scattered bag of molding fertilizer. Nothing obvious. Yet, the smell was repulsive and strong.

After poking around behind things, Ruby lifted the lid of the washing machine and the stench jumped at her, making her gag. Ruby slammed the lid down. But then she opened it again and, with some caution, reached in and pulled out a garment—her long, loose-weave sweater vest with pockets, now stained and molding. Ruby reached for a garbage bag and began stuffing the vest into it when she remembered she'd gotten Gardner's blood on it as she'd knelt beside his body. She'd tossed it off in the bedroom and somebody must have put it in the washing machine instead of the garbage.

With a quick pang, she remembered something else. She'd been wearing the vest at the drug store around noon the day he died. Quickly, she checked the pockets and yanked out a receipt for the small items she'd purchased at the drug store. Despite the condition of the sweater vest, the receipt was unharmed and easily readable.

Her alibi. She exhaled a ragged breath of relief. A simple piece of paper which supported her claim that she'd been buying clips and junk for her hair while Gardner was dying. The receipt had the date, the time, the cashier's name, the itemized list of various hair and cosmetics and her credit card number. Ruby hadn't even remembered she'd used her credit card and then she realized she hadn't seen the bill, or any bills. Damn, she'd have to track down the mail, pay the bills, get the lawn guys out here, and hire a maid.

But first, Ruby needed to tell Golder she'd found this one last thing that would guarantee the charges against her would be dropped. She held the receipt carefully as if some sudden force of wind might blow it away.

Golder nearly drove her mad pushing her to find the receipt. A receipt that, for all she could remember, she might have left on the counter of the store. Well, here it was and she owed the man who kept asking about it a quick phone call. To let him know she could prove, at least beyond a reasonable doubt, that she'd been shopping and not shooting her husband the hour he died.

As she hurried back to the kitchen phone, Ruby studied the little piece of paper. How small to be so important.

In black and white ink, there it was: 12:43 P.M. Just about the time the experts finally settled on as Gardner's estimated time of death.

If at 12:43 she was as far north of the St. Anne's house as the receipt indicated, Ruby could not have killed Gardner. She was grateful that Fred and Danni lived in a neighborhood north of Desoto Cove, on the bay, almost in the adjoining county. While staying with them, Ruby had gone to the nearest store, which was even further north of Desoto Cove, in the Whitfield Plaza. No way could she have driven from a drug store that far north of Desoto Cove to the house at St. Anne's in the heavy November traffic on the Tamiami Trail in anything under forty-five minutes to an hour, let alone in fifteen minutes.

Of course, the state attorney would put on witnesses who would testify that the time of death is not an exact science. He might even buy an expert witness to say she could have driven to the house in fifteen minutes. But the receipt created reasonable doubt. That, and the fact there was no solid evidence against her, guaranteed the charges would be dropped.

She dialed the phone and for once Golder was in his office. He told her to sit tight, he'd be right out to pick it up. He wanted to talk to her anyway.

The late afternoon sun shot bright beams through the kitchen window and Ruby poked around in the cabinets until she found a bottle of vodka. She poured a straight shot and gulped it down. She debated a second shot.

Instead, Ruby called Nathaniel at the office. He was out. She tried his house and no one answered.

She poured and drank the second shot, not so much a gulp this time.

As she picked up the bottle for that third shot, she remembered what Hank had said. Heard the disgust in his voice. Heard him tell her she stank.

That she wouldn't last long on her own as a drunk.

Ruby dug out the phone book and looked up the number for Alcoholics Anonymous.

But she didn't pour out the vodka.

***

Dave came with her to her first AA meeting for no other reason than she'd asked him to come.

Earlier, when Ruby had returned to her ratty little apartment, he was there, waiting, sitting in his car. They spoke and went inside.

"You should get a phone," he said.

"Yeah, I keep meaning to." She didn't want to be rude to Dave, but she wanted to ask him why he was there.

Instead, she offered to fix him some coffee or a drink. Wouldn't have minded a drink herself, but when Dave said no, she didn't want to look like she needed one. Also, how classic would it be to wolf down a vodka on the way to an AA meeting. She didn't want to be some drunk cliché.

Instead of sharing a drink, they sat down and he went through a rambling kind of conversation.

When she didn't talk back, maybe Dave got the point.

"I've got something to bring back to you," he said.

"Something? Of mine?"

"Yes. Remember, when Fred drove you to his house, the day you ...that Gardner...that you left the firm."

"Yes, Dave, I remember that day. You don't need to be shy about mentioning it."

Dave reached into his pocket and pulled out a necklace and a barrette. Hers. She recognized them. The necklace with her bright, hard ruby that she'd worn every day until Billy hurt her with his rage that last visit at the prison. The barrette, the one Gardner had made for her. The one with the seed pearls.

"These were on the library floor. I, er, picked them up."

Ruby reached out, opened her hand, and took them. "The library floor?"

Yeah, on the barrette. Sure. She'd had it on that day. Had forgotten about it, but it made sense that it was knocked out of her hair and fell on the floor.

But not the necklace.

Ruby remembered standing half naked in front of her mirror, looking at the ruby, thinking about how ugly Billy had been to her. Taking it off then. She wouldn't wear it anymore, but couldn't get rid of it either. She'd put it in her jewelry box.

The jewelry box in the bedroom Gardner and she had shared, in the room where somebody came and shot him.

Ruby studied the necklace and the barrette as if she could find some answer in them. Then she looked up, studied the man who had given them to her.

He's trying to tell me something.

And she wanted to hug him. And protect him.

Instead, Ruby asked him if he'd go with her to her first AA meeting.

"Might be a good idea," Dave said.

***

"I'm sorry to call so late," Ruby said to Nathaniel, ever so grateful it wasn't Lena answering the phone, "but I went by my house, met with Golder." She planned to tell him about the receipt and maybe the AA meeting when she saw him.

"All right."

"Did you get the money?"

"Yes. Lena's out tonight, visiting Katie and the grandkids. You can come over."

"Okay. I'll be there as soon as I can."

Leaving the payphone at the Sugar and Spice Restaurant near the hospital where the AA group had met, Ruby drove away.

221

Her hands felt shaky, but when she looked at them they looked steady enough. On the outside. Her mouth was dry and she had a weird, creepy feeling, like small things were crawling around under her skin. She was having trouble with the lights, not that they were blinding her, but the brightness irritated her. She felt like cussing at the street lights for having the raw nerve to be shining.

Ruby pulled into an empty parking lot and sat for a moment. She fumbled in her purse and pulled out a small plastic bottle. Carefully she broke a yellow Valium in half and swallowed it. She lit a cigarette and smoked it to a nub. Finally, she pulled back onto the Tamiami Trail.

Remembering that the young detective had been following her the night before last, Ruby changed lanes and made a few false turns, trying to see if anyone was tailing her. When she was sure no lights followed her, she turned on the road near Nathaniel's house. Just to be sure, she parked on the street in front of another house a few blocks away and waited. When no other car appeared, she drove on to Nathaniel's house.

He opened the door before she knocked. He looked stooped and worn out. Ruby followed him inside to the den and neither of them spoke, nor acknowledged the other.

In the den, Nathaniel turned on a small reading light on a desk which left most of the room in a kind of shadowy half-light. He went to a safe sitting discretely in a corner beside the desk and opened it. Ruby stood in the doorway, unsure of what to do or say. Nathaniel pulled a briefcase out of the safe.

"Here." He walked to her and thrust the case at her.

Ruby took the briefcase. "Nathaniel," she started.

"Don't." He tapped the briefcase with his fingers. "Be sure to dispose of this. Thoroughly. Don't just toss it in your trash can."

"I can do that."

"Yes, I figured you could. Stay sober. Can you do that?"

"I'm going to try."

There were a hundred things Ruby wanted to say, but Nathaniel's tone and look stopped her. "Thank you," she said.

He nodded and switched off the light. She found her way through the darkened house to the front door by herself.

Instead of going either to her house or her apartment, Ruby drove to a Denny's and had a cup of coffee. The creepy feeling under her skin had eased off. She felt, more or less, all right, but she did not want to go either to her house or to the apartment. Ruby had a sudden gnawing need for something sweet and ordered a chocolate sundae. After licking up the last of the melted ice cream, she had a second cup of coffee. Feeling vaguely ill, she got in her car and headed up U.S. 41 toward Tampa.

Ruby checked into a hotel in the sprawling Brandon area, a suburban extension of the City of Tampa, far inland and away from the elite doctors and lawyers living on the shorelines of Tampa Bay. Once inside her hotel room, she opened the briefcase and counted the money. All there, just like he'd promised. She wondered how much trouble Nathaniel would be in from the other partners when they discovered he'd withdrawn firm money. Then she took the other half of the Valium and sat down on the bed, staring at the briefcase, wishing she hadn't eaten so much sugar and drunk so much coffee.

Unable to sit still, she hopped up and inspected the money, looking for anything like a mark or a code.

Nathaniel wouldn't do that, she told herself. He'd never mark the bills, never work with the cops.

Still, she'd looked, hadn't she?

Meticulously she wiped down the briefcase and anything inside it that might provide prints. Now it was a matter of waiting until tomorrow and delivering the money to Billy.

Ruby paced in the small room. Billy will be just fine with $150,000 and a head start.

Past midnight, Ruby tried to settle down. She was sorry she didn't have a toothbrush, but using the hotel soap, she lathered a wash cloth and used her finger to push it around in her mouth as best she could. A trick from her years of half-homelessness. Eyeing the clock, she sat back down on the bed. Ruby spent the next four hours on the bed, staring at the air around her, waiting for daylight. After the first half hour, she made no pretense of sleep.

Ruby had planned to stay in Brandon until time to meet Billy at the park at 3. But by dawn, she was too restless and thought she could finally face her house again. It would better than killing time in a hotel room, after all. Leaving nothing in the hotel, she drove straight back to Desoto Cove. She headed to her house on St. Anne's. Before entering it, she smoked a cigarette in the car, watching. Wouldn't help things one bit if Hank or that Wilson found her with a briefcase full of money. But no one was staking out the house or following her, she decided after a few minutes. Still, she sat in the car. A shaky feeling enveloped her and the sense of small things crawling on her skin threatened to overtake her. With unsure hands, Ruby found and swallowed a whole Valium this time.

"First stop the booze, then the pills," she said, gathering up the briefcase and her purse and going in the house. She'd worry about those cigarettes she'd started smoking again somewhere down the line on another day.

***

Hank picked up the phone around 10:30 that morning and sat listening, nodding. Then he hopped up and headed out the door, half-jogging, half-walking rather than driving to a bank on Main Street. Subpoenas, phone calls, harassment from the state attorney's office, and finally Gardner's bank records were available. Luther and Wilson were both off someplace else, so Hank went for the records.

An hour later, he sprung the report on Luther when he drifted back in, Wilson tagging along. "Here's a twist." Not bothering with hello or any polite chitchat, Hank shoved some papers toward Luther, while Wilson craned his head to see.

Luther studied the bank printout, squinted at the figures, and read it all over again. "You sure it was Gardner took that money out of the bank? Not Ruby?"

"Yep, I made damn sure the bank was damn sure when I was over there this morning. His account only, she couldn't reach it."

"Fifty-thousand? Wonder what in the world old Gardner was gonna do with that? A big withdrawal." Luther looked at the date again. "Whoo. You don't think—."

"I think it is mighty interesting that Gardner cashed out a bank CD, took the penalty and all, just one day before he drove over to Starke and visited Billy at UCI." Hank shook his head, hoping some of his fatigue and anger would shake off with the gesture. "But the problem is, why? Nothing we know suggests Billy could be blackmailing Gardner. And how could Gardner get the money to Billy? I doubt he would try to just walk it into the prison."

"Ask me, the only question is why. There'd be plenty of ways of getting him the money. Leave it in a locker in the bus terminal, worse come to worse. But why give Billy that much money?" Luther handed the paper to Wilson and frowned at Hank. "Well, anyway, I reckon that explains how old Billy Boy seems to be doing so good out there on the lam and all. He's well financed."

"Yeah, I guess so." Hank rotated his head and rubbed his sore shoulders. "Of course, could be we're just reaching at straws. I suppose there'd be lots of reasons Gardner would cash out that CD." Hank wondered where Ruby had been last night. She'd never been to the apartment. "I'd like to call Golder, set up another interview with Ruby, get her to confirm this, explain it."

"Reckon we might as well try asking her. But, could be, maybe, her husband might've been up to something she didn't know about." Luther tugged his tie loose as if it was choking him. "I'm just real tired of this case, you know. Now we gotta go back to Starke and re-interview everybody and ask if anybody knows anything about Billy coming into money and nobody will, of course. Then we gotta start checking around to see if there's any sudden new bank accounts for a Billy Dittwilder. Like he'd be that stupid, but we don't check, somebody be ripping us a new one. Damn."

Yeah, damn, Hank thought. And Luther thought he was tired of this case. Luther didn't even know the best parts.

***

Ruby was standing in front of the bar at her house on St. Anne's, sipping from her third cup of coffee and eyeing the vodka. One small, well-measured shot glass would steady her, but she made a deal with herself. "Wait one hour and see how you feel." She spoke out loud as if addressing the bottle of vodka. Still, she stood there, wrestling with the equally persuasive forces telling her to drink or not to drink. The doorbell rang.

Running her hands through her tousled hair, Ruby glanced in the hallway mirror as she walked to the front door. She looked terrible.

Peeking through the view-hole, she saw Golder. Reluctantly Ruby let him in.

"Don't you answer your phone here?"

"Not anymore and good morning to you, too."

"Sorry." Golder sniffed her coffee, not bothering to hide it.

"Straight coffee. I stopped at Publix and got some supplies. You know, coffee, milk, sugar, the basics. But no liquor. Want a cup?" Ruby was already moving back to the kitchen to pour him a mug. Golder followed her.

With his hands around the coffee, Golder eyed Ruby. "Will the center hold?"

"Yeah. I'm sober, tired, but sober. The center will hold." Ruby tried to smile, but only managed a slight twist to her lips. "Thanks for asking."

"Police want to see you again. You don't have to talk to them, you know. But you damn well need to talk to me. They are intimating there's something new going on."

"No, I'll talk to them. Just not today."

"I'm advising you not to. And I'm ordering you to talk to me."

"Set something up for tomorrow morning. Then we'll chat."

"After I call, you're going to sit down and tell me everything about Billy. I'm not talking about a little chat here, you understand, but a full, total disclosure. You can't keep me working in the dark." Golder glared at Ruby as he reached for her kitchen phone.

Ruby half-listened to Golder doing his beleaguered lawyer thing with someone at the police department. Golder put the phone down. "Tomorrow, at 10 A.M. At the police department. They're not happy, want to go over it today. Won't say what it's about, just that it's new info."

"It's probably about the money Gardner gave Billy. One of the tellers I know at our bank called me this morning, told me the cops had come around with papers, and they'd had to release Gardner's and my banking statements." What Ruby didn't see the point of admitting was that she knew Gardner had given Billy some money before he died. She learned about it the day she was transferring some of the joint account funds to her own, private account. Chatty folks, those bankers. She'd never asked Gardner why, but she could guess.

"Gardner gave Billy money?"

"Yes."

"And you didn't tell me?" Golder scowled at her, but Ruby was used to that from him by now. "Mind telling me why?"

"I imagine that's what the police will want to ask me, too."

"All right, sit, talk." Golder pointed to the couch in the living room. Ruby looked at the clock. She had to be out of here by 12:30, 1 P.M. at the latest. "And I need for you to tell everything, for once. You hear me?"

"I'll give you the condensed version," she said, moving out of the foyer into the living room, ignoring the frustration in Golder's tone.

***

After pushing Golder out the door and eating a hasty lunch, Ruby stepped into the shower in the guest bathroom. She planned to leave for Tampa early to make sure she was at the park in time to meet Billy.

When she came out of the shower into the guest bedroom, Billy was waiting. Ruby stopped and instinctively wrapped her damp towel tighter around her.

"What are you doing here? How'd you get in? Didn't I say I'd meet you?"

"Yeah. Sure. That's what you said. But I got to thinking. No telling what I might be walking in on at that park. So, I just helped myself, came in using an extra key I'd picked up when I was here before. Easy enough. This way, I don't have to worry you setting me up, or whatever you might've had in mind."

Ruby began to ease back to the bathroom where her dirty clothes were piled on the tiled floor. "You think I'd set you up? Don't you understand I know what I owe you?"

"Nope, not sure you do."

As Ruby rushed to pick up her clothes, Billy lunged at her and, grabbing her arm, he dragged her back into the bedroom. Billy's hands tightly gripped her arms as she tried to pull away from him.

"You sure do take long showers. I already found the money, put it in my car."

"Then get out of here, go." Ruby tried to control her fear, forcing herself to breathe slowly, to relax and not to pull against Billy.

"Nope. Not yet." But as Ruby relaxed, she felt Billy's grasp soften. She leaned slightly forward toward him, her lips parting. When he released her arms and moved to pull her into an embrace, Ruby kicked out at him as quick and hard as she could, her right foot snapping against his left knee. When he crumpled, she ducked down for the towel, spun around and ran as fast as she could toward the hallway where her car keys were thrown on top of a bookcase.

Keys and towel in hand, Ruby ran to the garage and was almost in her car when Billy thundered out after her, holding a .38 in his hand.

***

Hank couldn't wait. It was that simple. He needed this to be over. Luther and Wilson had demanded to go with him, but he'd shaken Wilson off. But not Luther.

"I don't like this. I do not like it one bit." Luther grumbled as Hank drove, speeding as much as traffic would let him. "You know she's lawyered up and we're not supposed to talk to her without her attorney."

"We can go arrest her." Hank steered sharply around the last curve of the driveway to her apartment on Dolphin Beach. "Got to be new charges. Withholding evidence, tampering with a police investigation, conspiracy."

"Yeah. The-jerking-around-cops charge. Hell, Hank, you know it won't stick."

"Then why are you here?"

"I'm along for the ride. Keep an eye on you."

"Yeah, yeah, yeah."

"Her car ain't here. Maybe Wilson was right and we should've gone to her house on the Key."

"Let's just check. I want to ask that manager I've been paying good money to if he's seen Ruby." Hank pushed open the car's heavy door and heaved himself outside.

"You think Wilson'd go to her house by himself?" Luther slammed the passenger door and followed Hank. "He sure seemed raring to go."

"He's not that stupid."

"You sure about that?"

Hank shook his head as they stomped across the parking lot toward Ruby's apartment.

***

Ruby held the towel in front of her with one hand, the other hand strangled the keys in her fist. She shifted her eyes toward the car, the horn, the side garage door, weighing her options before she glared back at Billy. Gauging his expression, trying to guess if he would shoot her, Ruby studied Billy's face.

Pointing the gun straight at her chest, Billy advanced until he was just a couple of steps away from her. "You killed him, didn't you?"

"Please, Billy. Put the gun down. I'm no threat to you."

"You killed him, didn't you? Once and for all, you tell me."

"Why? What difference does it make now? You've got the money. Just go."

"You go with me. I ain't taking no chance on you setting the cops on my trail."

By now he was so close Ruby could feel his breath on her skin when he talked.

"Besides, I miss you." With the barrel of the gun, Billy lifted the edge of the towel off her breasts.

Right hand at her side, outside of Billy's sight, Ruby shifted the keys so that the longest key protruded firmly between her index and middle finger like a short, dull knife. It wasn't much of a weapon, but it was all she had.

"I got a right to know, all you and me been through. You kill him, or not?"

What was he thinking, what did he want her to say? Ruby tried to think. Maybe she was less of a threat to him if she *had* killed Gardner.

"Yes."

"Say it, bitch, say it."

"I killed Gardner."

"Good for you." Billy lowered the gun and eased back a step.

Cat and mouse. Ruby waited. No sense trying to jab him with a key if he was going to let her go anyway.

***

Hank picked the sandspurs off his socks and fought down the urge to kick something.

"Nobody at home, bud. Not even the damn manager. Let's get back to the station." Luther headed toward the car.

"Let's just run by her house."

"Bud, that's driving out of the way. You think maybe we ought to work on some of our other cases today, not chase down this wild goose."

"I'll drive." Hank opened the door and slid into the driver's seat.

***

The doorbell was rigged to ring in the garage as well as the house and Ruby and Billy both jumped at the sudden, loud chiming.

"Damn it. You stay put. Right there." Billy raised the gun again, easing another step back from her and glancing toward the garage door.

"Is that my gun? From our bedroom?" Ruby didn't move, but her mind tumbled over itself thinking in short, tangled bursts.

"I guess so. Found it on the floor next to Gardner. He was still twitching some. I hope the bastard could see me. Not smart of you to have left the gun there. So, yeah, I took it."

"What are you going to do?"

"Stand right here till whoever is at your door gives up and goes away."

"And then?"

"I ain't going down alone this time. You're gonna sign a confession. Mail it to the police and then you've leaving with me."

"No, I'm not."

"The hell you ain't."

The doorbell rang again. "Don't be thinking you can answer that, you hear."

They faced off, waiting, each tilting their heads listening for another bell, or the sound of a car starting up and leaving. Ruby started thinking about testifying and closing statements. "Men and women of the jury, he held a gun to her head. Of course, she signed that confession. At gun point. If the police held a gun to her head, no one would believe that confession. It wouldn't even be admissible." Yeah, that could work.

Still, it'd be better not to have to explain it.

The side door to the garage opened and she spun around. Wilson was standing there, a bewildered and frightened look on his face.

"Ruby? You all right?" His voice sounded as puzzled as his expression. He dangled a gun in his right hand.

Billy's finger tightened on the trigger and Ruby lurched at Billy's face, the key extended between her fingers. She jabbed at his eyes, missed as Billy jerked away from her, but managed to rake the key across his face. He screamed and brought the barrel of the .38 down across her face. As she stumbled back from the blow, Billy again raised the gun toward Wilson.

Ruby screamed at Wilson, an inarticulate, guttural cry of warning. As she fell, she tried to direct her fall against Billy to wreck his aim. In the brief bit of a second that she'd had to look at Wilson, she knew he'd never fire his gun in time. Billy would kill him and the police would never let him get away. They would track him relentlessly. And if they tracked him, they would be tracking her too.

With her arms flung out to grab at him, Ruby fell against Billy's leg just as he fired. The towel fell from her. Wilson's gun went off. Aimed wildly, Wilson's bullet crashed into a trash can on the other side of the garage. Wilson stood, a stunned, white look on his face. Then he went down. Crumbling in a strange, slow movement, grabbing a moment at the door, at the handle, at anything to hold, but falling down anyway.

"Don't kill him," Ruby shouted, struggling to get up from the garage floor. Billy knocked her down again.

Wilson moaned. From the corner of her eye, Ruby saw his right hand groping for the gun he'd dropped, his left hand clutching at the air. He seemed to be trying to form words, but his lips wouldn't cooperate.

From the garage floor, not trying to stand this time, Ruby looked up at Billy. "Don't shoot that man. He's a cop. They'll kill you for sure if you gun down one of their own." Her words sounded oddly calm, even reasonable to her. But inside her chest, a marching band was banging against her ribs, crushing her lungs with its force and fury.

"All this over Gardner." Billy's voice also sounded calm.

"Get out of here. Now. Forget Gardner. He's dead."

"Yeah, so I killed him," Billy shouted. "So that's it. I killed him. You got your happy ending."

He shouted again, but Ruby stared at Wilson, not Billy. Blood bubbled up on him, a bright red frost on his chest.

"That's what you want everybody to think isn't it? That I killed Gardner." Billy raised his fist at Ruby. But he stopped, held his hand in the air aimed at her, but frozen.

"Damn it, Billy, you shot a cop. Get out of here. Run. Now."

Billy twisted around and stared at Wilson. He had to know his only chance was to flee and that dragging a naked woman into a car would slow him down.

To her great relief, Billy bolted out the side door of the garage.

Ruby scooped up the towel and ran to Wilson, who lay flat down on his back. Shot in the lung, she guessed from the spreading stain on his chest. He gurgled like someone drowning in their own fluids. In a flash that came and went all but simultaneously, Ruby remembered her grandmother dying of pneumonia and the sounds she made. She remembered her father holding Grannie upright from behind, trying to help her breathe. Ruby curled behind Wilson and lifted him up, hoping to clear his lungs and mouth so he could breathe better. With him propped against her, she pressed the towel against the wound with one hand to slow the bleeding and spoke to him in the quiet, soothing voice of a mother urging a child to wake up. With her other hand, she reached out for his gun. Once she had a grip, she fired it at the garage door until it was out of bullets. *Please God, let someone hear it and call the police.*

She held him, willing him not to die. Wilson moaned, struggled as if he were regaining consciousness. His eyes opened half way, then quivered shut. Blood was still pouring out of him and she couldn't get it to stop no matter how hard she pressed.

"Wilson, I've got to call 9-1-1. I'm not leaving you. I'll be right back." Ruby made her voice calm. She pulled his hand over the towel. "Press down." She couldn't tell if he were conscious or not, or even if he were, whether he'd have the strength to press down on the towel. For that matter, she wasn't even sure it was the right thing to do. "I'll be right back."

When she saw Wilson's eyes tremble slightly, Ruby leaned over his face and kissed his eyelids. "You hang on." Jumping up and running, she went inside to the phone.

The 9-1-1 operator answered at once. "Police officer down, shot in the chest," Ruby said. Her voice sounded unnaturally calm as she gave the address, but the individual cells on her skin seemed to scream. Still naked, she dropped the phone, ran to open the garage door, and rushed back to Wilson. He sounded like he was drowning. She pushed herself behind him again and cradled him in her arms, willing him to keep breathing.

She was so covered with his blood when the ambulance came, the EMTs thought she'd been shot too.

***

Luther, Hank, and Butterfield stood off in a corner, watching the Tampa detectives go through their routine. Hank could barely hold himself back while they worked, but he appreciated that Butterfield had called him and Luther to the scene.

A woman at the hotel identified Billy from the artist drawing in the *Tampa Tribune*. A bloody, naked woman and a cop in a garage with a bullet in his chest caught everybody's attention. The newspapers couldn't get enough of it, printing what gory details the reporters could get or guess at. Police all through the state had the basic information on the shooting. Tampa police were handing out copies of the artist's drawing of Billy and asking around. Billy had triggered a standard rule of practice: You shoot a cop, the man hunt intensifies.

A hotel maid also agreed the man who been staying in room 310 looked a lot like the drawing. The hotel manager let the police officers into the room. Nothing much there of interest except a couple of shirts, some toiletries, and some brochures on Los Angeles with a receipt for a bus ticket to L.A. stuck between the pages.

"Well, I reckon that just about does it, don't it, Hank? Can't be any doubt now."

"I guess so," Butterfield said. "Still, we all might want to catch the bastard first. Kinda hard to convict somebody unless you got them."

"Yeah," Hank muttered, walking away from them and back into the hotel room where Tampa evidence technicians were still dusting for fingerprints. "Just the one ticket receipt?" he asked the Tampa detective standing around in the way.

"Sure, just the one," the officer said to Hank. "Just like I already told you. Not but one ticket. I'm sure. You want to look, you look. But you wait until our guys are done."

Hank nodded. He'd look all right, even if he'd have to wait until the evidence technicians finished.

"Yeah. Now all we gotta do is catch him," Butterfield said.

"Aw, come on, bud, how hard can that be? Every cop in the state of Florida is looking for him." Luther nodded at Hank.

***

Everything was repetition now and the only game left for the police detectives was to try to wear her out into an inconsistency or an admission.

She needed to keep the center from fraying apart and to keep her lies straight.

What she wanted most was a drink and a chance to lie down, maybe to sleep.

She didn't even want Hank anymore. That was one ache lost in all the others.

"Again, how'd Billy get in the house when he came after you? No sign of breaking and entering. For a house with serious deadbolt locks, people seem to come and go at will." Hank paced behind Ruby as she sat rigid in a chair in one of the interrogation rooms.

For the third day in a row, Hank and Luther pounded Ruby with questions about why Billy was at her house and what had happened there. Ruby consistently answered them by insisting Billy came to ask for money. After that basic lie, she gave a point by point description of what had happened, starting with Billy slipping into the house while she showered. Leaving out, of course, the cash he'd put in his car and later drove off with. "How'd he get in?" Luther seconded Hank's question.

"I told you. Billy took a key when he was there before, you know, the day he killed Gardner. At least that's what he told me."

Ruby looked down, ignoring them all. Her hands twitched in her lap, but the table hid that from Hank and Luther. Her back was straight. Across her face, a purple gash throbbed where Billy slugged her with the gun.

Golder stood up and stretched. "Don't you think we've been at this long enough?"

Ruby didn't feel good and she appreciated Golder's protection. The cops had given her hell at the house. But the EMTs took her to the hospital, where the police later arrested her for shooting Wilson and threw her back in jail. Judge wouldn't make bail on this one and she'd sat in jail, freaked and desperate for a Valium and vodka. Shaking for real. And now, this stupid cop bullshit harassment stuff. She didn't care if one of their own had been shot, she wanted to slap Hank and Luther both.

Three hours yesterday alone on what had happened in her garage and six hours the day before when she was still in custody. And now this. Like it mattered anymore. This was just bullying her and Ruby knew it.

"Tell us about the money again." Luther folded his arms across his chest and tucked his chin.

Ruby stood up and pushed past Hank to walk over to the only window in the room. Outside, some police officers were taking down the Christmas decorations. She couldn't remember which day had been Christmas, or what she had done.

Luther stood up and followed her. "You may as well tell us."

Ruby moved away from Luther and the window, drifting slowly toward the door with her head down. Hank blocked her way, forcing her to stop and look at him.

"Get out of my way."

"Ruby," Hank said, staring at her with a hard look she couldn't stand. "Sit down."

Ruby glanced around the room briefly, dizzy, confused. Then she bolted out the door and ran down the hallway. She'd finally been *nolle prossed* after Wilson woke up and backed up her story. Freed now because of what Wilson said in the hospital, she could leave this room and they couldn't stop her legally.

Outside in the hallway, Ruby stopped at a drinking fountain and gulped water in stuttering gasps. But she was crying so hard she had difficulty swallowing and water ran down her chin, spilling out in a wet stain across her green shirt. Luther put a hand tentatively on the back of her neck and, though surprised, she leaned into him till he cradled her head in his hand.

"Come on," he said. "Let's you and me get out of here for a bit." As Ruby let go of the handle on the water fountain, Luther took her other hand and led her out of the police station. The chill in the air blew into her face as they stepped outside, but the sun was so bright she squinted into the morning.

"I'm sorry about Wilson." She truly was—he was a sweet guy even if he wasn't much of a cop.

"Yeah, you already said that. A lot. Appreciate it," Luther said. "Shall I take you home?"

"Please."

Ruby followed Luther until he stopped in front of an older model Chevy. He opened the passenger side door for her before settling himself into the driver's seat. Ruby didn't have anything left to say as she stared out the window at the traffic.

Luther took her to her house on St. Anne's. "This ain't no police protocol that I remember," he said, pulling up into her driveway. They went into the house without speaking further.

Ruby went to the bathroom to wash her face. When she came back into the kitchen, Luther fixed them both glasses of ice water. Ruby took a glass and walked out to the screened porch. The ice cubes had a stale freezer taste to them, but she drank the water anyway.

"Wilson did everything right. But he's just a kid," she said. "Billy was tougher."

Luther shook the ice cubes in his glass and took a sip while she watched him.

Luther and Hank had arrived at the garage only minutes after the ambulance. Everything had been chaos, shouting, blood. One EMT had her, two others were working on Wilson. IV's, oxygen, straps, and gurney. By the time they had Wilson ready to transport, Ruby was wrapped in a blanket. Luther escorted the first ambulance to the ER, while Hank stayed behind. But he wouldn't touch her, wouldn't look her in the eyes.

He thought she'd shot Wilson, Ruby realized. They all thought so.

Ruby was never sure why the EMTs brought her to the hospital in the second ambulance, but they did. An hour later, dressed in a hospital gown, but disheveled and with traces of blood still under her nails and on her face, Ruby stood vigilance with Luther and the rest of them in the waiting room. Every cop on the force with B positive blood soon loitered in the hallway, waiting to donate. Reporters, cameras, and microphones clustered and were thrust at anyone even remotely involved in the shooting. Then some detectives she didn't know arrested her and took her away while the nurses and doctors hovered over Wilson in the operating room.

Trying to block the scene from her mind as she stared at Luther calmly sipping water, Ruby's heart beat so hard she felt it in her eyes and stomach.

Luther put his glass down on the patio table. "Look, if he'd died, you know you'd still be sitting in the jail. Your word about what happened wouldn't cut it. But Wilson told the same story. Claims Billy confessed. That he heard him say he killed Gardner. No doubt in Wilson's mind. He saw you throw yourself against Billy. Thinks you saved his life messing up the guy's aim."

"I'm glad he's going to be okay."

"Yeah. I know you are. Hard not to like Wilson, ain't it? He's like this big puppy dog always getting in the way. He went out to your house against orders, trying to show us he was a good detective. Told me when he saw this old beat-up car parked nearby, he got suspicious. Peeked in the garage window when nobody answered the door and saw Billy with a gun on you. Busted in."

Ruby nodded, too tired to talk. She wondered if the bottle of vodka was still in the house.

"Why don't you tell me about that money? That's what started this round."

For a moment, Ruby thought Luther meant the money Nathaniel had gotten for her. Then she realized he was still talking about the cash Gardner had gotten for Billy.

"Look. Why do we have to keep doing this? After all this? Who gives a shit about the money? Gardner gave him some money, so what?"

Luther shook his head. "Because it's a loose end. Because there are still those who think you and Billy were in it together. That you put him up to it."

"Even after what Billy did to me?"

241

"Yeah, well it wouldn't be the first time criminal conspirators had a falling out, you know. I'm not sure how that all connects up with the money Gardner gave him, so maybe you can tell me?"

"Luther, I don't really know. Honestly. I can only guess."

"Well, take a guess then."

"Gardner was probably trying to pay him off. Bribe Billy to stay away from us. He was terrified of Billy, afraid he'd come around and make trouble for us. That's all. I didn't know he was going to do it, I don't know details. I don't know how Billy got the money. But it wouldn't have been that hard, really. I mean, they were both smart guys." Ruby finished her water and glanced around for the vodka she thought she'd left on the counter top.

"Why didn't you tell us that when all this started?"

"I didn't know about the money being withdrawn. Not until you and Hank started asking questions about it."

"Well, you are one fine liar," Luther said, the snap in his voice making Ruby rock back from him.

"What do you mean?"

"Got me some bank folks that can document you knew Gardner had taken that fifty thousand dollars out of the bank account the day before Gardner was shot. Something that came out when you were transferring some funds. You knew Gardner took the money and so you had to be figuring well in advance of Wilson getting shot that Gardner tried to buy off Billy. You had to be figuring on that *before* Gardner got shot."

Ruby couldn't think of anything to say and wondered if she shouldn't just ask Luther to leave.

"Why wouldn't you tell us that much at least?" Luther asked. "Try to help us out, help get you off the hook?"

This time, Ruby heard kindness in his voice. Yet she didn't think she had the energy to explain. Luther's expression invited her to try anyway. "Because I knew how that would make it look. For Billy. That maybe he was blackmailing Gardner. Or threatening him somehow. With everything else, I thought this would make the case against Billy seem stronger. I mean, you know, before he confessed and shot Wilson."

"I don't guess I understand that. Billy tried his damnest to kill a cop and he killed your husband. You might have been looking at jail yourself for that murder. Yet you try to protect him?"

"Yes. Before he shot Wilson. Not after. Not anymore. But when Hank and you first asked about Billy, yeah, I wanted to protect him."

"Like I said, I don't get it."

"No. I'm not sure I understand myself. Maybe because once Billy meant more to me than Gardner did. I loved Billy. I never really loved Gardner. I was just swept away by him for a time. Can you understand that?"

"Not from what I know about Billy, no."

Ruby wiped her hands on her jeans and eased out to the patio until she stood at the edge of the pool. There was trash floating in it and mold beginning to grow on the tile. She turned back to Luther.

"I've known Billy all my life. He was my brother's best friend growing up. Even if I was baby sister, I went almost everyplace with them. I figure somewhere between third and fourth grade, I fell in love with him. We double dated, Billy and me and my brother and his girl, at the prom. But we left the dance early, just went driving out in the country." She tried to close her mind to the memory of that night, the spring air, the dancing to the car radio in the woods at the edge of the lake, skinny dipping, floating in the cold dark waters and staring at the sky. Of being seventeen with the boy you love, with the whole world and the rest of your life in front of you.

Ruby'd never be able to put into words what she was feeling, had felt. She couldn't explain it. Not anymore.

"So he was an old boyfriend. Hank and me wondered. Figured y'all knew each other in Louisiana."

"More than just an old boyfriend. He was everything to me after my father died. Billy was friend, protector, lover." Ruby paused, gathered herself together for a moment. "I had a tough time. My mother never got over my father's death. She took it out on my brother and me a lot. Billy ran interference and when he couldn't do anything else, he'd hide me out."

All the hours she'd spent at Billy's house with him holding ice packs on her face or carefully dotting iodine on her wounds, Ruby recalled against her will. She remembered how he broke into houses to steal money for her so she could buy a prom dress when her mother took the cash Ruby had saved from waiting tables. He ran with a tough crowd after school, always had. Didn't interfere with his running track and the burglaries kept him in pocket change. She'd been glad he stole money for her dress. But she doubted she could make Luther understand.

"Billy wasn't this bad guy, you know? Not then. He was a track star. Got on the honor roll a time or two. Good looking, popular, and the thing was, he chose me. Those snooty town girls couldn't figure it out when he took me to the prom." She decided to leave out the part about Billy being an accomplished thief by the time he was a senior.

"But he got drafted. When he came home right before being shipped out to Nam, we talked it all out, planned things before he left. I wanted to marry him then and there. He insisted I had to stay and finish high school. Truth is, I basically moved in with his folks my

244

senior year. They're both dead now." Ruby looked down at her hands as if they were a mystery to her, saddened by her memory of good people who'd been kind to her and died in a senseless car crash.

"Billy had a bad time of it in the war and afterwards. When his parents died, that hit him hard. I wasn't very good at handling it, I guess. I mean I was just this girl, you know, this kid, and I didn't understand what he'd been through and I was focused on me. So, when he got back home, we didn't stay in Louisiana too long. We went to Tampa. And things just got worse."

"So you were willing to go to jail for him? Because he was a good guy before he got drafted?"

"Oh, please. Come on, Luther, you know in your wildest dreams no jury was going to convict me on what y'all had against me. You didn't have any hard evidence and damn little circumstantial. And that receipt gave me an alibi. I wasn't risking anything by trying to cover for Billy."

"Okay. I guess the answer is 'no,' you wouldn't risk jail to protect him."

"Damn you, Luther, you're as bad as Hank."

"Well, thank you, ma'am, Hank's always been kind of my hero."

Ruby moved toward the phone in the kitchen. "I'm going to call Golder. You should leave now." The small window of connection between them was closed now and she knew it.

***

Luther slouched in a folding chair out in his backyard, working his way through a six-pack and staring at the moon. *Things didn't add up, not by a long shot, thank you.*

Nora came out and stood by him. "Okay, Luther, what's wrong?"

"Nothing. Just admiring that full moon. Look at that beauty. A harvest moon to beat all I ever seen." He took a long drink from his beer, then offered the can up to her. His wife shook her head.

"You don't sit out in the yard staring at the moon unless something is bothering you. Now, what is it? Can't I help?"

"Picked up this junkie once, long time back, on a full moon night like this. He was a street poet. I ever tell you this story?" Luther looked over at Nora, who shook her head in a noncommital way. "He, the junkie that is, points up at the big moon and says to me that God is a junkie too and the moon is the hole where he shoots up."

Nora eased closer to him, resting her hand on his shoulders and giving him a soft massage. She wasn't much for street poetry, Luther knew, but she made a pleasant noise in the back of her throat as she rubbed his sore neck muscles. Luther tilted his head up toward her.

"By God, you sure look pretty in this moonlight. Why don't you come sit with me?" Luther patted his lap with his free hand and sipped his beer with the other.

"Put the beer down first," she said. He did. Nora smiled and slipped onto his lap. Luther wrapped his arms around her and buried his face in her thick, honey-colored hair. "You look pretty in the broad open day light too," he muttered to her hair. Luther knew Ruby and Hank would never have a moment like this. He pulled his face out of Nora's hair long enough to say, "By God, woman, you sure do smell good."

Later, walking into the house, Luther squeezed her hand. "I know there's been some rough spots. But by God, you ain't a lightweight, that's for darn sure."

"Likely to be some more rough spots before it's all over."

When Luther turned to kiss her, Nora opened her lips to him and wrapped her arms tightly around him.

***

For five consecutive nights Ruby went to Hank's house, but the lights were out. Neither his city-issued official Chevy nor his personal truck were in the shed or driveway. Each night she rang the bell anyway and knocked. On the fifth night, she walked around the house, looking for some sign of occupancy. His boats were still there. Ruby tinkered with the doors to his house, but the locks were complex and solid.

When Ruby couldn't get into the house, she pried open the door to his room in the shed. That lock was cheap, rusted. Ruby walked around the room, studying the weights, the tools, the tossed about things. She ran her fingers down the barbells, traced the indentation of Hank's body on the weight bench. Years of sweat left a clear mark. Ruby barely breathed as she pulled her fingers off the outline on the bench. She sat, unmoving, on his bench.

The night's chill pulled her out of her dazed silence and she rose from the bench, taking one final look around. As she was headed out the door, she spotted a rusty tool box with a brand-new lock, tucked away in a corner behind a larger tool box. The new lock made her curious.

Ruby took a long time to break open this lock, but years ago Billy had taught her well. If she'd had more energy, she might even have gotten into Hank's house. She opened the box, already with a sense of misgiving. Under some loose nails and screws, she saw a folded sheet of paper and a cassette tape. She pulled them both out, recognizing Gardner's handwriting on the tape's label. A label that said "Billy Dittwilder."

A bolt of nausea hit her as strong as if someone had kicked her in a kidney.

Chapter Twenty-Two: Harlan

Ruby was hunched over on the hard, wooden bench in the front room of the police department when Luther came out to see her.

"Receptionist said you asked to speak with me." Luther didn't greet her, nor respond to her gesture to sit down.

"Yes. Thank you for seeing me. I want to know where Hank is. I need to talk to him."

Luther shook his head slightly as he spoke. "Hank's in L.A. Taking some of his vacation days and paying his own way so he can show Billy's photo and that drawing of him around. Trying to pump up interest in catching him. Nobody here, like the chief, thought he needed to go out there, but he's determined to try and find Dittwilder."

"Damn." Ruby pushed herself up from the bench. She looked over at the receptionist who was blatantly watching her.

"Why 'damn'?" Luther rocked back on his heels as she rose in front of him. "You mean, 'damn' you don't want him to catch Billy, or 'damn,' it's a waste of time. Or what?"

"Just damn. I need to see him, Hank I mean." Ruby glanced around the room. "Can we go somewhere else and talk?"

Without speaking, Luther nodded toward a hallway and ambled off in that direction. Ruby followed him down the hall into a kitchen. Two uniforms were sipping coffee and laughing over something in a magazine. Luther motioned for them to leave and they picked up their cups before strolling out of the room.

"Why'd he go to L.A.? Can't the L.A. cops handle finding Billy?" Ruby leaned against the wall, her shoulders rounded in.

"Yeah, well, maybe yes, maybe no. We sent them the info, the photo and the drawing. But how many requests like that you reckon the L.A.P.D. gets in one day? One week? They got their own murders. Ours won't be a top priority. If Wilson had died, yeah. Even just shooting a cop makes Billy's case stand out a bit more, but probably not enough." He poured a cup of coffee and offered her one. She nodded.

"From the day we got his ID on the prints, we've had reports out to our police at every roll call and I personally sent out teletypes to police agencies 'round this area of the state. After he shot Wilson, we went whole hog, put the word out everywhere. But you gotta know, local, state and national teletype networks are swamped. And looking for a skinny 40-year-old white guy wanted for killing a lawyer, well, in a flooded system, it ain't like it's gonna be a high priority, even with Wilson."

Ruby sipped the coffee, wincing a bit at the bitterness. Luther had not offered milk or sugar. She nodded as he continued.

"Usually the only thing the average cop is gonna remember from roll call is the red ball cases. The heartbreak kid cases. The cop killer. I don't mean to be snide, but a lawyer killer ain't gonna stay placed in their minds too long. And 'cause Wilson's okay, that part of it will slip away after a few days or weeks. You know what I mean?"

"Yes. You mean the odds of Billy ever being caught are pretty slim."

"Yeah. That's exactly what I mean. You know, unless they pull him in for something else and run his prints. So, it's kind of up to Billy now whether he gets caught or not. Hank couldn't live with that, so he's got to go out there and try this macho cop last ditch thing on his own."

"Only he won't find him either, will he?"

249

"Probably not." Luther put his cup down on the counter with a loud thud. "But I get the feeling you'd be just as happy if your old boyfriend gets away."

Ruby didn't answer. Luther held the door open for her.

Walking toward Luther, Ruby asked when Hank would be back.

"Leave him alone."

The two of them glared at each other for a strained second before Ruby stomped out the door.

***

In a chair on the deck in Hank's backyard, Ruby sat still and stared at nothing in the gloom around her. A few fireflies skittered about in the air. She was thinking she might as well give up and go home when she heard a car turn into the driveway. She kept her seat, watched the pattern the headlights made on the shed wall, and listened as a car engine stopped and the door slammed. When heavy footsteps neared her, she glanced up, a sheen of sweat on her face in the cold night.

"Well, damn, Mrs. Randolph, you like to startle me." Luther stopped in front of her, his expression guardedly bland.

"I parked down the street. If Hank saw my car, he might not come in."

"How'd you know he was due back tonight?"

"I'm not without my lawyer tricks and guile." Truth was, Ruby hadn't known until Luther just told her.

Luther stepped onto the deck, pulled up a chair and sat down close to her. "This won't do you any good."

"But it's over now. Everybody knows Billy killed Gardner, not me."

"We do, do we? Everybody?"

"Look, I'm so tired of saying this. I didn't kill Gardner. I wasn't in on it with Billy. And I didn't put Billy up to it. All right?"

"Sure. You're probably right. But you got to admit there's a whole bunch of loose ends on this one."

"You say so." Ruby wiped her face with her sleeve and wished she could stop sweating. "So what do I do? I mean about Hank? I want to straighten it out. But how?"

"Look, damned if I know. Best I see it, you're about screwed either way. Even if Billy Dittwilder came in and confessed and said you didn't have nothing to do with it, Hank's never gonna for 100 percent sure trust you not to have been part of killing Gardner."

Ruby rose out of the broken-down plastic lawn chair and wandered over to the railing. "I'd like to see him alone when he comes in. I'm asking you please to leave now."

"I could do that. But first, you're gonna make me understand about you and Billy. In Tampa. When he got in trouble and all. You explain that to me and I'll leave."

"I told you. We came down from Louisiana together. We lived on the streets for a time, then I got a job. Billy would do day labor now and then, mostly he just took downers and drank. We met some people down by the college and we crashed with them."

"What about the bars? Drinking at the bars?"

"Why do you ask about that, Luther?"

"I want to know."

"We were broke, so we took up hanging out at the college bars."

"But you just said you were broke?"

"Oh, come on. You know how it works. I was 18, I looked good. Billy and I'd split up in the bar. Some guy would buy me a drink. Then Billy'd drift back over. Worst that happened would be the other guy would leave and Billy'd finish off my drink. But if we were lucky, the guy would buy us both a few rounds, maybe score some dope from

251

us, take back a tale for the next day at the office or the class room. Usually there wasn't any harm in it."

"Usually?"

Ruby looked at Luther a long time, a hard look. An image struggled in the back of her subconscious. She half-closed her eyes, imagined him younger and without the moustache. Thinking about the bars, why he asked about that. Thinking about what came after the bars.

"You were skinnier then." Her voice had a hint of surprise.

Luther's eyes narrowed and his lips parted a bit under the heavy droop of his mustache. He was seeing it too, she believed, the fuzzy image struggling from the back to the front of memory.

"Yeah, damn. So were you."

"I don't think I ever thanked you for your kindness that night."

"No, as a matter of fact, I think you did." He paused, frowned. "You weren't really hurt, were you?"

"No."

"But we talked, didn't we?"

"Yes. For a few minutes. I just wanted to get out of there."

"Yeah, Saturday night at the bars. What was the cause, now, I can't quite remember? Not a classy bar, but not a dive either."

"The bar? I meant the laundro—." She stopped, a wary look slipping over her face.

But Luther caught the sudden pause. He stared at her without speaking so long that Ruby began to sweat again. Maybe she should go, try to catch up with Hank another night.

Just as Ruby was shifting to leave, Luther stood up, walked over to the back door, fidgeted through the collection of keys on his ring until he found the right one, and unlocked Hank's door.

"Come on. I'm supposed to be checking the house and mail and stuff for him." Luther waved Ruby toward the door.

Ruby wanted to see Hank alone, but something in Luther's tone and expression made her follow him in.

Luther turned the lights on and rambled in the kitchen, pulling out three glasses and a bottle of whiskey. With a quick, polished motion he poured a shot into two of them. He offered one to Ruby. She started to say no, but she took the glass and swallowed the whiskey in one hot, burning rush. Luther followed suit, then refilled their glasses, holding the bottle in his hand as he stared at Ruby. She gripped the refilled glass in her hands as the whiskey from the first shot seared down her throat.

An odd, strangling sadness crept over Luther's face. "Damn it to hell and back." He slammed the whiskey bottle back on the counter and spun out away from her, throwing his fist in the air and striking at an imaginary foe.

"In the laundromat, you and two men. Somebody called the cops the way the three of you were slugging it out, wrecking the place. You. And that guy from the bar. The college professor guy. He'd been beating you up." Luther twisted back to Ruby. "Damn. The third guy, I reckon that'd be Billy, wouldn't it?"

Ruby was too tired to lie anymore. "Yes."

"The professor disappeared, didn't he? Just being a street cop, I didn't hear about that." Luther shook his head. "Damn. I didn't know that he'd gone missing until just a few days ago. You were questioned. But the first suspect was some guy who shot the professor's dog. Then the investigators decided the professor up and left. No evidence of foul play, the report said."

"The report?"

"Yes. I read through the professor's file back in Tampa."

"Why?"

"Let's just say your path and the professor's crossed. 'Sides which, Hank asked me if anything in the missing person's file tied you, Billy, and the professor together. I can't believe I didn't put it all together, didn't remember that night until you said laundromat."

Car lights beamed in through the window. "That'd be Hank, I reckon."

"Leave me alone with him, please. You promised."

"Yeah, maybe I did. But I ain't done here." Luther tapped his fingers on the whiskey bottle, eyed Ruby's still full glass, and sloshed a half shot into his glass. "I should have arrested all three of you that night. Or least ways the professor. But it was near the end of my shift. I just wanted to get home. Nora'd just had our first child, a girl, and I didn't want to be caught that close to quitting time filling out damn arrest forms. My partner that night didn't care one way or the other. It was up to me. So, I let y'all go. Forgot about it. Till now."

"You should forget about it again. And leave."

"No. Hellfire and damnation, I want to know the whole story. This man is beating crap out of you in a laundromat and then he disappears off the face of the earth and Billy was involved somehow. Y'all hired Gardner to defend Billy, only that went South in a big way."

"Gardner sold Billy out." Ruby didn't figure she was telling Luther anything he hadn't figured out, but in a strange way it felt good to say it. "He wanted Billy convicted and sent away."

"I reckon I know why." Luther flicked his eyes up and down Ruby's body, fast, but not so quick Ruby didn't read the message.

"He wanted Billy sent away, but he didn't connect Billy or me to the professor." Ruby craned her head around to watch the door, waiting for Hank, but Luther's voice drew her attention back to him.

"Way I read the missing persons report was just that the cops looking at it dead-ended and figured the professor was a creep

254

anyway. Maybe the lost professor is no big deal in the overall scheme of things. But why do I think this has something to do with your late husband's blackmailing you? And with Billy?"

Ruby felt strangely relieved. She'd been expecting this moment for almost sixteen years.

Hank opened the back door and came in.

"What are you two doing here?" He threw down his carry-on luggage and glared in turn at both of them.

"I don't reckon you found Billy Dittwilder?"

"No, Luther, I don't *reckon* I did."

Luther poured whiskey into the third glass and handed it to him. Hank took the glass but didn't drink it. "I'm tired. It's a long flight from L.A. I'd appreciate it if you would both leave my house."

"Nope, bud, I think we have some unfinished business. Ruby and me, we might be on the brink of a kind of a break-through. Tired as you are, I think you better take a seat and play this out."

Ruby eased past Hank into the living room. Clutching her glass of whiskey without spilling any, she slid down into one of the worn, stuffed chairs. Luther and Hank followed her.

"Ruby here was just fixing to explain about her and Billy and this professor in a laundromat."

"I don't think I have anything else to say. Not without Golder present and probably not even then." Her lawyer face dropped back in place as Ruby settled her features into a blank.

"Well, then Hank, damn it, why don't you finish the story for me? You do know it, don't you?"

Ruby dropped her head, unable to even glance at Luther. Of course, he was angry. He'd no doubt put together his revived memory of the fight in the laundromat with his puzzlement over Hank's question about whether the missing person's report linked Billy, Ruby, and the professor. And if Luther had connected that, he'd probably figured his partner withheld something from him about her.

Like the tape she'd found in Hank's garage, with Billy spilling his guts to Gardner. She wondered where Hank found it, but it didn't really matter.

Billy hadn't known Gardner recorded it all until he threatened to use that tape to keep Billy from appealing his harsh sentence on grounds of ineffective counsel. Gardner made things worse for Billy at the trial, pissing off the prosecutor and the judge and never bothering to defend Billy on the arson—or anything else. If there'd been a transcript, anyone could have seen the ineffective counsel defense. But Gardner told them they didn't need a court reporter to transcribe the trial. But the real kicker was the tape—even if Billy appealed without a transcript, Gardner would have dropped the tape on him.

All so Gardner could have Ruby for himself. Not so much of a bargain, really. Certainly, not in the end.

Ruby made herself look up, first at Hank, then at Luther. She licked her lips, prepared to explain—if she could. But Luther spoke first.

"Tell me, bud, or so help me God, I'll forget you're my partner."

Something in Hank's expression collapsed as Ruby watched, her own face hot and sticky with sweat.

"Damn it to hell and back," Luther said, "Let's put it all on the table. What happened that night? And how is it you know, Hank?"

Hank glanced at Ruby and all but imperceptibly she shrugged.

"I found these notes Gardner wrote. And a cassette tape of Billy. They weren't dated. But they indicated that Billy and Ruby killed the professor and buried his body in an orange grove," Hank said. "It was in the storage unit. When you and that other lawyer went out for a smoke, I went back and got the tape and the notes."

"By God I ought to punch you out. When was it you were planning on telling me about this?"

"Never." Hank lifted the glass with the whiskey toward his face, glared at it like he didn't know what it was, but then took long, slow swallows till the glass was empty. He never glanced at Ruby or Luther.

Luther muttered something too muffled for Ruby to hear. Though she couldn't hear the words, she could sense the anger in the tone.

"Gardner's notes started off strange. He indicated that Ruby and Billy Dittwilder approached him recently for advice on moving a body they had hidden." Hank spoke in a steady monotone, almost as if he were reading something boring. "Housing developments were going up all around that orange grove. Said that they were afraid the building in that area would unearth the body and the police would open a murder investigation. Notes went on to say that because his clients, Billy and Ruby, were seeking his advice on committing a crime— moving a body—which also was meant to defraud the legal system, that the attorney-client privilege didn't apply."

Luther cut his eyes over at Ruby. "Is that true? I mean about the attorney-client thing?"

"Yes. There are exceptions to the attorney-client privilege and that's one of them. That is, if a client asks for advice or assistance in committing a crime before the crime is actually committed, there's no privilege. But it's not true that Billy and I asked for Gardner's advice about moving the body. We might've been stupid enough to trust Gardner once, but not twice. But it wouldn't matter. It'd just be Gardner's word against ours. Given that tape, he'd have been more believable."

"So now what?" Hank asked.

"I want to hear her side of the story," Luther said, turning to Ruby.

Ruby shook her head. "I didn't come out so good the only time I told it."

"Try us," Luther said. "We're not Gardner."

Ruby didn't figure she'd come out any better this time, but she was ready to tell it, to put the truth into play, and see how it turned out. She was tired of almost sixteen years of lying. She wanted to come clean and find whatever redemption she could. Telling the truth was probably a good place to start.

Chapter Twenty-Three: Ruby Tells her Story

That summer Billy came back from Nam was so blistering hot we walked around feeling like we'd been rolled in peanut oil and dusted with corn meal, only it was just the usual dirt blown up off the roads and from the fields. You can't know what it was like for us when he came back. He'd killed a child over there, or that's what he said anyway. A little boy with a home-made bomb tied to him, running toward him and his group of soldiers. Nobody else would shoot the child. Billy didn't want to die there, not blown up by a child. The boy would've died whether he shot him or not—so Billy said. I never knew if I believed that story. He only told it to me once.

Other people had almost killed him for no good reason Billy could figure out. It certainly couldn't have been personal because they didn't know him and he couldn't understand why they would try so hard to kill him. But he had the scars to prove it. After Billy went crazy, the Army just booted him out with a medical discharge and a refillable script for some serious downers.

Billy was scared but he couldn't admit it. Being home didn't help. One night, we'd been out at Casey's Bar drinking, playing pool, the usual screwing around not amounting to anything night. We came back to this trailer we were staying in with some other folks and crashed out in the bed. Summer in Louisiana is so hot that even at night things stick to you. Pillow cases, sheets, tiny bugs, dirt, dust. It all just gums into the greasy film on your skin you can't wash off for more than a couple of minutes. We had a fan going by the bed and the window open to catch any night breeze, even though it wasn't safe to sleep with the windows open. But safety had stopped being a concern for us.

I woke up drenched, not just in sweat, but in urine. His. Billy's. He'd dreamed he was back in Nam and the fan sounded like a copter blade and the heat and humidity and the drunkenness all conspired against him. He was scared enough to wet the bed like a little boy. At first he didn't even know he'd done it and groggy as I was, I couldn't figure it out either, why I was this wet.

He told me he'd spilled a beer. In the bed. That's why it was so wet, Billy said, just spilt beer. And like milk, there wasn't any sense crying over it. Go on back to sleep. But I got up, went into the living room, and crashed out on a filthy couch. That was the night when I began to question my resolve for the long run. A long haul with a man who dreamed about killing a boy and woke, wetting the bed.

Got to the point neither of us slept. We just passed out. He got downers from the V.A., we got street drugs, beer and whiskey and God-knows what, and we swallowed it all. We'd cringe out of bed around noon, pissing and moaning and not even knowing what day it was. I remember going over to Casey's sometimes as early as 2 P.M. and we'd drink.

We didn't even try to have jobs after the first few weeks. Times were not booming in Louisiana. Even if they had been, we weren't the types who'd get hired. Straggly and long-haired, red eyes we wouldn't look anyone in the face with. So, we stopped looking for jobs.

Billy'd run with a tough crowd even before Nam and had become good at breaking and entering. Locks didn't stop him and folks we met those days taught him some more tricks. He taught me. We broke into stores, homes. We also got some money here and there selling drugs, shoplifting, but mostly we didn't have money. And that didn't matter so much as it might have because we had a big circle of people, friends of a sort, just like us. Somehow between us all we managed a trailer at the park by Casey's, beer, cigarettes, pot, and a few Quaaludes and Seconal.

I guess it was the inevitable next step, though, to finally begin losing even that much. So, we did, kicked out of the trailer first.

We ended up way out in the country, back in the woods in a shack of a house. A group of us. I don't remember how many. There wasn't any electricity, but there was water from a well. Somebody'd rigged up something that pulled power off somebody else's line. Don't ask me. They'd just done it and it was a joke whether we'd have water day to day.

Billy and me and the rest of them had been up most of the night, drinking, smoking pot. He and I crashed out together on one of the few mattresses. There were no sheets now. No pillows or pillow cases to stick to us. Now we stuck directly to the filthy mattress with its smells and stains of God-knows what. I remember mildew and spider webs grown together and hanging in gray clumps from the ceiling like moss in the live oaks. The place smelled worse than a swamp.

I woke up early, or early for our crowd. I was sleeping in the same T-shirt I'd been wearing for days. My jeans were kicked off and lying on the floor by the mattress. I wasn't wearing, didn't own, any underwear. Like sheets and pillow cases, nightgowns and underwear had all just slipped away. I don't even know where they went, how I'd lost them.

But I still had the ruby pendant Billy gave me before he left for Nam. I'm surprised we never tried to hock it.

That morning, I remember my head hurt and I was thirsty and desperate for a cigarette, so I went prowling in the living room. I fumbled around in the ashtrays looking for a butt long enough to smoke. Some kind of disgust finally broke through in me. I went back in the bedroom and I woke Billy up and I said we're getting out of here, we're going to Florida, we're going to do better than this, and I don't want to listen to any crap.

For the life of me, I don't remember how we got back into town. But we did. And I begged my brother for money for bus tickets and we took showers at his house. He gave Billy some of his clothes and his girlfriend gave me some of hers. They were good people and maybe I told them so, thanked them. We took the extra clothes and wrapped them up in an A &P grocery sack. If I hadn't watched him, kept the money tight against my hips in the side pocket of my jeans, Billy would have spent the bus ticket money on beer. But I saved it, I got us to the bus station, and I got us tickets and on that bus. For the thirty hours that bus took traveling south to Tampa, stopping in every God-forsaken place every half hour to pick up people as wretched-looking as us, I kept us sober. We took some downers, but we were okay enough to know when to get off the bus.

It was foolish of me to think things would be any better for us in Tampa, but I thought all I had to do was get us out of Louisiana and somehow we'd be all right. We weren't.

Ruby stopped talking, looked down in her lap and was surprised to see the white knuckles on her hands wrapped tightly around the glass of whiskey. Her mouth watered as if she were salivating at the smell of fresh baked pound cake. Almost involuntarily, like a thing removed and separate from her body, her hand rose bringing the glass to her mouth. Ruby smelled the whiskey.

"Steady, gal. You lived through it and it's over now. Telling it is just talking." Billy's voice came to her so clearly that Ruby jumped, cast her eyes around the room until they came to rest on Luther, sitting opposite her. In Luther's red-rimmed, tired blue eyes, Ruby saw something like compassion—the same look of concern she remembered from the day Gardner had been killed and she sat in an interrogation room at the police department. Ruby put the drink down on the table.

262

"Luther is a kind man."

When a blush spread across Luther's face, Ruby realized she'd spoken out loud what she only meant to think. She tried to smile at him but could not. Instead, she glanced at Hank slouching against the wall, but still on his feet. When she looked him in the face, Hank's eyes narrowed and he pushed off the wall and went in the kitchen and refilled his glass of whiskey. When he came back into the room, Hank slunk down on a worn couch, exhaustion evident in his face and the way he moved.

Ruby went into the bathroom and rinsed her face, which was sticky with sweat even in the cold. When she returned, she suspected the men had not spoken to each other. She took her seat in the chair across from Luther. Glancing at him first, she continued.

All we had was some traveling money my brother gave us, the clothes, and a stash of downers. We hung out around the bus station, eating crap out of the vending machines for breakfast until we met up with some folks like us. We sold them half of our stash and they told us the best place to hang out was around the college, University of South Florida. Not knowing our way around, it took us a while to hitchhike out there, but we got to the edge of the campus and crashed out that night in a county park across from a trashy, run-down trailer park. But the county park was clean, there was a breeze, and we could wash up in the public restrooms. They were locked after 6, but it was easy enough to break in. We took a couple hits from the dwindling stash of downers, a little panicked at how few were left, and slept on the cool, damp ground.

Next day, we set out to get some money, dragging our little A & P luggage with us. We picked up junk at a construction site, day labor, and got some cash. We had enough money to get a room, a cheap nasty efficiency. We did day work, not steady, but enough to keep the room. Then we met up with another couple who lived in that trashy trailer park and we moved in with them. I borrowed a decent enough dress from the girl to get a job—washing and folding clothes at one of those laundromats that advertises "drop-off" service. I took the clothes, washed and dried them, and folded them. It was easy. A lot of college people came in.

Sometimes Billy hung out with me, helped fold clothes. We met people. Soon enough we were running a little part-time drug store, dealing nickel and dime stuff. In those days, you could get a good two finger bag of pot for $15 and a pound for around $300. We'd get a pound, break it down to so-called ounces, steam it in a colander over a boiling pot of water to add weight, body and make it look real fresh. Sell it at a profit and hold back enough to keep us high. I thought things were looking up.

One night when Billy was passed out early at the trailer and didn't come to the laundromat, this man came in, very handsome. Dark hair, black eyes, tall, but filled out, not skinny. He was so beautiful I couldn't take my eyes off him. But he was too clean-cut looking for the evening trade and I thought he might be a cop and I played it cool with him. He was asking about drugs, pot or crystal meth, either one. I played dumb and he left.

But he came back. Not that night, but a few nights later, and we talked. He helped me fold clothes and we laughed at silly stuff. You know how it is when you first meet somebody that turns you on and you act stupid about it. By the time he was coming in regular to see me, Billy was too messed up to help at anything and he stayed away from the laundromat.

That long haul with Billy started looking too long. I took up with the good-looking man. His name was Harlan LaSalle and of all things, he taught biology at USF. I thought I was in love all over again and when he invited me home with him, I went. And I stayed.

Teacher or not, he was into drugs, serious stuff. Crystal meth was his thing. Sometimes Angel Dust. You know how messed up Angel Dust makes you? The meth wasn't much better. He'd stay up night after night and just talk about blood cells and bones and I was fascinated by it all.

Harlan was also broke. He spent money like he really had it. He blew a lot on meth, so the only sensible thing for him to do, he said, was to go into business.

It was 1972. Everybody sold drugs.

At first I didn't like the idea of selling street drugs on a bigger scale with Harlan. I was looking to get out of that life, but even I saw how easy it was. All Harlan had to do was front me the money and I did the rest. By then I knew people who were connected to the right people and with Harlan's money and his car and apartment, I branched out from breaking up pounds of pot into $15 baggies. I got nervous about the laundromat. Anyway, now I was making enough money off dealing that I didn't need the base salary and I didn't have to pay rent living with Harlan. I quit the laundromat and focused on a smaller, but more profitable clientele.

But the thing I'd missed those first few weeks of being new in love was that the truth of the matter was Harlan was a sick, evil man. By the time I knew it, I couldn't seem to pull loose of him. He was turning violent. The meth brought it out in him more and more.

Harlan liked to humiliate me. First he'd take me to parties and make me look stupid—the hick girl who never went to college, you know? He also liked to take me someplace and then leave with another girl. I remember walking home in the rain one night back to his apartment. I had to sit on the back porch until he was done with the other girl and let me back in.

Then he got where he didn't want me going anywhere with him. But he liked having me at home waiting. He liked having me deal his drugs for him. I took it, I guess, because it wasn't that different than all my growing up years. And I didn't know what else to do.

Harlan had a lot of other girls. He had this one other girlfriend, a blond girl who seemed a serious sort, one of his students. She got pregnant and when she started pressuring him, Harlan started losing all control. Her damn father came after him. Shot his dog. Harlan was scared and it wasn't the first time he hit me. I fought back. I was a good fighter, but I was never any real match for him. Especially when he was on the Dust.

When I saw how it was playing out, that it would just get worse, I started making plans. I didn't want to leave empty handed, not after all I'd been through. One night after my bruises healed, we were out drinking at a bar and this other girlfriend came in and asked me rather nicely to leave them alone. Then with me just a few feet away, she demanded Harlan marry her or else her daddy would kill him. He was as nice and sweet as any man could be and calmed her down and promised to come see her at her parents' house. I could hear him when he promised to marry her. If I'd thought for one minute he meant it, I'd've followed and tried to talk her out of it. When she left, he called her a stupid slut and laughed about it. That made me mad. She was just a scared little girl. So, we lit into each other. This time I fought back like I meant it. Bad enough that the police came and had to pull us apart.

Truth was, Harlan was losing it and the meth was making him weak and stupid. His weakness made me sick in a way his abuse hadn't. I wasn't going to lay in wait much longer and the next day I rooted out the extra key to his car and hatched my plan. Three days later while he was teaching, I took his car out of the faculty parking lot and drove it to his apartment, where I filled up his luggage with a stash of crystal meth, pot, and his whole damn inventory. For once in my life, my timing was perfect because just a week before he'd cleaned out his bank account to make a big score. It was the end of the semester and he wanted a big stake so he could leave town.

All that meth. The refrigerator was full of it. I was the one who was supposed to sell it. I figured I had a right to it.

So, I took it. I hauled it right over to Billy's trailer. By now the other couple had left and the power had been cut off. Billy was just lying around waiting to be kicked out. I paid up some back rent, hid the drugs, and took Harlan's car back to the parking lot.

A couple of days later, Billy and I were right back in business. He was too messed up to be as angry at me for leaving him as he should have been and took me back. We started selling off some of Harlan's stash. Just a little, here and there.

Where we made our mistake was going back to the old laundromat. I didn't want to sell Harlan's drugs to my new customers because most of them knew Harlan and I was afraid they'd tell him where I was. Billy wandered around in his haunts and sold some, but we decided we needed to get rid of it as quick as possible and quit town. I was hoping to find somebody to buy the whole inventory at once. Key West took on a whole mythical proportion to us and that's where we decided to go.

Only we ran into Harlan in the laundromat. He'd come there looking for me. Crazy as shit on the Angel Dust.

Ruby stopped talking, wondering if Luther wanted her to leave him out of the story. Studying his face, she saw him nod as if giving her permission.

Harlan started in on me right away, hitting me, knocked me down before I even had a chance to get a kick in. He had me on the concrete floor, beating hell out of me when Billy jumped him. We all got into a big fight. Harlan was hopped up on Dust and fought like a demon even though he'd lost strength. Billy had lost strength too. Maybe I was the only one who hadn't, but I was a girl. It took Billy and me both to get him down this time. But he'd come back up, hitting and swearing. Somebody'd called the cops. A car with two policemen came and pulled us apart.

Ruby nodded at Luther. "One of those cops was you."

Hank moaned and turned to Luther. "You remember this?"

"Not at first. It took me hearing a few more pieces of the puzzle before it came back to me. Kinda smashed me, the memory. She was beat up, bleeding. And I told the guy to leave her alone." Luther's voice faded off. "I just told him to go on home. And the hell of it was, I'd just separated them before, in a bar, not that long before. So, I knew there was a pattern. The man would keep coming after her. Until one of them killed the other. Isn't that how it usually plays out?"

"And, you didn't—" Hank started to say.

"No. I didn't. I was young and in a hurry to get home and didn't want to fool with all the arrest reports. I didn't do what I should have done. Instead, I left Ruby to clean up the mess herself."

"No, not quite," Ruby whispered. "You left me with Billy."

***

After Luther broke the fight up and Harlan left, Billy and me thought that'd be that and we'd leave town the next morning.

I'd count that as my biggest mistake, not leaving right then, right out of the laundromat, taking what we had money wise and leaving on foot, thumbs out. But I was messed up and bloody and wanted to go back to the trailer, wash up.

Billy helped me clean up some and then we tanked up on some booze and meth. And when Harlan tracked us down somehow, I never knew how, we were part crazy anyway. Harlan had a gun and if he'd tried to shoot me, I guess I'd be dead. Thing was, Harlan was more messed up than we were and he never got a shot fired, but tried to pistol whip me instead. He got in a couple of good hits on the back and side of my head, in my hair, and I went down, blacked out. When I came to, Billy had him on the floor, pounding his head. I picked up the gun and smashed his head with it. When I stopped, Harlan was dead. It was that quick and that stupid.

The only thing that made sense to us at that point was to drag his body out into his car and take it far away and bury it. Crystal meth gave us great violent energy, but not good sense. It was self-defense, but who'd believe us? Maybe we had no choice at that point but to get rid of him. So, that's what we did.

Of course, we waited to make sure anybody who'd heard the fighting had gone back to sleep. Even high, I had sense enough to look around the trailer park before we dragged him out. Must have been two, maybe three in the morning. We stole some shovels out of the maintenance shed at the park and drove a long way south of town in Harlan's car, going down U.S. 301 for about an hour till we took an old orange grove trail called Moccasin Wallow Road and we buried him in the grove. As deep as we could. Deep. The sun was trying to come up by the time we finished.

After that we drove the car due south, then east for a whole day until it was night again and we were in someplace north of Miami. We drove the car into a bad neighborhood, left the keys in it, and walked out of there as fast as we could. By then we were sober enough to wipe down the car and the trunk for prints, but mostly we figured the cops would never see that car again. We caught the bus back to Tampa to get our things, our stash.

Next night the cops came for Billy while I was out getting a pack of cigarettes. I hadn't taken but a few bucks with me, just walking to the store on the corner. I was even barefoot. I'd walked because I needed to figure things out. Billy offered to get the cigarettes because my face was still messed up, but I wanted to go.

Mostly I just needed to get away from Billy for a little bit. We still had tons of the meth and it was still right there in the trailer when the cops came. I was just about half a mile away when the bust started. Billy fought with cops, broke the shoulder blade on one of them. In the fight, he knocked over a candle and the whole damn trailer burnt up. But it didn't burn before they'd taken most of the meth out as evidence.

A week or so later, a guy at the jail recommended Gardner for a lawyer.

You know the rest of the story. I don't know why I told Gardner, how it was he talked me into telling him, but I did. Billy too, spilling his guts into a damn tape recorder. When Billy got the max sentence and started a jailhouse appeal on grounds of ineffective counsel, Gardner said he'd play that tape if Billy didn't stop. See, Gardner wanted Billy out of the picture. For a long time. To get me. And when we started falling apart, Gardner used that tape against me too.

I wouldn't have killed Gardner, don't you see? Or had Billy do it, knowing that Gardner had that tape and wrote everything we told him down. And I did know about that tape and that it was all written down someplace I couldn't find. That's why I made Golder fight you every step when you started looking through all his papers, afraid y'all would find it before me.

Which Hank did, didn't he?

When Ruby stopped talking, neither Luther nor Hank spoke. Hank sat with his head in his hands and Luther drooped over in his chair, looking down at his feet.

"All right. You do what you have to do. I'm going home now. I'll be at the house on St. Anne's." Ruby stood up. Feeling light-headed, she stumbled a bit, but made it to her car and drove home. There, she showered and lay down on the couch in the living room and waited.

Chapter Twenty-Four: Eulogies

When Luther drove up in his official police Chevy, Ruby was pointing out things that needed to be done to the yard man. She led Luther back inside and held out her hands, palms down.

"I didn't come to arrest you."

"No, why not?"

Luther shook his head. "Because of Hank. He took that tape and those notes of Gardner's out of a file during an official police investigation and he hid them. That's enough to ruin his career if it ain't enough to put him in jail. I won't ruin Hank. Not just to dig up a dead guy in an orange grove."

"I wouldn't tell anyone Hank hid those notes."

Luther snorted, a quick sputter of noise that sounded rude. "Of course you would. Or you'd threaten. You'd use it to bargain. And if that didn't work, Golder would use it to try and defend you. Ruin Hank to discredit him. The spurned lover. The bad cop. Whatever. Before it was over Hank's career as a cop would be dead."

"No. I wouldn't hurt Hank."

"Sure you would, Ruby, even if you didn't mean to. Only I'm not gonna let you."

There was more to it than that. God knows, Luther didn't understand the half of it himself. That maybe some part of him at least wanted to give her a chance to redeem herself. That Hank chose to protect her over his being a good cop told Luther how much Hank loved her. That, and maybe she'd been punished enough without the legal system's intervention.

And his guilt too, Luther had to admit. If he had done what he should have that night in the laundromat, they wouldn't have had to kill Harlan. If Luther had been a good cop that night, Harlan would have been locked up. Billy and Ruby might have made it to Key West. Maybe had a chance at a decent life. Luther didn't think Billy could have pulled it together, but he was sure Ruby would have.

Maybe the bottom line was even simpler than any of that: He and Hank both needed to be done with Ruby, free and clear. The quickest way to do that was to let her and Billy keep their secrets. Lord knows the dead man in the orange grove could have cared less by now.

Luther closed in on her, catching and holding her eyes with his own. "Thing is, Ruby, you got to promise to stay away from Hank. He can't come and tell you that but I can. Maybe you put Billy up to killing Gardner, maybe you set him up for it. I don't know. But Hank and me are hereby officially wiping our hands of you. You hear? File is closed. Billy Dittwilder murdered Gardner Randolph as far as the police department and state attorney are concerned. Wilson heard him admit it. The bullet from Wilson and the one from your late husband both came from the same gun. Belt and me will issue a joint statement. Wilson'll be at the press conference. We're gonna make him out a hero if we can. Then we're gonna transfer him some place he won't get hurt again."

"Why won't Hank come here and tell me this?"

"You're too smart to ask that." Luther edged toward the front door, eager to leave.

Ruby stepped in front of the door as if to block Luther from leaving. "I don't get it. I mean, I really don't. Why's Hank so angry with me that he can't come here, that he can't even talk to me? I call him and he hangs up. I don't understand."

"Of course you do. You just don't want to admit it."

"Admit what?"

"Why he's so mad. You took away the one good thing he thought about himself."

"That's absurd."

"No, not if you really understand that Hank's basically a loser. Don't get me wrong, I mean the man's my partner and my best friend and he's the only man I'd let take my little boy if something happens to me and Nora, but he's still basically a loser."

"How do you figure that?"

"Jez, think about it, Ruby, will you? If he's not a drunk, he's a hog's hair away from it. Been divorced two times. His house is about four hinges and a screen away from a shack. But he's a good cop. Thing is, he's a damn good cop. Okay, so that's his one good thing, see? Now you come along messing up that. Wrecking his one good thing."

"Because he hid Gardner's notes and that tape?"

"Yeah, that's part of it. But see, right from the first his cop head said you're the killer. Plain and simple. But he loves you so he can't accept that."

"He loves me? Did he tell you that?"

"No. He wouldn't. But I got me a street degree in reading people. Same as you, learned on the same streets, but we just practiced it on different sides. See? And during the whole investigation he can't figure what to do about you. He goes hot and cold. But when he stole that report to protect you, that's when he destroyed his one good thing. Now he can't think he's a good cop."

"That's it?"

Luther could see how tightly she held herself together and how bleak her expression was. Even her voice was controlled, grim.

"Yeah. That's it. I don't figure you're getting off entirely scot-free. Still, I reckon if it weren't for Hank, I'd have to call the Tampa P.D. on this thing. But who knows? Maybe not."

Ruby stepped away from the front of the door and Luther walked outside into the fresh air and sunshine. She didn't follow. Neither of them bothered to say goodbye.

***

Ruby pressed her hands against the closed door of Nathaniel's office, willing herself to face him. Bad enough being back in the building, let alone going into Nathaniel's office. The few remaining secretaries and lawyers were milling around, boxing up things and closing up shop. They looked harried and unhappy and she sensed a certain hostility toward her, though for what reason she couldn't imagine. Perhaps because she had been the wife of the man who destroyed them. But it didn't matter. Nathaniel was what mattered.

Ruby straightened her shoulders and walked in.

Nathaniel wilted on the couch, a glass of whiskey in his hands and a gray pallor on his face. His skin seemed sunken, his lips colorless, and his white hair longer than she'd ever seen and unkempt. He didn't look up when she came in.

Ruby sat down beside him. For a moment, she didn't know what to do. His law firm was destroyed. The partners had officially dissolved the corporation. Lena had left him. The law firm's creditors had taken everything they could get except Nathaniel's homesteaded house and some retirement annuities. He looked sick and old. Broken.

Ruby wanted to pull him into her arms, to hold him, to stroke his head. To promise him things would be all right.

But she kept quiet until he turned his face toward her and lifted his whiskey glass as if to toast her.

"What brings you here?" he asked.

Ruby tried to read his face and tone of voice but couldn't tell if he was angry with her or not.

Why should he be angry with her? She'd saved him from Hank and Luther and Belt.

And left him to these other, perhaps bigger losses.

"You can get it all back, you know. Lena will come home to you, just give her time. Start another law firm. You and Dave. You did it once, so do it again."

"Doll, I'm an old man and I can't do it all over again."

"Why not?"

Nathaniel silently stood up, poured Ruby a drink, and offered it to her.

Ruby watched him pour the liquor, even reached out her hand to take it, imagined the bite of the warm alcohol on her tongue, the spark in her belly, the click in her brain. This was going to harder than she'd thought, she realized with a shudder.

One day at a time. One drink not drunk at a time. Every time you say no, you're a little stronger. Clichés, yeah. But there was a lot of truth in the old sayings.

Ruby put her hand down, shook her head. "No, thank you. I quit."

"Since when?"

"Since I've been going to AA."

"Good for you."

"Do it again. Build your law firm back. Dave'll help. He's fine now. You aren't too old."

"I can't. Because it's not worth it anymore." He poured the whiskey from her glass into his own and stepped back toward the couch, but didn't sit. "What can I do for you today?"

So, that was the way he wanted it. Like the nights at his own house, all business. Okay, she could be that way too. "I'll have the $150,000 soon to pay you back. Fred's about cowed the insurance company into paying me on Gardner's other life insurance. He had to file a lawsuit to get their attention. He's settling the estate for me, but maybe you knew that. Looks like Golder will get most of what's left for his legal fees after I pay you back, but he earned it. Anyway, as soon as I get the money, I'll see you get what I owe."

"Some of the partners here were actually going to have me arrested for stealing that money. Fred and Dave shamed them out of it. Because I was the one put up my personal property to keep us afloat. And because I told them I took it for Lena, gave it to her so she'd have something to live on." He paused, breathing heavily like a man who'd been running.

Ruby was glad the partners had that much decency left in them.

"Of course when Lena heard that I lied and said I took the money for her, she wouldn't deny it. Too much of a lady for that. But she was furious I used her as a cover for what I'd done for you. She left me because of it. She won't be back." With a sudden violent motion that made Ruby cringe, he reached down and grabbed her, pulling her up off the couch.

She came to her feet and into his arms. Nathaniel crushed her to him, tightening around her until he pulled her head back and put his mouth on hers. Ruby had no desire left for this man, had to face the fact she never really had, that all that sex once between them was just a part of the bargain she'd made with him, love me, teach me, protect me, be my mentor and my father-figure, and I'll help you remember when you were a young man.

But she let her lips part, let him kiss her, searching out her tongue with his while he pressed his body against her. And then like somebody had pushed the stop button, he shuddered back from her.

277

"Damn. That's what started all this." He shoved her away from him.

"Don't be blaming me. Gardner would have gone after you sooner or later anyway. He was a jealous, possessive son of a bitch, yeah, but you were in his sights from the minute he made partner. He always wanted to control this firm."

"If that's what you need to believe."

Ruby started to point out that it was him, Nathaniel, who had made the first move sexually, Nathaniel who had pursued her, but there didn't seem to be a lot of point in kicking at a dog when it was down.

"Before I forget, I've got something to give back to you. Don't even know why I took it." Nathaniel went over to his desk, opened a drawer, looked in, shoved things around, muttered, and then looked in the other drawers, slamming them shut after he'd riffled through them, leaving scattered papers everywhere.

"Damn, I guess I lost it. Or the cleaning crew stole it. Or Jacob got it and pawned it. Sorry."

"What? What did you have?" But Ruby thought she knew what he meant.

"That ruby pendant you used to wear."

No explanation how he might have gotten it, but Ruby could guess. And she knew who had taken it from Nathaniel's desk.

Dave. Trying to protect Nathaniel. Dave must have found the necklace in Nathaniel's desk and sensed the implications and risks. Everybody knew it had been Ruby's signature piece of jewelry. Anybody finding that necklace in Nathaniel's desk would have had questions. Questions that could have been dangerous.

So, Dave found the pendant, took it, and gave it back to her so nobody would be asking Nathaniel why he had it in his desk drawer.

That answered one of the few remaining questions Ruby had. Which left her with one, last thing to find out.

"There's one thing I have to know, Nathaniel. I have to ask. Why?"

"Why? What do you mean why?"

"Why kill Gardner?"

"I've been wondering when you'd get around to asking me that."

"What happened?"

"Man never goes home for lunch. I had the key you'd given me, you know, back when we were together, and my noon meeting canceled so I went to the house to look for the second set of books he and Nancy were keeping. It's was a spur of the moment thing. Find out where he'd been putting the money. Get it back. That's all I wanted. When I heard him come in I was in the main bedroom so I hid in the closet. He came right into the bedroom. He got out a gun from beside the bed. I could hear him loading it. Then he went into the bathroom and I came out of the closet and saw the gun on the bed. All I could think of was that he intended to kill you. I didn't know about Billy, didn't know he was out and had called Gardner."

"No, neither of us did, did we?"

"When he came out of the bathroom and saw me, he seemed almost relieved. I mean, I can't really explain it but it was almost like he was glad I was there."

"Maybe he was. He was terrified of Billy. That's why he got out the gun."

"Yeah. That's how I put it together. Later, that is. And if I'd waited, let him talk, maybe I wouldn't have killed him. Who knows? But when I saw him, I just exploded. I picked up the gun and shot him."

"Because of me?"

"Maybe. It was a hard thing to watch him rub your face into that table. But I shot him for me too. And to protect Dave. I promised myself to take care of Dave after he fell apart and I couldn't let Gardner push him out. Dave needed the firm, at least for a little while longer." Nathaniel held out his right hand and looked at it. "I took a gun in this hand and shot your husband. I went crazy. Can you understand?"

"Yes. I doubt Golder could have made a case for temporary insanity, but at least I understand. All Gardner had done to you. And me. Kind of like self-defense."

"Maybe I was trying to save the law firm too. He was destroying it. Hell, he did destroy it. These last two years, ever since he found out about you and me, that's what triggered it." Nathaniel shook his head. "But I was wrong to blame you a minute ago."

"Blame Gardner. All of it, 100 percent, his fault, blame him." That's what she was trying to do.

"I would never have let you go to trial. You know that, don't you?"

"Yes."

"And when you came for the money and I saw what you were up to, I let it go. I let you set up Billy. I should have had the guts to come out and admit it then. Save you and him both everything you went through on my account. Now Billy's out there with a murder warrant on him."

"Don't feel sorry for Billy, okay. Just don't. He came out this about as good as somebody like him could. Better than he had a right to. He shot a cop, all right? And Billy went to the house to kill Gardner. He told me that himself and I believe him. Gardner was right to get out the gun, but it wouldn't have done him any good. Billy would have killed him. Gardner wasn't any kind of match for Billy in terms of physical violence."

"So you think justice was done here?"

"Nathaniel, we've both been lawyers long enough to know justice is in the eye of the beholder."

"Do you think justice was done here, Ruby?"

Ruby backed away from Nathaniel and moved toward the door. "I'll get you the money as soon as I can. If I were you, I'd keep it, not use it to pay back the firm's debts. Screw them."

"I'm going to give it to Lena. If she'll take it."

Yeah, that'd be classic Nathaniel.

"One last thing. How'd you know?" Nathaniel asked.

No reason not to tell him now. Maybe if she'd confronted him sooner, Wilson wouldn't have gotten shot.

"When Hank asked me who else had a key to the house the day Gardner got killed, I thought of you. I'd given you a key to the house that time Gardner was trying the case in Miami, when we were still together. You never gave it back. Thing was, I kind of liked knowing you had that key—that is till Hank started asking about keys. But then Billy's prints showed up in the house and I figured he shot Gardner. That is until I saw how sure Billy was that I'd killed Gardner, which pretty much took him off the hook. And there you were, with that key I gave you."

Ruby didn't tell him that there for a brief time she'd thought Dave had killed Gardner. Because Dave had wanted to and because he'd had the necklace from her bedroom. But a few days of hard, sweaty, painful sobriety helped her understand and accept that Nathaniel had been the one after all. More than the key, it was the money, that $150,000 he stole from the firm, that proved it to Ruby. Nathaniel wouldn't have given her that money unless he'd been guilty. Paying Billy off was something he'd done as much to save himself as to save her. Same as shooting Gardner. Saving himself.

"How'd it play out?" She was tired of the damn key, tired of the money, tired of lying, but wanted that last piece of information before she got out of town.

"Billy must have come in right after I left. I shot Gardner. Then I wiped off my prints, cleaned the gun, called 9-1-1. I left the gun lying on the bed. But he had your necklace out, on the nightstand, and I took it. Getting sentimental in my old age, I guess. I'm sorry I lost it."

"It doesn't matter."

"Maybe not, but it was still sloppy of me to take that ruby, sloppier to have lost it. Anyway, like I was explaining, I got out of there fast as I could. I'd parked my car out of sight on the next block. Figured I had a decent chance of getting away with it. Figured you did too, even when they charged you."

"Sure, I know." She ran her fingers through her hair, wanted to rub her temples, wake up eighteen and do it all over—but differently, better. "And we did, didn't we? See, we're pretty good lawyers, aren't we?"

"Did we get away with it?"

Ruby studied Nathaniel for a last moment, then turned and left without answering him. Once his door closed behind her, she stood there a second and wondered if there wasn't something she could do to help Nathaniel. After all, she did love him, her friend, her mentor. But she didn't go back into his office. Instead she hurried down the hallway toward the world beyond the law firm.

Outside in the bright cool day, the Florida sun seemed to bounce off the concrete and into her eyes. It was almost spring. Back home, the Amaryllis and Narcissus soon would be curling out of the grounds around old farm houses. In the fields, the first nudges of green would be poking out of the dark loam and the dogwood trees would be in early bud. Ruby stood in the parking lot and faced north. Time to go home. Time to start over and see if she could do better this time around.

On the way out of town, she stopped by a homeless man with his cardboard sign and she handed him the ruby necklace. "It's real," she told him. "Pawn it for whatever you can get."

A note from the author:

Honest book reviews written by readers are a vital part of any book's success or failure. Not only do reader–driven reviews at such well known locations as Amazon, Goodreads, Bookbub, B&N, and similar sites help encourage others to buy and read the book, but the number of reviews often goes into complicated algorithms some booksellers use to decide which books are promoted or not. Therefore, please consider drafting a short, **honest** review of *Privilege* (and all other books you read!) and posting at book review sites and on social media. The key word here is "honest." The review can be short, just tell other readers what you honestly thought and what you liked (or didn't) about the book. Please remember not to give away the ending or otherwise be a plot spoiler. Thank you for myself and for all other writers.

Claire Matturro

CPSIA information can be obtained
at www.ICGtesting.com
Printed in the USA
BVHW031355200422
634823BV00004BA/682

9 781945 181597